Midnight In Hope

Also by Michael Andrew Marsden

The House in Harrison
The Man in the Closet
The Black Dog Bed & Breakfast
A Walk in the Rain
Sam d'Bear

Midnight In Hope

Michael Andrew Marsden

ISBN: 978-0-9851763-2-7

Published by Marsden Publishing
www.MichaelMarsden.com
Coeur d'Alene, Idaho

Printed In The U.S.A.

Printing by Gray Dog Press
Spokane, Washington

Acknowledgements

This story is set in the town of Hope, Idaho. Hope is a unique railroad town that has seen days of glory when steam engines ruled the rails. Today it is a sleepy town with fewer than 100 residences. The hotel building is still there but it no longer serves as a hotel. The railroad water tower and roundhouse are both gone. The ghosts are beginning to limit their visits to town except for special occasions. You should plan to visit Hope on the night of the Harvest Moon if you want a chance to encounter one of them.

Judy Pederson lives in Sandpoint, Idaho and is a respected watercolorist with a special passion for capturing old buildings in their present condition or their former glory. She has done an excellent job on the old Hotel Hope for the cover of this book. She shows it on the night of a Harvest Moon waiting for a midnight visitor. You must read the book to share the fun.

As with my other novels, I must thank the Idaho Writers League and the Spokane Authors and Self-Publishers for their support. I must also thank David Hibber for reading an early draft and informing me about the Mormon religion. David, I hope I got it right in this draft. George Washington a special thanks to you for your excellent job of line editing. I also must thank Bob Manion for his comments and suggestions on the main characters who like Bob was a marine. Last but not least I wish to thank Russ Davis of Gray Dog Press for making this an attractive book.

Prologue

Aunt Betty looked every bit as old as the hotel in Hope. Her voice was like the fog drifting on the lake in early morning. "You may see a ghost or two while you are in Hope. They return for many different reasons." She closed her eyes for a moment. "Some spirits come back to tell loved ones something they failed to tell them when they were alive. Others come back to right a wrong done years ago. But most come back because they are simply lonely."

She opened her eyes, those deep, dark green eyes that never looked directly at me. "They were lonely in life and now they are lonely in death. They wander between the two worlds looking for someone or something. They did not choose this fate, just as you do not choose what awaits you in Hope."

Part I

1969

Chapter 1
Anna: October 1969

In the summer of 1969, after my father died, my mother and I moved to Hope, Idaho, to live with Aunt Gladys. At first I hated the place. It was too small to be called a town. I felt alone and deserted. All my friends returned to the university in Moscow that fall, but I remained in Hope. I was promised to Sam Chapman, the most wonderful guy in the world, but he was off in Scotland on his mission for the church. We were both members of the Church of Jesus Christ of Latter Day Saints, and although I supported his mission, it was his absence that led to this adventure in Hope.

I tried to make friends with Betty, or Aunt Betty as Gladys called her. She was not a relative but just an old woman who lived in one of the smaller houses below the road. The first time I spoke with Betty she tried to frighten me by saying that there were several ghosts in Hope. I didn't believe in ghosts but still her stories frightened me. Of course I didn't believe her when she told me that those who disappeared in the lake years ago returned with the full moon. Yet, late at night when there was a bright moon, I would sit in my room looking out the window at the lake and imagine someone coming out of the cold water and up the steep hill to our house. It was frightening and yet not as frightening as being alone. I told myself I just had to suffer through the next two years until Sam returned. But that fall I met Kurt, and he changed everything.

Aunt Gladys, like my mother, was a widow. Her husband died in the Vietnam War just two years prior to my father's death. Today, Gladys works at the small café on the ground floor of Hotel Hope.

I remember it was a Friday morning in October, Gladys' day off. She asked me to go with her to Sandpoint. On the north end of Lake Pend Oreille, Sandpoint was the only town of any size. It was also seventeen miles of a windy two-lane highway from Hope. She had a neat little rig, half car and half truck, a 1965 Ford Ranchero. It looked like a Ford Falcon sedan from the front, with bucket seats, a stick shift, and a pickup bed in the back; I called it a Tr-car.

Gladys let me drive that morning. We had just left town and headed up the road near Trestle Creek when it happened. I was watching the winding road ahead. Most motorcycles you can hear before you see them. I never saw him in the rearview mirror; the bright blue motorcycle just appeared on the road beside me and roared past. I jerked a little to the right and then straightened back into the center of the lane. I floored the gas pedal but Gladys put a hand on the dash and said, "This is not a road to race on. He won't get far at that speed."

She was right. Several miles later I caught up with the motorcycle. It had slowed behind a logging truck. I got a good look at the rider. He sat upright, not slumped like most bikers do. Near the end of the Pack River Flats the highway took a long curve to the left. He shouldn't have tried to pass on that curve even though you can see well down the road. As soon as cars quit coming from the north, he leaned to his left and the bike moved over into the oncoming lane. I heard the engine roar again as he darted forward. The brake lights of the logging truck came on. It all happened so fast. The rear end of the logging truck swung left and jack-knifed across the road. I slammed on the brakes. We came to a stop, our front bumper resting against the dual rear tires of the logging truck. The load of logs was dumped into the swamp like a pile of sticks. The truck driver was cussing a blue streak. Down the road a few yards a big bull moose just stood there looking like he wanted to charge, but instead he turned and ambled off the north side of the road.

Gladys called out to the truck driver, "Where is the motorcycle?"

"What motorcycle?" the man shouted back.

"That big blue motorcycle that passed you when you slammed on your brakes."

The man just shrugged. Gladys and I walked past the cab of the logging truck to the other side of the road.

"He's under there," Gladys said. She turned to me and nodded. "Anna go down into the slough and see if you can find the rider."

The Corps of Engineers had started to lower the lake level and the flats looked like a field of mud with a dozen little sloughs and a meandering stream in the center. The driver of the logging truck called over the radio for an ambulance. Following Gladys' directions I waded out around the logs, not knowing if I was looking for a motorcycle or a dead body. I fell several times going through that mess of mud and shallow water. I was sure the rider would be pinned under that pile of logs, but I was wrong. In an S-shaped slough I saw what looked like a blue ball floating. I waded out to it. The rider was laying face down in the water. I reached under his shoulders, lifted his head out of the water and started to drag him to the shore. He was stuck. I became frantic. I pulled harder. I lifted his arms higher. He was still stuck. Finally I knelt down in the water and pulled him straight toward me. Whatever his feet were caught on released him, and I was able to pull him up onto the soggy, grassy shore.

His leg jerked when his feet reached the shore of soggy grass. He was a muddy mess when I rolled him over. There was water inside the helmet. I unsnapped it and pulled it off. Then I started to panic. If I hadn't gone down there, he would have died. If he had a broken neck, I would have made thing worse by turning him over on his back.

I yelled at him but he didn't react. I leaned my face down next to his and didn't feel any breath, so I turned his head to the side. I know you are not supposed to move an unconscious person, especially if they may have a neck injury, but my lifeguard training told me he might have swallowed a lot of water before I found him. He wasn't breathing, so I rolled his head to one side and pushed on his stomach. A gush of water came out of his mouth. I heard him cough. It was like singing. He was alive. I didn't do anything else but kneel beside and until the ambulance arrived.

They put an inflated raft in the water and floated him over to the road. They were very careful putting him on a stretcher to stabilize his neck before loading him onto the raft. I told them I dragged him out of the slough because his head was face down in the water. They assured me they would have done the same thing.

That is how I met Kurt.

Chapter 2
Kurt: October 1969

I awoke in a white room with only a dull gray light coming in the window. When I moved my eyes, the bed floated to the right and tipped. I put out my hands to brace myself. A man in a white smock reached out and took my hand.

"Awake now?" He asked.

His voice was like someone talking in a long hallway. He laid my hand down across my chest and he stood up straight. I could not tell if he was talking or praying. I tried to move my fingers but they remained limp. Like an electric shock, the thought of death raced up my spine to my ears. I had cheated death in Vietnam. It was a constant companion; like a bad cold that spread from one member of Charlie Company to another. I closed my eyes tight, and then slowly opened them. The room was still foggy but I could hear more clearly now. The man in white turned to face the door and two angels entered the room. They had wings, big white wings that raised them off the floor as they approached the bed. I put up both my hands to shield myself from then. I was not ready to die just yet. The fingers of my right hand curled into a fist, I was still alive.

The two angels stopped at the foot of the bed. The one with golden hair was a little taller than the silver-haired angel, but they both were beautiful... not glamorous or dazzling but a simple yet powerful attractiveness, like the morning sunrise.

"Angels? I don't want angels. I'm not dead yet."

"Not even close," the man in white told me. His smock slowly transformed itself into a white lab coat as he spoke. "I'm Doctor Brian Joseph. You were in an accident. Broke your right fibula. I set it. From the X-rays, it appears you fractured the tibia once before. You won't be putting weight on that leg any time soon. You were unconscious for more than ten hours. This is the second time you regained consciousness. Do you remember our first conservation?"

I shook my head slowly. "No. Where am I?"

"Bonner General Hospital. I have another patient to see. I'll return to talk to you shortly." He stepped back from the bed. "The anesthetics are slowly wearing off. You will have to stay here over the weekend. I'll be out of town tomorrow but I will see you again before I let you leave." He paused as he reached the doorway, "Keep this visit short, he needs rest."

When Doctor Brian Joseph left the room, I turned and looked at the two angels. Their wings had folded behind them, completely out of sight. The older angel stepped forward and spoke.

"You don't know us. I'm Gladys Williams and this is my niece, Anna. We were in the pickup behind you when you went off the road."

I didn't recall the accident at all so I listened as she told me what happened. Anna, the taller angel, stood quietly at the foot of the bed. She was so beautiful and I couldn't think of a single clever thing to say. I told Gladys that I didn't remember the accident or how I got here.

"Perhaps you will tomorrow," she said. "Is there anyone we could call for you and tell them what happened to you?"

"No, thanks. I'll take care of that later."

They left and I went back to sleep. Every time I awoke that afternoon and the next morning, I looked to see if they had returned. The next two days passed slowly and painfully. A deputy from the sheriff's department came in and helped me fill out an accident report. Some memories returned and I told him I was pulling out to pass a logging truck when it jack-knifed. He said he would send me a copy of the accident report. After the sheriff left two men stopped by; Art Blackbushman, the manager of the BB

Logging Company, and his driver, Hank. Art did all the talking at first. He asked about my insurance and gave me a slip of paper with his lawyer's name on it.

"They tell me you don't remember the accident. That right?"

I had dealt with men like Art before. He was hoping I'd say that I didn't remember the accident and he'd have a witness that I didn't remember. That would leave the story entirely in his court.

"You the guy who hit me?" I replied as I looked at the name on the slip of paper he'd handed me.

"Hit you? Hell no. You drove off the road." He looked over at Hank, who nodded.

I managed a slight smile and looked directly at Hank. "Then you hit me?"

"I didn't." Hank shot back.

I turned back to Art. "I got some people I need to talk to." I patted my leg and added, "Including the doctor. This could be bad."

Art raised both hands. "Now let's not get a bunch of lawyers involved. Accidents happen every day. We have insurance and if you do too, maybe we won't need any lawyer guys getting involved."

It was a fast switch in posture. He came to the bedside and shook my hand. "We are really glad you're on the road to recovery." He stepped back and looked over at the slim man who had been standing at the doorway and nodded. "It was all that damn moose's fault. Right Hank?"

The two departed. I now had two motivations to get back on my feet. I was going to make these two pay for running me off the road, if that was what happened. I also wanted to be able to stand up if that blonde Angle ever returned. I had been through the broken leg routine in the Marines. I looked down at the white cast on the ankle. It would be tough, but the sooner I got back on my feet the better.

The second day I was able to hobble to the bathroom on my own. The nurse taped a plastic bag over the cast and helped me shower. That was embarrassing but I felt so much better after a shower.

The two angels returned late Sunday afternoon. I was sitting up in bed when I heard them in the hallway. I pulled the blanket up to my waist. Those hospital gowns are simply indecent.

They didn't have wings but it was like a visit from heaven. Anna was a natural beauty and she had a smile that would lift any man's spirits. Gladys, who had eyes as blue as the Colorado sky, did most of the talking.

I thanked them. "I really appreciate this. It brightens an otherwise dull day. I hate hospitals."

Gladys pulled up the only chair in the room and sat close to the bed. "We gave the sheriff a statement about the accident. I hope he gave you a copy."

"Someone on his staff came by with a statement for me to sign. I told them I wanted to read it first. I'm trying to remember just what happened. I know I didn't just ride off the road."

Gladys looked over at Anna who was standing at the foot of the bed. I had pulled the blanket over both of my legs now.

"It wasn't your fault," Anna said. "We told them the truck jack-knifed and hit you."

"Art Blackbushman will be by to see you if he hasn't already," Gladys said. She quickly added, "That man never spent a dime he didn't have to. Do you have a lawyer?"

"No lawyer. I do have insurance. The local insurance agent, Ken Weiser, stopped by yesterday. He said to not sign anything without checking with him."

Gladys smiled, "Ken is a smart cookie. You may not need a lawyer with him in your corner. When we were here last time. I offered to contact your family but it looks like you are well enough to take care of such matters. If I am not being too nosy, what are your plans?"

I shrugged, "Get out of here. Check into a motel and find my bike. I haven't thought beyond that."

"Your bike is in Hope. Art had one of his loggers pull it out of the mud when they were pulling out their load of logs. It isn't pretty but it's all in one piece. He was going to take it to the wrecking yard but I insisted he leave it in Hope with us. I told him that I'd tell you he saved it from the junkyard."

"Thanks. I'll make arrangements to have it hauled to town and I'll pay you for your efforts."

She smiled, "I didn't get a full answer when I asked what you were going to do. Are you going home or staying in town until you can ride again?"

I swore I saw Anna smile at Gladys' question. I measured my words carefully in reply. "I planned to stay awhile. If the bike can be fixed, I'll do that. I don't want to leave it. Quite frankly, I don't have any place I'm in a hurry to get to. The doctor says it will be weeks before I can ride."

Gladys leaned forward. "Tomorrow, when they release you, why not come back with us and stay in Hope while you recover. We're a small town but we're friendly." She nodded. "I have some houses in our neighborhood that are vacant for the winter. The owners have gone to Arizona; they would just sit empty all winter." She glanced over at Anna. "We'll clean one up for you this afternoon."

I started to argue but Anna quickly added her opinion.

"There is one rancher with all the rooms on one floor, so you wouldn't have steps to contend with. We already put your bike in the garage. The house is small but it has everything— a kitchen, living room and bathroom."

I sputtered a few counter statements but neither was listening. Gladys stood up and put a hand on my arm. "It's settled. I'll drive you there when they release you. If after a day you don't like it, I'll give you a ride back to town."

"Wait!" I called as she turned to leave.

"What?"

"Two questions. How much and why?"

"You have the questions in the wrong order. Why? Because my late husband was career Navy. He was injured and spent two months recovering at a hospital in San Diego. I couldn't afford to stay down there for two months, but some good Christians did visit him often and even invited him to their home on occasion. Now it's my turn."

I really made a fool of myself just then by saying, "You didn't tell me how much?"

Gladys looked at me and shook her head slowly. Anna walked past her and up to my bedside. "Please come. We can help with your recovery. If you can't cook, I can teach you a few things."

"I can cook."

"Then you'll come."

She had such an honest smile, but still I persisted. "And what will it cost?"

She glanced back at Gladys and then leaned over toward me. "You don't pay us, you pay it forward. Someday you will have the opportunity to help someone else."

Hell, I couldn't say no. If she had asked me to jump out of bed and walk down the hall on my broken leg, I'd have done it.

Anna was a puzzle. She looked younger than me but she acted like a big sister. Anna was a beauty but despite her insistence I come to Hope, I didn't feel she was flirting. She and Gladys actually wanted to help me. After they left, I told myself the moment they tried to get me to go to church, I was leaving.

I asked the girl who brought my dinner what she knew about Hope, Idaho. She told me it was a small town on the other side of the lake— a good place in the summer for fishing and boating but deadly dull the rest of the year. She said the only things in Hope were a hotel with a small café and a bar called the Soiled Dove Saloon.

"When I turn nineteen my sister promised to take me to the Soiled Dove Saloon. She said it is really neat and it's haunted. Won't that be a kick to be actually drinking in a bar and know someone is watching you? Someone you can't even see?"

I assured her it sounded exciting.

Chapter 3
Anna: October 18, 1969

Every time you go to a new place you are tested. What will you be expected do? How will you be treated by those who have lived there for a long time? Aunt Gladys went out of her way to make me feel at home. She knew my father's death had been a blow, and not going back to college was another. Gladys did all she could to encourage me to stay busy. She was a kindhearted woman who tried to help anyone whom she thought was in need. Betty Nietzy was one such person who Gladys had taken under her wing. Betty was very old and her house was a small one just below the road. A fear I hadn't felt since reading Hansel and Gretel swept over me the first time I went there.

Each day Gladys would fix a meal for Betty and I was given the task of taking it to her. Gladys also asked me to stay and talk with her so the woman wouldn't feel so alone. Betty had what I called some major faults. She smoked and she told stories— not stories of family or friends, but ghost stories. Perhaps she could sense my discomfort at her little house by the way I stayed near the front door and out of the dark hall that led to her kitchen. As she ate her lunch she would tell me a story of one of the many ghosts who haunted Hope. The ghosts weren't always human either. The story about Morgan was rather amusing.

She told the story as if she were there and had witnessed all the events but for that to be true Betty would have to be more than a century old. Hope was a town borne of the Northern Pacific Railroad in 1882. On the shore they built a roundhouse and shipping yard. From there engines would be added to the trains going east and taken from those going west. When the railroad was being built, the veterinarian who cared for the horses for the railroad was named Hope. The story of Morgan began when the railroad was being built.

When the Northern Pacific was laying tracks along the Pack River Flats area, the work crew would ride to the end of the rails, get off and start work leveling the ground and laying ties. Early one morning when the crew arrived, they saw a moose standing on the just completed portion of the line. The engineer sounded the whistle, but instead of running off the moose lowered his head and charged. His antlers got stuck in the cattle catcher on the front of the engine and the moose was dragged backwards down the track. When the train finally came to a stop, the workman jumped off and ran up to see what the train had hit. The moose was a bloody mess but still alive. His antler was stuck, and he couldn't pull away. One of the workmen took a saw and cut off the right antler. The moose jumped back and limped off into the woods. The workmen were sure a bear or the wolves would get the animal, but that didn't happen. The moose with one antler was often seen near the mud flats of the Pack River. They gave him the nickname Morgan, the one-sided moose. Now a moose sheds his antlers each winter and grows a new set in the spring, but for years Morgan was seen with his big, unbalanced rack, the right antler being sawed off in a straight line making it a foot shorter than the left.

It was a harmless ghost story, so when on my next visit Betty offered to tell me another story, I said yes. I wish I hadn't. Her story about Annette was not amusing at all. Annette was the widow who watched the lake by night; waiting for her long lost husband, Brad, to return. There were gold mines and timber camps along the steep slopes of the Green Monarchs, on the east side of the deep arm of Lake Pend Oreille. Brad had worked in one of the logging camps and was gone for weeks at a time. One spring he just disappeared and was presumed to have drowned in the lake. Annette was a beautiful woman and had many suitors, but she was afraid to remarry less Brad would somehow return. He was a big man with a violent temper. The following winter she was found beaten to death in her own bedroom. Some said it was one of her many suitors; others say Brad returned and found her with another man.

Betty didn't stop with that story. "The lake is possessed by spirits. They claim all who drown. Some they keep, others: they throw back. Not only men like Brad are sent back, but sometimes a woman is made to return."

She had a slow way of telling a story, which often included a bit of history of the area.

For many years Hope was a water-stop for the big steam engines of the six transcontinental trains that passed through each day. There was also a roundhouse for turning around the extra engines needed on the eastward route over the Northern Rocky Mountains. The Northern Pacific built a swank resort, the Highland House in 1886. There were about 3,000 souls in Hope when Jeannot built his hotel in 1897. Today, it is the grand old lady in white that sits on the slope above the lake. It looks today like it did when Teddy Roosevelt stayed there. Betty told of another person who stayed awhile at Hotel Hope— Vicky Anna O'Sullivan.

In 1915, Vicky came to Hope on the Northern Pacific. According to Betty, she was tossed off the train for cheating at cards in an all-night poker game. She only had one suitcase but she had more than one deck of cards. Vicky checked into the Hotel Hope and stayed there several months. She was a regular at the nightly poker games at the Soiled Dove Saloon. She was either very good at cards or she cheated. Betty said that you must be good at cards to get away with cheating. Vicky also used to invite men up to her room at night for a price. That got her kicked out of the hotel and banned from the saloon.

Prohibition came to Idaho in January of 1916. Vicky joined in a venture with a man called Whiskey John to sell whisky to the camps along the lake. John was from Canada and he made regular trips up North. The local bootleggers could not compete with real Canadian whisky. Try as they did, they could not stop John from smuggling it either. They made a pact with the only federal agent in north Idaho. They would deliver Whiskey John and Vicky if he'd stop looking for their stills. Five times they helped the federal man locate the boat they used. Each time it was empty. Vicky would taunt the law by leaving an empty whisky bottle in the boat. She would claim that she won the money they had by playing poker.

The south end of the lake was deep. Drop anything over the side of the boat there and it was gone forever. But up here at the north end there were some shallow bays. Ellisport Bay, where Hope is located, is one of them. When John brought down a fresh shipment of whisky from Canada, they would take it out into the water to a spot off of Hope Point. They had to fill the crates of whisky with smaller rocks so they would sink. They would then lower the boxes into the water and return to Hope. Once they felt it was safe to make a trip they would leave late at night, sail out to the Hope Point and drop the anchor. Vicky would take off her dress and put on an iron belt. She would then take a rope and a gunnysack and dive down into the water. She would pull the bottles of whisky out of the crate and stuff them in the sack. After a few minutes, John would pull the rope up with a sack of whisky bottles and Vicky holding on tight. She would have to have been part otter to survive in that cold water. They then wrapped the bottles in a blanket and stored them in the bottom of the boat. From there they would sail south and make their rounds to the camps along the lake. They would be gone from town for three nights at a time when they had whisky to sell.

One week in October they were gone for five days. Most folks in town blamed it on the wind blowing out of the north. On the night of a full moon, the wind changed and came from the south, bringing with it a storm unlike any Hope had experienced. It blew down trees in town and pushed the lake water up to the level of the railroad tracks. That night the men went down to see the waves crash against the docks. They claimed they heard a woman's scream in the wind. Betty said she told them it was Vicky trying to swim ashore after her boat sank. No one in town believed her, but neither Vicky nor Whiskey John were seen again that year.

When the full moon came in October of the following year a logger was found after midnight wading in the lake and yelling for Vicky. He was drunk, of course, but he claimed he had met Vicky at the Soiled Dove Saloon. They had had a few drinks and went up to his room. He stuck to the story that her name was Vicky, and his description fit the woman who had disappeared a year before.

There was not another Vicky story that year, but a few years later a man who had just gotten off the train walked across the tracks and down along the lake. There he met a woman who, he claimed, came right out of the lake carrying a bottle of whisky. He admitted to going up to the hotel with her, but she had gotten up in the middle of the night and left. She told him she was going for a swim in the lake and wanted him to come with her. The man couldn't swim so he didn't go down to the lake. He looked around town for two days but didn't find her.

I asked Betty why Vicky was seen some years but not others. She told me that Vicky returns every year, finds a man who is lonely, entertains him as only Vicky could, then lures him into the lake. The years during which there were stories of Vicky's visit are the same years that a man drowned in the lake.

That night I dreamed I was swimming out in the cold waters of the lake just beyond the dock at Hope. There were several men standing on the dock watching me. I called to them to come join me. "The water is not so cold. Come. See if you can catch me. I must warn you I'm a good swimmer."

One of the men jumped into the water and started to swim after me. I turned and swam away, out toward Cottage Island. Several times I stopped and looked back. If he was gaining on me, I swam faster; if he was slowing down, I too slowed my pace. We had just made it to Cottage Island when I suddenly awoke. For a while I lay in bed wondering how the dream would have ended if it had continued. The moonlight was coming in through the top half of the windows in the widow's watch. I got out of bed and looked out at the lake. The reflection of the moon on the lake circled Cottage Island.

The next morning I wanted to ask Aunt Gladys if anyone lived on Cottage Island, but she was busy convincing my mother that to bring Kurt to Hope was a charitable thing to do. I smiled and thought of how he looked the first time we went to the hospital. He was propped up in bed like a doll on a shelf in a toy store and now we would be taking him home. He was going to stay in the small house just below the road from our house and next to the one where Betty lived. I was happy and looked forward to a better companion to talk to than Betty. I didn't want to hear any more ghost stories.

Chapter 4
Kurt Comes to Hope

I didn't know if my leg was broken because the wheels of the truck knocked me off the road or from a log falling on it. Nothing went right the morning Gladys and Anna came to get me. I could not get my pants on with that cast on my right leg. I only had two pairs of pants for this trip and one was in the saddlebags of my motorcycle, somewhere in Hope. I asked a nurse to get me a pair of scissors to split my pant leg, but before she got back to the room Gladys arrived. That woman had thought of everything. She had with her a pair of old boxer shorts that belonged to her late husband and a pair of jeans that she had already cut off just above the right knee. She made Anna stay out in the hall while I got dressed. Next, the nurse wheeled me down to the front door in a chair. Anna carried my sack of clothes and items from the hospital. Gladys carried my leather pants and leather jacket.

I balanced myself on a pair of crutches, turned and sat down in the back seat of the station wagon.

On the way to Hope I told Gladys about the progress that Ken Weiser had made. I was not even given a ticket for speeding or passing on a curve. My insurance would pay for the repair of my bike and they were splitting all the hospital expenses between the two insurance companies. I would not get lost work pay.

"That was my fault," I explained. "I quit my job before I set out on this trip."

I didn't want them to think I was a bum, but I wanted them to know I was about out of money. I was also very uncertain of what I had gotten myself into by accepting their charity.

When we arrived in Hope, I took one look at the house and

said, "This is too much. I need to pay you for this. After all, I could be here for weeks."

Gladys told me I would just have to pay someone else. "God expects us to help one another. In the New Testament the good Samaritan did not ask for repayment."

"I don't know what kind of religion you belong to, but if you are planning on converting me you can forget it."

Anna was quick to answer. "Brace yourself. We're Mormons and we don't just forget anyone. See that lake? We put it there just so we could baptize you any time you get the urge. If you can't walk, we'll carry you down. We don't want you to have time to change your mind."

I laughed. "No way. I bet that water is freezing."

"No not freezing, but maybe a little cold."

I hobbled on the crutches into the house. I didn't want to sit down on the couch in the living room. It was so low I didn't think I could get up again; I hobbled on into the next room. At the kitchen table I slowly turned and sat down. The front of the house faced the road and the kitchen had a view of the lake. Anna walked over to the window and looked out.

"See that lake down there? I went swimming there this summer. I have my lifeguard card, so if you want to swim just give me a call."

I patted the white cast. "I wonder if this thing floats."

She came back to the table. "Give me the key to your bike and I'll get the rest of your things."

I pointed to the leather jacket. "Check the inside zipper pocket. The keys should be there unless someone at the hospital lifted them."

Gladys brought my jacket to the table. I unzipped the pocket and took out a set of six keys.

"See?" Anna beamed. "You have got to work on that suspicious mind of yours. We are honest people up here." She left and returned with the two saddlebags.

Gladys took the bags from Anna and said, "Kurt, let's open these and take your clothes up to the house to be washed."

The two saddlebags were packed tight. I was glad I didn't have anything illegal in them. As best I could I sorted the personal items from the clothing. Gladys opened the kitchen closet and took out two paper sacks. She put light color clothing in one sack and the dark in the other then looked up at Anna. "Give the man his keys and take this up to my house. I want to talk to Kurt alone."

Anna picked up the sacks and pouted. "I'm just the washer woman around here."

I smiled. "And lifeguard."

I was stuck with Gladys, a woman I had just met, taking over my life. It was a hopeless feeling to know that for a while I could only go where someone else let me go and do what someone else let me do. They may be treating me with kindness, but I had lost my independence.

Gladys told me that Anna Chapman and her mother lived with her in the big house above the road. Anna's mother was a widow, as was Gladys. Her husband had fought in the Vietnam War. She had recognized the tattoo on my shoulder— Chester the bulldog with a helmet was the Marine Corps mascot. Her husband had been in the Navy, and when she visited him in the hospital in San Diego he had a Marine as a roommate who had a similar tattoo.

"What does the tattoo on the other arm mean?" she asked.

"*Di bo Chet*. That only means something to a Marine."

Gladys shook her head and gave me the rules of the house. There was to be no smoking or drinking in the house. I could fix coffee and cook meals in the kitchen. The house was in a quiet neighborhood where everyone knew everyone else. Anna would come every day to see that I was doing all right.

She gave that 'mother knows best' look. "I'll fix a noon meal the first week, and Anna will bring it down to the house. She does the same for your neighbor Betty. After you are back on your feet, we will make other arrangements."

She nodded toward the house next to this one. "Now, I must warn you about Betty next door. She is an old woman and in some ways rather odd. She knows more about the early days in Hope than anyone else around here, but some of her stories are rather far-fetched, to say the least."

Gladys smiled and stood up. "As for Anna, she is a beautiful, Christian woman. No doubt you will find her attractive. That's natural. Anna is promised to Sam Chapman who is away on his mission. He will return, so don't let yourself get too infatuated with Anna. Once you are back on your feet, I expect you to leave Hope and return to your home. Do we understand each other?"

I assured Gladys that getting back on my feet and heading home was my goal too. It would include fixing my bike. The first step was for my leg to heal. The doctor had said in three weeks he would remove the cast, and it would take at least another three weeks to regain enough strength to ride.

Before she left Gladys showed me the items she had put in the refrigerator; milk: juice, cheese, butter, and a bin of vegetables. There were two boxes of cereal on the counter beside the sink. She asked what else I needed. I told her I'd make a list tomorrow. I wanted to see what her lunch would be like first, and I knew she wouldn't bring me a six-pack anyway.

That afternoon I hobbled around the house on my crutches and explored what was to be my home, or prison, depending on my mood of the day. The house had a very small, square living room and a kitchen about the same size, hardly enough room for a stove, refrigerator and a table. There were two bedrooms. One had two single beds with a small dresser between them. The other was crowded with a queen-size bed but it had a large closet. Shelves had been built into half of the closet. I chose the room with two beds. I could put my clothes on one and sleep in the other.

The garage was detached from the house. I ventured outside and around the side of the house. Across the road was a larger two-story house. Because of the steep hillside, it loomed over the road and the smaller houses that lined the road. The door to the garage opened upward. It was not locked but it was hard for me to balance on one leg and lift it to full open position. My bike looked like it had been dragged through the mud. The front fork was bent far to the left. A broken chain lay beside it on the floor. I walked around it and checked the engine. It was dirty but it didn't look like it had suffered from the crash with the logging truck or landing in the swamp. This was a Honda CB750, the first of the super bikes. I swore aloud that we would both be back on the road again.

Shutting the garage door was as difficult as opening it. Both my legs hurt but I was not going to go lie down. I was going to keep active and hopefully recover sooner. Instead of going back inside I walked down the road and looked at the houses, both above the road and below it. One must always know his environment, area of operation and discover any threat before it discovered you. The road went in a northwest direction as it curved around the hillside. I could not see very far but I recalled when we were driving here there was a large white building nearby. That would be Hotel Hope with the Soiled Dove Saloon. If I was to do any drinking, and I wanted a drink badly, I would need to go there. I glanced up at the big house. Gladys may be watching me. I decided to postpone exploring in that direction. The first house I saw the other direction down the road was about the size of my new abode, only it had a front porch. There, in a rocking chair, sat an old woman. I could tell she was watching me so I walked down the road a few steps, stopped and waved. She waved back and called out, "Come here."

I struggled down the paved part of the road on the crutches. There was a single, low step up to the wooden porch where the woman waited in an old rocking chair beside a wooden bench. Dark brown boots, not shoes, poked out from under the long black dress she wore. A gray jacket was tightly buttoned up to her skinny neck. I was wondering where she parked her broomstick when her voice cracked a greeting.

"I'm Betty. Come sit here and tell me how you ended up here. Some people call this place Hope, but at times it is a place for the hopeless. I hear they pulled you out of the Pack River Flats."

I was careful with my story for I was not sure if she was just curious or had some friend working for the BB Logging Company. She used her thumb when she gestured as she spoke, as if there was an unseen crowd standing on the porch listening to our conservation.

"You may see a ghost or two while you are in Hope. They return for many different reasons."

She closed her eyes for a moment. "Some come back to tell loved ones something they failed to tell them when they were alive. Others come back to right a wrong done years ago. But most come back because they are simply lonely."

She opened her eyes wide. The deep, dark green pupils scanned left and then right as if to include all those on her porch. "They were lonely in life and now they are lonely in death. They wander between the two worlds looking for someone or something. They did not choose this fate, just as you do not choose what awaits you when you came to Hope."

I awoke with a jabbing pain in my leg. I yanked off the blanket to free my foot, which was being held captive by the sheets twisted it. I turned on the light, sat in bed and massaged the leg. I moved my foot back and forth until the circulation was restored. Swinging my legs over the side of the bed I stood and hopped on one foot into the bathroom. I noted the time on my watch. It was just before midnight. I last took a pain pill at eight so, it was okay to take another. When I reached for the small plastic container the whole room shook. I grabbed the doorjamb and watched the container of pills roll off the counter. The lights in the bathroom flickered, the window rattled. I put out both hands to brace myself in the doorway. The window stopped its rattle, the lights came on and the house stopped shaking. Holding onto the counter I leaned over and picked up the container of pills. I swallowed one and washed it down with a full glass of water. Doctor Brian had told me it was best not to take the pills on an empty stomach, so hobbled into the kitchen. In the refrigerator I took out the milk and fixed myself a bowl of Shredded Wheat.

A train whistle called in the distance, and in minutes the house shook as the train rumbled by. It wasn't a violent rumble like the one at midnight. I went back to bed and lay still waiting for the pain pill to take effect so I could sleep. I thought about what Betty had said. I should have died in the mud flats after that accident. Anna had saved my life. What if I had died and she had snatched me back from the grave? I imagined my body lying there, cold and stiff, with Anna kneeling beside me, kissing me gently until warmth flowed again in my veins. Now that was a ghost story I could really get into.

Chapter 5
Anna Visits Kurt

I felt ashamed of being so happy Kurt had moved into the house just below the road. It was all right to want to help him, I told myself. Wasn't I obligated to do so since I had saved his life? But in truth I found him attractive. I had just turned twenty last summer, a week before my dad died. Mother was devastated, so I dropped out of summer school at the U and returned home. Dad had been a hard-working man and made a good wage when the Forest Service let them harvest some of their precious trees. They had to let some contracts after all those fires. Sun Dance was the worst. It was also why he died. He had just finished working a double shift the morning he drove into the bridge abutment.

The week following the funeral, Aunt Gladys came to visit and insisted we sell our house and move to Hope to live with her. She too was widowed then and said she needed the companionship. Mother agreed and told me we had to move for financial reasons. Mother had no love for Hope. To her it was the end of the world. There wasn't even a ward there. Still isn't. As for Gladys, Hope was her home. I remember Mother considered her the black sheep of an otherwise good Mormon family. She had joined the faith just to marry her brother, Peter. His father had insisted they be married in the temple. Mother often said that it was Gladys' fault Peter remained in the Navy, only to die in Vietnam.

Sam and I understood that kind of family pressure. Mother insisted that Sam complete his mission before she would consider letting us get married. He made a promise to me and to Mother that we would be married when he returned. He gave me a CTR ring just before he left. He wanted to buy an engagement ring but his father told him to complete his duty to the church first.

Gladys' house set on the hill high above the lake. There were two bedrooms downstairs and two upstairs. One was used for storage; I stayed in the other. It wasn't really a bedroom. It was a sitting room. Gladys called it the widow's watch. The room was octagonal in shape and had windows on the front four sides. The man who built the house was from New England and he had an interest in the whitefish fishing in the lake.

I was sitting there one night with the lights off, watching the house below and wondering what Kurt was doing. Gladys came up to my room late and knocked lightly at the door.

"Anna, are you asleep?"

"No. I'm just looking out at the lake."

Gladys came in and closed the door behind her. "And what has your interest?"

I couldn't tell her I was watching Kurt. "What's the island out there?"

"Cottage Island. I thought I told you the names of the islands. Warren is the big one. Cottage is much smaller. From here it is almost hidden behind Warren. Beyond it is Pearl Island. Here let me help you look."

She opened the closet and took out a box from the top shelf. Opening it, she took out a large telescope. In the dark we assembled the stand and mounted the telescope. There was an almost full moon that night and we centered our sights on Warren Island.

"You can see the dock but no boat. The island is rarely visited in the summer and never this time of year," Gladys informed me.

I took my turn looking and asked, "What of the little island?"

I slowly shifted the telescope to the left until I could just see the smaller island above the trees on Warren Island. "I can't even see a dock on Cottage Island."

"Oh, there is one, or there was one. Cottage Island is where the cribs were. When the railroad was being built, they kept prostitutes out there on the island. They didn't want them in town and they didn't want the workers traveling all the way to Sandpoint. Cottage Island was close and yet out of sight."

"So there were no prostitutes in town?"

"Now Anna, I didn't say that. Cottage Island was an attempt to keep the town looking upright, and to a degree it worked. At least that is what Betty tells me. You see, at one time Hope had a population of almost two thousand, mostly railroad workers but some miners and loggers too. Women were in short supply."

I left the telescope set up by the window and after Gladys left I turned it down to the house where Kurt was staying. After refocusing it I could see right into the windows of his house. The living room was dark but light came in from the kitchen. He must have been in there. I turned the telescope back to Cottage Island. Was that where Vicky was taking her men? No one could swim that far in the cold waters of Lake Pend Oreille.

It seemed ironic that men would boat out to Cottage Island to be with the women back then, and today I sat alone in my room. Hope once had too many men and not enough women; now it has too few men. I wondered if Kurt were here eighty years ago would he have taken the boat out to Cottage Island.

I stepped back from the window and sat on my bed. The rat. I bet he would. He's not like Sam. Sam would save his money, writes his sweetheart back home and wait for her.

The next day when I took meals down to Betty and Kurt, Betty looked at the basket.

"So you're going to feed that soldier too?"

"He's a Marine, not a soldier," I countered.

"No difference. They both make their living killing people and breaking women's hearts."

"Kurt's not like that. He has a broken leg. I saved his life and now Gladys and I are helping him recover."

I left Betty and hurried down to Kurt's house. I knocked twice and then looked through the window. I hear a door slam just before I saw him hobble through the living room to open the door.

"Sorry to keep you waiting. I was in the bathroom." He smiled, "Shaving." He pointed to his face. "I got tired of the dark, shadowy look."

"Gladys fixed you a lunch."

He let go of one of his crutches to take the basket.

"No, let me take it to the table," I insisted. "I have to take the basket back home."

He held the door and I walked through the living room to the kitchen. I set the basket down and began to unpack it. There were two bologna sandwiches, a small salad, a cup of hot soup, a piece of gingerbread cake and a container of milk. I sat down at the table and took out a piece of paper and pencil.

"Have you turned on the refrigerator?"

"Gladys did that. I checked the stove. The burners get hot but I have no food that needs to be cooked."

I smiled. "That's my next task - a grocery list."

He unwrapped one of the sandwiches and took a bite. "I like this."

"Fine. I'll make bologna sandwiches again tomorrow. Now for the list of food that you are going to fix for yourself. You can cook, I hope?"

Between bites he made suggestions, mostly simple stuff - a box of cold cereal but not Shredded Wheat, a loaf of bread, peanut butter, a quart of milk and a case of beer. I wrote down most of his order but substituted cans of soup for the case of beer, and then showed him the list.

He read the list, chuckled at the cans of soup, took the pencil and added two items - rags and a book to read.

"Oh, I have just the book for you," I said.

He shook his head, "Don't bring me a Bible. I read it already. Make it a James Bond novel."

We talked as he ate his lunch and then I told him I had to go back home and get ready to go to work. Starting that day I was now a waitress at the café, working the late afternoon and evening shift. He walked me to the front door and thanked me for the food and the company.

Chapter 6
Kurt in Hope

The second week in Hope things had settled down to a routine for me. I tried to keep my house looking neat because Anna came to see me every day and Gladys made unscheduled visits. I looked forward to Anna's visits; she was like the sunshine that burned away the morning fog. After her visit I would go to the garage and work on my bike. The main task was cleaning and trying to start it again. To my surprise, the engine started up after I had cleaned all the wiring, drained and refilled the oil. Anna purchased the oil from the local gas station in the north end of Hope. She told me there was a Mobil station in Sandpoint that sold Hondas. I told her I'd like to stop by that station and order some parts for my motorcycle when we went to Sandpoint to get my cast taken off. The following morning I had a visit from Gladys.

"Anna tells me you want to stop at the Mobil station to buy parts for your motorcycle. What kind of parts are you talking about? You don't have to take that thing with you, do you?"

I shook my head. "The front fork is bent. I tried but I can't straighten it. It would be best to just replace it. There are some cables I want to replace also. The engine seemed to have survived. It even starts. Needs new plugs and a tune-up, but I can do that myself."

"So how long before you can have that cycle ready to ride?"

"A week after I get the parts. You could be rid of me pretty soon."

She shook her head. "Kurt, you remember that leg. The doctor will take the cast off this week but I don't want you trying to ride that motorcycle until you can walk from here to the resort down by the lake, and back up again."

"How far is that?"

"Just over a mile, and it's uphill coming back."

"You sound like a drill instructor."

"I'm someone who cares about you. I want you to make it home not just leave Hope." She smiled. "Anna cares about you too. You're making quite an impression on her. Can I trust you two to go to Sandpoint and back alone?"

"Hey! Don't worry. She is my G.A."

"Your what?"

"Guardian Angel. She saved my life."

"Okay. Do you have enough money to buy the parts for your motorcycle?"

"I have some money. Ken Weiser said for me get the bike repaired and send him copies of all the receipts. He'd see that I am reimbursed."

"Do you have enough money?" Gladys asked again.

"That's my problem."

"Kurt, I said we care about you. We want you to be physical able to ride before you leave, and we want you to have enough money to make it back home."

"It will be close but I've been through tough times before."

Gladys stood up and walked to the front door. "Kurt, I talked to a friend here in town. She needs a night man at the gas station. It's more of a little store than a gas station but she likes to stay open late. Are you interested?"

"I can walk down there; it will be practice for walking to the resort and back."

"Exactly, and this way you will have some money in your pocket when you are ready to leave."

"Once the bike is fixed and I can walk, what else is there?"

Gladys smiled. "Something in God's control. The weather."

Anna was all excited when she brought my lunch. She told me she was going to drive Gladys' pickup, or Tr-car as she called it.

There would be plenty of room to put pieces of the motorcycle in the back.

"Anna, this is a new model. They may have to order parts. I'm sure they won't have a new front fork for a CB750."

My comments didn't dampen her enthusiasm. When she left, I watched her actually skip as she went up the road to the Hotel Hope.

I shared her feeling and whistled while I worked on my bike in the garage. When I finally took a break, the clouds had moved in and it looked like rain. Gladys was right. Weather could ruin my plans for a quick departure. I had several passes to go over. Motorcycles and snow don't mix.

I walked out onto the road and looked west. The mountain range in the far distance was hidden in clouds.

A voice behind me squawked like a crow. "A storm is coming."

I turned my head and looked at Betty. She sat, as she always did, in that old rocking chair on her front porch. I was still feeling positive about my future, at least the next few days, so I walked over to see her.

"My, you're in a grand mood. What did Anna give you for lunch?"

"Don't think bad thoughts of Anna. She is my G.A.," I scolded her.

"G.A."

"Guardian Angel." I gripped the rail to the porch. A train rumbled by on the tracks below the hill. "Those trains will shake this house down some day."

"Oh, the trains we have today are pussycats. You should have been here when the steam giants ruled the north county."

She rocked back in her chair. "Hope was the center of the railroad back then. We had a full station, complete with a roundhouse. Sometimes there would be five big iron engines down there at the same time, huffing and puffing smoke like you wouldn't believe."

She nodded toward north. "Hotel Hope was a busy place indeed, back then. They had a tunnel that you could go through to get to the station. When one of those big steam engines would start up, it shook the town. Back then Hope was loud and exciting. We would laugh when the engineer on one of the big iron horses used the engine as a brake as he rolled into town."

She began to rock slowly. "Hope was a booming town back then. The railroad was built by the Chinese, pigtails. They also worked some of the mines, but the real miners didn't like that."

I shook my head. "I bet they didn't. The Chinese built the railroads in the West but no one wanted them to dig for gold. Hell, they might get rich."

"Pigtails were strange people. They worked here but sent most of their money back to China. That was their home, not here."

"Well some of them made this their home," I protested.

"Oh no! They wanted our money, but China was their home and that's where they wanted to be."

I shrugged and started to leave.

"Don't run off. Listen. Building the railroad was dangerous work. So is mining. When a Chinaman died he wasn't buried in the cemetery with the Christian folks. No, he was buried in a shallow grave in their own place. You see, the pigtails wanted their bones returned to China. That was their home, not here. So they would save some money to have their bones shipped back. That's when Lazy Jack played a fast one on them."

I leaned back against the post and watched her. Betty stretched her arms out and looked around the porch as if she was addressing a crowd.

"Jack told the head pigtail that he could ship the bodies back at half what the railroad was charging. They had to bring the bones to the rail yard at midnight. He would have them loaded on one of the flatcars. They had to pay him in gold."

She clapped her hands together. "He lied. He didn't work for the N. P. It was all a lie. He took their money and loaded the boxes of bones on the last flatcar of the train headed west. Then when the train started across the trestle that crosses where the Pack River enters the lake, he tossed the boxes off into the lake."

I shook my head. "So, he took the gold and went to Seattle."

"That's how the story goes but that's not the end."

"Let me guess," I said. "The Chinamen got even when he arrived in Seattle without the boxes?"

The old woman grinned. "I don't know about that but I've watched the midnight train come by. It's a steam engine, just like the one that took their bones away. It stops on the siding just like it did when the station and roundhouse were here. The ghosts of the pigtails bring boxes of their dead to the last flatcar. After the engine is watered and the wheels are oiled the train chugs off. Just like it did that night. It's called 'The train to China.'"

I felt like laughing but she seemed so serious. She kept looking around and nodding her head, as if there were a dozen other people on the porch listing to her tale.

"If a train wakes me in the middle of the night, I'll know what it is," I told her.

She raised both her hands up, looked to her right and then to her left. "You won't hear 'The train to China' unless you listen for it. You will not see the pigtails or the boxes they carry unless you are down by the railroad and look for them."

I left the porch a little afraid to look back, for I might see a dozen ghosts from the past watching and listening to the old woman. I awoke that night just before midnight and listened for 'The train to China,' but it didn't come.

Chapter 7
Anna: Back to Sandpoint

I was very excited about getting the chance to go to Sandpoint with Kurt. He was scheduled to have his cast removed on October thirtieth. Mom said it was far too early for his leg to have healed. Gladys stated firmly, "Doctor Brian Joseph is a fine physician, and if he says the cast is ready to come off, it's ready to come off. We had better get Kurt back to the hospital this Thursday."

Since Gladys worked the morning shift, I was selected to drive Kurt to Sandpoint. Mom didn't want me to take her car so Gladys lent me her Ranchero. I parked on the road in front of his house while he hobbled out using both crutches. Last week Kurt had been hobbling along on just one crutch.

I asked, "How come two crutches today? Did you hurt your leg again?"

"No, I have to take them both back to the hospital," he replied. He turned his head toward the garage door that was open. "I got a few things in there I'd like to take to town. If it's not too much trouble, I'd like to stop at that Mobil station."

I followed Kurt down to the garage and we loaded the bike chain, some other parts and the front wheel into the back of the pickup. Kurt put a pair of jeans in the cab of the truck. I was so used to seeing him in those shorts that Gladys gave him, but he was anxious to have on some warmer pants. When I opened the passenger door, Kurt spun on one crutch and backed into the seat. He handed me the crutches and I put them in the back of the truck. I told him to put on his seat belt.

"Hey, this isn't comfortable." He complained.

I reached over, found the other end of the seatbelt, and pulled it across him. "I want you to be safe when you're with me."

"Do you think you're safe with me?" he asked.

I turned and looked at him. "That's what my mother asked." I laughed and added, "I trust you."

I then started the truck and backed up to Lake Street, turned around and headed west on Main. I knew my Mother was watching from the window. Kurt must have thought the same thing because he waved out the side window.

As we drove over to Sandpoint, Kurt asked if I knew of a place that he could take me to lunch.

I told him, "You don't have to buy me lunch."

"But I want a real lunch. I mean those sandwiches your mother makes are good, but I want a full meal with a dessert. Besides, I don't often have a date with an angel."

I smiled, for it was nice to have a man flirt in a kind way. "I'm not an angel. You just have to forget that I pulled you out of the mud. Anyone who came along that day would have done the same thing. Next week I'll ask Mom to bake a pie and bring you and Betty each a piece."

I drove first to the hospital. He fretted about leaving the parts from his bike in the back of the pickup, but I assured him Sandpoint was a safe town. The doctor came in and talked to Kurt before he cut the cast off his leg. Kurt then asked me to leave the room so he could put on his jeans.

I shook my head. "First, I want to hear what the doctor has to say."

Doctor Joseph laughed. "I knew I didn't have to send a nurse over to Hope to check on you. You've got the Saints taking care of you."

He examined Kurt's leg again and had him flex his feet and bend his knees. He told Kurt to be careful about putting his full weight on the right leg for a while. "The bone is healing nicely but the muscles are weak. Start using it but don't push it. If you have any severe pain let me know."

Kurt slipped off the examination table and took a few steps. He turned around and looked over at me. "Guess I don't need those crutches anymore."

Doctor Joseph insisted he take one of the crutches with him. Kurt shooed me out of the room so he could change his pants. I'm sure he and the doctor had more to say after I left.

It was almost noon when we went to the Mobil station. Kurt looked different in long pants. He acted different too. He put the crutch in the space behind the seats of the Ranchero and he walked tall. I knew he was in pain but he held his head high. He told the man at the station about his bike and how he was trying to fix it. I wandered off and looked at the new shiny bikes in the front room. Some of the parts Kurt needed had to be ordered.

We left the Mobil station and went to a restaurant just a few blocks from the hospital. I felt so proud when Kurt took my arm and walked with me to the table. He walked differently. Like... well, like a Marine was supposed to walk. I could feel everyone watching us and I was so glad he wasn't limping or leaning over as he did when he first came to Hope.

Kurt ordered a hot turkey sandwich with cranberry sauce, mashed potatoes and dressing. I ordered a hamburger. That was dumb of me. I should have ordered something special like he did. For dessert he had a piece of apple pie. We talked about silly things such as what it would be like if we could fly. Not in airplanes but with wings, like birds. People wouldn't need roads or bridges, if they could fly. It was foolish but relaxing, and I just felt so grand being there with him.

At first Kurt had been just a relief, someone to worry about instead of thinking about myself. When the doctor took off that cast, Kurt put on pants and he changed into a man. I hung onto every word he said. I bet we spent two hours just talking at that table.

We talked about flying but it soon changed to riding. Kurt said riding a motorcycle was the closest thing he'd done to being a bird. On his bike he was free. He admitted to being scared when he first started riding. It was intense. You had to watch the road for obstacles. Even a small piece of tire was dangerous. You had to watch traffic and never assume they saw you. People misjudge how fast a bike is traveling. Even a short ride can leave you exhausted.

He told me of riding down the Going-to-the-Sun highway in Glacier National Park. It was so exhilarating he turned around and rode back up the pass. On the way up he'd pull off at all the viewpoints and look around. When he reached the top, he turned around and just rode down the mountain.

His vivid description made me feel like I was riding with him, around one turn and then banking into the next. I could see the waterfall coming down the side of the mountain as if I was really there.

Mother was not at all pleased we didn't get home until after four that afternoon. I explained that we went to the Mobil station to order parts for his motorcycle and that he took me to lunch. She gave me a stern lecture about helping someone but not becoming involved with him. When I told her he needed a real meal with vegetables and dessert, she asked what he had to eat. I told her I just had a hamburger, and then I described the meal he ordered. She seemed to accept the long trip to town as not a total waste, but she was still concerned.

Kurt had changed. He had a different view of himself, and I saw him in a different light too. The next day my hours were changed to the afternoon shift and I had to work through the dinner hour at the café. When we closed that night, I walked down to this house. He wasn't there so I asked Betty if she'd seen him. She said he was up at the Soiled Dove Saloon. I'd never been in there, although it was right next door to the café. I walked back to Hotel Hope and looked in through the big glass windows. Kurt was sitting at the bar. I wanted to go in and tell him to go home but instead I ran back to Gladys' house. That night I turned off the lights in my room and watched the road for Kurt. He had to walk down Main Street to go home, and I should be able to see him as he crossed below Lake Street.

I reasoned that he had to go to the saloon because Gladys forbad him from drinking at the house. I knew his leg was not strong and I feared he'd fall and hurt himself if he had too much to drink. I was so worried about him I couldn't sleep, so I snuck downstairs and slipped out the front door. I walked down to Kurt's house and banged on the door. He didn't answer and there were no lights on inside. I then reluctantly walked up to the Soiled Dove Saloon. It was closed. I started for home when I heard someone cry out. I walked around the front of Hotel Hope and saw Kurt struggling to get to his feet. He took two steps down the road but he looked strange, like he was leaning on one of his crutches, but there was no crutch.

"Kurt," I yelled, "Are you all right?"

He fell flat on his face. I ran to him and lifted his head. He looked right at me. His eyes were wide with fear. I tried to help him get up. He spoke and his voice was low as if he were out of breath.

"Vicky, listen. I have a story for you."

Once I got him up on his feet, I put his right arm around my shoulders. We limped together down the sidewalk past the café and the saloon. He stopped, turned and gave me a hug. Not a friendly hug either. I felt myself shaking. Then he called me Vicky again.

"My leg hurts. I can't go down to the lake. Let's go to my house. You will like it. I know what you really want."

I was more afraid of leaving him than of taking him home in this condition. I put my arms around him and held him closer. He closed his eyes and began to cry. I managed to turn and we shuffled along. We walked a ways, hugged, he would say something, and then we'd start off again.

This is a strange thing to say, but I knew that night I had fallen in love with Kurt. When we crossed below Lake Street, he stopped and looked up the hill.

"Anna, I see you. Anna."

He was calling and crying at the same time. I hurried him across the road for fear that he'd wake Mother or Gladys. The front door was unlocked and we managed to get down the narrow hall to his bedroom. There I lay him down in bed. He begged me not to leave. He had no idea who I was. He called me Vicky one time and Anna the next. He wouldn't let go of me so I lay down beside him and kissed him. He didn't try to undress me or anything like that. He just held me tight. After a short time his arms relaxed. He was asleep again. I rolled him over and climbed out of bed. I was afraid to leave him, and yet, I was afraid to stay. I have heard stories of drunks rolling over on their back, swallowing their tongue and suffocating. I said a prayer asking God not to let that happen, and went home.

He was not an alcoholic. I only saw him drunk that one night. The next day he came to the café about dinnertime. He told me he'd gone to the Soiled Dove Saloon the night before and had one too many. I didn't tell him that I helped him home. He said he's decided not to drink again, at least not at the Soiled Dove Saloon.

Chapter 8
Kurt at The Soiled Dove Saloon

When I got that damn cast off my leg I felt better. I put the crutch that Doctor Joseph insisted I take with me in the back of Gladys' Tr-car. My leg didn't hurt but it did feel weak. Anna drove me to the Mobil station and I ordered the parts I needed to fix my bike. The owner himself waited on me and gave me lots of advice, and a repair manual for the CB750. Next I took Anna to lunch. I don't remember what I had for lunch that day. It was great, almost like being high. A beautiful woman can be more intoxicating than any whiskey. She wasn't my woman. I knew that and so did she, but that afternoon we just enjoyed each other.

I hoped Gladys would not be upset when we got back to Hope that afternoon. Anna was late for her shift at the café. I walked down to my house and spent the afternoon reading and checking things in the Honda repair manual.

I walked up to the café to get dinner but stopped in the Soiled Dove Saloon first. Gladys didn't want me drinking or smoking in the house where I was staying. The people who owned it were teetotalers. I sat down at the bar and ordered a Jack Daniels on the rocks. One drink followed another. Not many. I was watching my money closely. Somehow the time just raced by and the few other patrons had left.

I sloshed the ice in my glass. There was one last swallow of that sweet amber liquor left when old Bill, the bartender, called out.

"Close in a few minutes. You want a nightcap?"

I jumped at his words. I must have been drifting off, a sign that I'd had too much already. Bill was a potbellied old man with a white apron. I raised my glass. "Sure, a nightcap."

In one of the rectangular-shaped mirrors framed in silver that hung above the row of whiskey bottles, I searched the bar behind me. *Last one to leave. Why do I do it? Can't they close a bar without me? Hell, they call this place Hope.*

I leaned on my elbows and watched as Potbelly dumped some ice in the short, wide glass, then turned his back and took a bottle from the shelf. With a slow spin he turned and held out the glass with the ice floating in dark amber. "Jack Daniels on ice. Three dollars."

I put a five on the bar.

As he turned, Potbelly picked up the bill and started down the bar. He paused to collect the trashcan from under the bar. With a limp he sauntered though the door at the far left end of the bar. Just as the door closed behind him there was a crash of broken glass. I jerked my head in that direction. Suddenly, I was back in Vietnam that morning when it happened. We had some early mail delivery. I had two letters. I opened the one from my girl friend first, and then I screamed.

"Rachel!" My eyes closed tight and my head bowed. The First Sergeant grabbed my hand and shook it.

"Get a bandage." He held my hand upright and squeezed my arm just below my wrist. I never believed I could break a water glass by squeezing it. My other hand held the letter, crumpled tight.

In the bar that night I had I yelled out Rachel's name, just as I had when I read that letter. I looked cautiously at the glass of whiskey and figured it was too stout to break. Then I heard a voice behind me reply, "There is no one by that name here tonight."

I raised my head. It took a few moments before my eyes could focus. I knew I wasn't in Nam, I was here in Hope. I looked into the silver-framed mirrors behind the bar, one by one. The room dimmed as all the lights but the one chandelier over the bar at my end were off. I sat up straight and carefully glanced to my left. The old grandfather clock in the lobby began to chime, Announcing the midnight hour. In cadence with the chimes I heard her voice again. "There is no one here but you and me."

I turned sharply to my right. She had eyes like fathomless green pools, raven-colored hair and small pink lips. "What are we drinking tonight?"

"Whiskey's too strong for a little girl like you." I grinned and carefully slid the fresh whiskey down the bar.

She raised the glass slowly to her lips, took a sip and then set it down on the bar, halfway between the two of us. She floated closer, as if the barstool had wheels. Her icy fingers touched my wrist. "What's your name?"

"Kurt."

"You have a last name? I never accept a drink from a man with no last name."

"Johnson. Kurt Johnson. You want to see a driver's license?"

She leaned back her head and laughed. "I'm Victoria Anna O'Sullivan. My friends call me Vicky. Did you just get into town?"

"Yeah, I'm on my way back from Spearfish."

She floated closer, her dark green eyes never leaving mine. The smell of lilacs overpowered the sweet aroma of the whiskey. "I was in Spearfish once. A long time ago." Her left hand slipped up onto the bar next to mine. Her small, icy fingers entwined around the broad thumb of my right hand. "What's your story, Kurt?"

"Got no story."

She squeezed my thumb. "Who is Rachel?"

I shook the ice round in my glass and raised it to my lips. I glanced in the dim mirror. "None of your damn business."

"Everybody has a story. I have a hundred of them."

I smirked. "I bet you do."

She shook her head and pulled her long hair back over her shoulders. "Don't be quick to judge people." She smiled. "Now, the only way to forget a lost love is to find a new one. Don't you agree?"

I set my empty glass on the bar. *The girls all look pretty at closing time. Hell! Why not?* I turned to face her. "It's closing time here. Let's go down to my place and finish this conversation."

She took a deep sip from her glass then set it down on the bar. "Vicky cannot be had for just one drink. Do you like to gamble?"

"Sure, life is a gamble."

"Poker is my game." She leaned to the side slightly. Her long, dark hair fanned out away from her face. She placed a deck of cards on the bar. "You can learn a lot about someone when you watch him play cards— especially poker for silver and gold. I only play for silver or gold."

I laughed. "Silver or gold! Hell, the most I got is a twenty. Is that enough to play your game?"

She finished her drink in one swallow. "Thanks for the drink, Kurt."

"Hey, wait a minute. How much do you want?"

I turned on the barstool and watched her walk toward the door. Her tight, black skirt moved with the rhythm of a forbidden song. At the door she paused and looked back before pushing into the darkness of the hallway.

My stool almost tumbled to the floor as I hurried after her. I hit my head on the doorjamb when I tried to push my way into the hall. I took a half-step back and pulled the door open.

As I stumbled up the stairs, the hotel seemed to shift from light to darkness, like a flickering oil lamp. I reached the second floor and staggered down the hall. The doors to the rooms were all closed. At the last door I heard laughter and I put my hand on the knob, the door swung open. The room was darker than the hallway. I felt her small hand in mine. She led me to the bed.

That night in the dark I had a crazy dream or dreams. It was like being in a big movie theater with a screen as big as the wall, but the show kept flashing from one movie to a different one. First

I was home with Rachel, and then I was in Vietnam. Next I was racing my Honda up endless winding canyons, fighting dangerous crosswinds and rumbling over towering steel bridges. Her arms tightened around me, her voice cried for me, "Faster, faster." I buried the speedometer well past the double zeros, and still I raced on. With a flash the road vanished and we jetted off into the darkness.

I jumped to my left and the bike sailed away. With a loud thump I made a hard landing on the floor beside the bed. Slowly I pulled myself up to kneeling position, my knees and arms trembling. "A dream? It was just a dream. But which dream?"

I climbed to standing and waited for my eyes to adjust to the dim light. Slowly the images of the room came into view – the queen-size bed, the bedside table and a chair by the large double windows. There she was, standing at the doorway, the light from the hall framing her figure in that tight, black skirt and silky blouse.

"Come with me Kurt. Hurry."

Seconds seemed like hours and I rushed to pull on my pants. When I reached the door, she was already at the top of the stairs.

"Where are we going?" I asked, out of breath when I reached her.

She took my arm and started down the stairs. "To the lake."

Cold air greeted my face like water shot from a hose when we stumbled outside. I held her tightly and we walked across the road.

"We must hurry," she whispered. "Down to the lake. Down to the lake."

One step off the road and I fell. She knelt beside me and whispered, "You must follow me down to the water. Come. You must come with me."

I forced myself to stand, putting all my weight on my left leg. She slipped my right arm around her shoulders and we started walking again. I heard my name being called, turned my head and fell.

The next morning when I awoke I was back in my own bed in the little house. It's all so weird. I could recall drinking at the Soiled Dove Saloon and I could recall meeting Vicky. How much of what we did at the hotel was real I was not sure. The strange thing was Gladys had told me Hotel Hope wasn't open, and hadn't been, for years. I had never been in the upstairs of that place but I was sure I had spent the night up there with Vicky.

Anna brought my lunch but she just left the sandwiches and hurried off. That afternoon I went up to the café and talked with her. I told her I had been out drinking the night before and would never do that again.

Later that afternoon I stopped over to visit with Betty. She asked me where I went with Anna the day before. I told her, and being the storyteller that I am, I included my visit to the Soiled Dove Saloon last night. For once she listened instead of interrupting to tell a story of her own.

I ended the story with leaving the hotel in the dark of night.

Betty nodded and looked around the porch at her invisible audience. She turned to me and asked, "Can't you swim?"

"Of course I can swim."

"But you didn't go with Vicky to the lake. Why?"

I shrugged my shoulders. "Don't know. Don't know how much of that story is real and how much is a dream of a Marine who had too much to drink."

She looked over her shoulder as if speaking to someone standing behind her. "Kurt will know some day. Yes, some day he will know. Vicky grows stronger with each conquest."

Chapter 9
Anna: Spanish Joe Story

I was concerned that Kurt would hurt himself if he went drinking again at the saloon. The next day I went to the café early to talk with Gladys. She had a visitor— Joseph Trevino. Everyone called him Spanish Joe. He lived in a shack down below the town. He had one of those metal detectors. Treasure hunting wasn't thought of very highly by the other folks in Hope. A thief is what some call him because he never tried to find the owner of something he found, he just sold it. He was showing us some of the things he had found that week and began telling a strange story.

In 1969, the Corps of Engineers lowered the lake early so they could inspect the dam. Every day Joe would walk the new shoreline with that metal detector, hunting for stuff. Out near Trestle Creek, he spotted what looked like a big turtle in the mud. He watched it for a week before the lake was low enough for him to walk out there. Joe wore big rubber boots three sizes too large. He walked like a toddler and sounded like a horse.

The turtle turned out to be an old wooden boat turned over in the mud. Joe checked with his wand the area near the boat and found some coins. Some coins! I should say a lot of coins. He also found a silver chain with a cross. He washed off the coins and the necklace as best he could and put them in the old bucket he carried. If there were coins around the boat there might be more coins under the boat. So Joe took his shovel and dug until he had one side of the boat clear. That took most of the afternoon. But Joe was sure he'd find more treasure under the boat.

He used the shovel to pry the side of the boat up and looked underneath. He had found something all right. It wasn't what he wanted. Under the boat was what looked like a man laying face down and wrapped in a blanket. Joe nearly jumped out of his skin. He lowered the side of the boat, picked up his bucket and his metal detector and squished his way back to his shack. The next day he came to the Hotel Hope, told Gladys his story and asked her to call the sheriff.

That morning they sent a deputy out and Joe took him to the boat stuck in the mud. The boat was still there but when they pried it up out of the mud there was no one under it.

The joke was on Joe. It wasn't a man at all but two dozen bottles of whiskey wrapped in a large blanket. The story that circulated quickly around town was that Spanish Joe had finally found what he had been looking for all year, but didn't recognize it. He imagined there was someone under the boat because his conscience was bothering him for stealing from the dead.

Gladys was a friend of Joe's and she helped him sell his little treasures. Joe also had a friend who sold things at the flea market in Sagle. Gladys knew the value of coins. You see she had traveled with Peter whenever she could during his military career. They collected coins from all over the world.

Gladys first scrubbed the coins lightly with a brush and then added some detergent to the mix. She rinsed the coins in warm water, dried them carefully and then polished them with mercury. She used tweezers to remove the coins, one at a time. "Well, these three are silver dollars. Looks like the date on this one is 1914." She held up the lone gold coin, "Canadian Maple Leaf a twenty-dollar coin. Worth a lot more today."

Joe grinned. "I knew when I saw it that it was the best find."

"No. This is the best find." Gladys held up a silver chain with an amulet. "You must try to find the owner."

Gladys handed the chain to me. "Here, Anna, what do you make of this?"

I told her I thought the amulet was the Greek letter tau and it might have belonged to someone in a sorority. I turned it over and noted there was something inscribed on the back. I showed it to Joe. "Look, there is a name here. Perhaps the owner."

Gladys took the tau from the chain and scrubbed the back lightly with a soapy rag, rinsed it and handed it back to me. The name Anna was engraved in fancy script.

I laughed, "My name is Anna. Can I have it?"

Joe snatched the amulet from my hand. "No way. I found it in the lake. If it was lost with these coins, it was lost long ago. Who knows, maybe she drowned in the lake? It's mine to sell now."

Gladys sat back in her chair. "I don't think it's the letter tau but instead a crucifix. The owner is likely Catholic. Just let me try to find the girl."

Joe blessed himself, kissed the cross and then smiled. "There must be a hundred Annas in Idaho." He pointed at me. "Just like her, they will all want it. She couldn't have dropped this in the lake when that old boat turned over. But if I start looking for Anna there will be a dozen like her claiming they lost a silver crucifix. I'll sell it at the market."

Gladys knew all about people who live or had lived in Hope. I thought she was going to launch into one of her stories but she didn't. She simply asked, "Did you find this in that boat on the Pack River Flats?"

Joe grinned, "No. Not in the boat. I found the cross and chain a few yards away closer to the docks here in town. It could have come from another boat. Maybe it was lost when the girl was swimming."

"What about the whiskey you found wrapped in that blanket?"

He shook his head. "The deputy took that away. He said it didn't have the state tax seal on it. Hell! It was old enough that there was no seal back then." His dark eyes grew wider, "You know what? I bet that boat belonged to a bootlegger. That's what I think."

Gladys nodded, "Good guess."

Joe smiled. "I'll keep the chain and crucifix until summer. There are no tourists here now anyway."

After he left, Gladys asked me to go tell Betty that Joe had found an old boat with whiskey bottles wrapped in blanket. I left without telling Gladys about Kurt's drinking. When I told Betty the story she said it was proof that the story she told me about Vicky was true.

I argued that finding the boat did not prove that she ever made it to Hope. On the contrary, it is proof they both drowned. Betty was quick to reply.

"They both drowned all right but only Vicky has been seen in town since then."

Chapter 10
Kurt: One Step at a Time

The week after getting my cast removed passed slowly. The happy feeling of being free was followed by dark thoughts. I could walk short distances without the aid of a crutch but I paid a heavy price in pain. My general rule was to avoid pain pills; I'd seen good men get addicted to all forms of narcotics. It wasn't going to happen to me.

I read the manual about my Honda and spent hours taking it apart and putting it back together. Until the parts for the front fork arrived, I couldn't move it out of the garage. Afternoons I didn't work on the bike; I spent them walking the town. I used my crutch but avoided the hills at first. Soon I became bored walking back and forth on the same few roads so I tried going down to the lake and then back up the hill. It was a long walk the first time and I was exhausted after the climb back up to my house. I took it as a challenge, vowing to be able to walk to the lake and back without my crutch in two weeks. The next morning I went down the hill to the city docks using my crutch, but abandoned it once I got there. The rocky shore was hard to walk on and a real challenge for my right leg. When I turned around and started walking back to the docks I saw Anna running down the road toward me.

When she drew near, she put her arms out. I raised my arms and stepped back. "I'm all right. I don't need your help to walk."

She put her fists on her hips. "Of course you don't. I was just going to give you a hug."

"Go for it." I spread my arms wide. She put her arms in front of her and stood still. I stepped closer and whispered, "Anna, I could really use a hug."

I didn't know how much that statement was true until my arms held her tight. She wore a winter coat and I had my leather jacket on but still a wave of warmth stirred within me. She must have felt something too, but she stepped back quickly.

"Just a hug," she said. Anna took my hand and we walked back to the dock where I got my crutch.

"I'm so proud of you. You made it all the way down here. I was watching from my window. Kurt, you are getting well so fast."

I put my crutch under my right arm and started back toward the hill. Anna went to my left side and took my hand. We walked all the way back to Centennial Street, crossed the railroad tracks and started up the hill.

"Did you ever see the China Train?" I asked Anna.

"No. What's the China Train?"

"Years ago when lots of Chinese lived in Hope, they used to ship the bones of their dead back to China. An unscrupulous guy who worked for the railroad made a deal. They would pay in gold and he'd put the boxes of bones on the midnight train."

"Oh no. This sounds like another one of Betty's ghost stories."

I shrugged. "It is. Anyway the guy took their gold, put the boxes on the train and then, when the train was going out across the inlet out there, he tossed the boxes off. Now, when the China Train comes at midnight you can see the Chinese come out of the lake and put the boxes of bones back on the train."

Anna laughed. "More ghosts. You don't believe in such things do you?"

"It was a neat story. Can't you just see an old steam engine chugging to a stop, at midnight of course? It would really shake the house."

"Sounds like I need to get you some more newspapers to read."

I nodded. "Next time we go to Sandpoint, I'll buy a novel. That Honda manual has no plot at all."

Anna smiled. "I hope it has a happy ending."

After that day I made it a routine to walk down to the docks each morning. I'd look for Anna before walking the shoreline a short distance. The days she came down to the docks were warmer, regardless of the weather. The days she didn't come, I forced myself to walk farther without the aid of my crutch. Saturday morning she was so out of breath when we met that she must have run all the way down the hill.

"Bill called this morning. The parts for your motorcycle are in."

I dropped my crutch and gave her a big hug. This time she didn't step away.

"I asked Gladys if we could go over to Sandpoint today."

She shook her head but her arms still held me tight.

"Monday," she said with a smile. "Sunday we have to go to Sandpoint for church. Mom insisted we go. Monday morning we take Gladys' Tr-car and go to Sandpoint."

I gave her a quick kiss on her cheek. "Monday it is."

She blinked twice. "What was the kiss for?"

"Always reward the bearer of good news."

She leaned back but her arms remained locked around me. "I thought the news was better than that."

I put my right hand behind her head and guided her lips to mine. I swear, despite the winter coats I could feel our bodies heat up. We stepped apart and looked up toward Gladys' house on the hill. I leaned down and picked up my crutch. Anna took my hand and we started back down the road. When we got to my house, she said good-bye and ran up to Gladys' house.

At noon Anna returned with my lunch. I had straightened up the living room and kitchen and hoped she would stay while I ate. She gave me the lunch at the door and left without a word. At first I was angry. Then, as I watched her walk back up the short road to Gladys' house, my anger vanished. She didn't want to come in because she too felt something had changed. One kiss was all it was. She was promised to another, but that kiss said 'I love you.' I heard it loud and clear. Most surprisingly, I knew I loved her too. It wasn't just a physical attraction, it was a deeper feeling. Anna was a beautiful person. She had been more than kind to me, but it was her nature to be kind. She expressed interest in my feelings. She was cheerful when I was down. Even while doing a simple thing like fixing my bike, she expressed concern and wanted to help. If a kiss was a message of thanks for good news, I knew what I wanted to do to express my love for her. But she was not mine. She would never be mine, and any strong moves by me would only make it harder for me to leave Hope.

That night I sat on the couch in the living room with the lights out, just looking up the hill at the widow's watch on the second floor of the house above the road. A few times I thought I saw someone at the window, but there was no light on in the room so I couldn't be sure. I must have fallen asleep, for when I awoke I heard a man yelling.

"Help me! Somebody help me."

I got up from the couch and moved silently to the window. A big man in boots and black overalls stood in the middle of the road. He shook his fist and waved a double-headed ax in the air, yelled for help once more and then walked on toward Hotel Hope. I checked to see if the door to the house was locked, then went back to the bedroom. As I got in bed I checked the time on my watch. It was just after midnight in Hope.

Chapter 11
Anna: Back to Sandpoint

That Monday, Kurt and I made a second trip to Sandpoint to get the parts for his motorcycle. We had been having a running discussion about religion. He acted like he had never been inside a church or had any idea why someone would go to church. It was all an act. When I gave him a copy of the Book of Mormon, he jerked his hands back like he was afraid to touch it.

He joked, "Now, I better stay clear of this. That Brigham Young guy had three dozen wives. That's far too ambitious for me."

"Brigham Young was a man. He was a strong man and a smart man. Without his leadership the church would have suffered greatly. He led them out of danger in Illinois and on to safety in Utah. And he didn't have three dozen wives, only twenty-seven."

Kurt scratched his chin with his fingers, "Now, Anna, how would you like to have twenty sister wives?"

"It's not the way we are anymore. It was necessary at one time. And Brigham Young wasn't the first prophet to have several wives. Have you ever read the Bible? Solomon had many more wives than that and he was a great and wise prophet."

"He may have had many wives but Sheba had no trouble seducing him. Of course if she looked anything like Gina Lollobrigida, I can see why he couldn't resist."

"Is all you know about religion what you saw in the movies?"

"Yul Brenner wouldn't lie."

"The movie was far from the truth. Sheba didn't seduce Solomon; he was the one who tricked the queen into his bed. She was hesitant to stay over night in his palace because she had heard of his lustful ways. He told her if she took nothing of his he'd take nothing from her. That night she awoke thirsty and drank some water from an urn in the palace. He awoke and told her now she had taken something of his; he was no longer bound by his words."

"I bet they had ham for dinner that night. It's nice and salty."

"The Jews didn't eat pork. Don't you read the Bible?"

"You do, so you tell me how many women did Solomon have?"

"According to the Bible his wives and concubines numbered in the thousands."

Kurt shook his head. "I would settle for one."

"Does she have to look like Gina Lollobrigida?"

He winked. "No, Gina is too short. I like them a little taller."

It was an interesting exchange. I knew he was just egging me on. That comment about height brought the discussion back to us. I was almost at tall as Kurt. My height bothered me with some guys but it never did with Kurt.

We stopped at the Mobil station to get the parts for his motorcycle first. Bob and Kurt checked the repair book for the CB750 to be sure Kurt had the wrenches and screwdrivers needed, as well as the parts. From the Mobil station we went shopping. Kurt bought another pair of pants and a sweater. He had not come expecting to spend the winter. We also stopped at a bookstore. He wanted some books to read because television was such a bore. He admitted that he hadn't read the book I gave him.

We shopped at a corner used bookstore. He picked up a copy of a Louis L'Amour book off the first rack in the store. We wandered around the narrow aisles bumping into each other. The books were sorted by subject, to a degree. He stopped at one shelf in the very back and selected another book. The first looked like a paperback novel but it was by Isaac Asimov, *The Human Brain*. The last book he selected was a paperback, but a size bigger, and it was an even bigger surprise—*Men of Mathematics*. I can't remember the author. I was shocked.

"Do you like science and math?" I asked.

He nodded, "I had a mixed major of math and biology. You read the bible; I read science and people like Louis and Zane."

"Zane?"

"Zane Grey. I highly recommend *Rider of the Purple Sage*."

We walked around town a little more just to window shop. Kurt had blown his cover; he wasn't the uneducated, former Marine drifter he first appeared to be. I should have guessed. He didn't ride an old Harley. He rode a new Honda. He didn't cuss or swear and he was polite and courteous. What he had hidden was his education. Math and biology. What was he thinking? Those two never mix. I was impressed. I struggled with algebra. His reference to *Riders of the Purple Sage* had a meaning too. He was like the gunslinger in that story who rode into a small town in Utah and stirred up everything. When we crossed the street, he took my hand in his. It was a simple gesture but it was so nice of him. We stopped to check out the marquee at the Panida Theater and realized we were still holding hands. He gave my hand a squeeze and asked, "What would your mother say if we went to the show?"

True Grit was playing and there was a matinee that day. It was an odd movie with John Wayne as the star. At first we sat close and shared popcorn. By the end of the show he had his arm around my shoulders. Mom was upset; as it was dark by the time we got back to Hope. She asked what took us so long and I told her we had gone to the movies.

"Did he try anything?" Mom asked.

I told her he was a perfect gentleman at the show. "Mom, we both know he's leaving as soon as he can get his motorcycle fixed."

That seemed to reassure her, but it snowed that week and we both knew he would not be leaving right away, even if he did get his motorcycle put back together.

I looked for Kurt every morning when he'd go for his walk down to the docks and back. Sometimes I would go with him; other times I'd just watch him through the telescope. Of course we spoke each day when I took Kurt and Betty their lunches. He was always working on that bike. A few times I stopped to help him with something that needed more than two hands to do. I worked the afternoon-to-dinner shift at the café. Some days he would walk up to the café. He'd come about two, just after the lunch rush was over and Gladys had gone home. I'd take my break and sit at the table with him.

Some days I'd bring Betty her lunch, and then hurry down to see Kurt. He was a real storyteller. He told me of his first trip on the big Honda. He went up to Rocky Mountain National Park. He described the little town up there—Estes Park. He must have spent a lot of time just walking around. He described it so well. He also talked of the ride. Riding that motorcycle was his release from the world. He didn't tell me then, but I knew it wasn't the war that sent him wandering. No, some girl had broken his heart. He needed me to listen because he didn't have anyone else. He was like a little boy who had run away from home, but he was a man.

I asked him about college. He had graduated from Colorado State University. His major professor tried to talk him into going on to graduate school. He applied to enter the College of Veterinary Medicine. He thought he was about to be drafted so he enlisted in the Marines. The college said they would hold his application until he was discharged. He could get his military obligation over and then go back to school. It didn't work out like he planned. The university scene changed to an anti-war atmosphere. After he was discharged from the Marines he took a job in Wyoming, but in spring he quit and took off on a long motorcycle ride around the West. He had no destination in mind when that moose made him stop in Hope.

He began to notice me, or let himself show that he noticed. It was cold that winter and I often wore slacks to work, but sometimes I'd wear one of my short skirts. When I did, I'd wear pantyhose too. After all, it was cold. Kurt would always say something not crude but complimentary, like, "Anna, you look like you are dressed for a banker's office. Lucky banker."

He got mail at our house. He got two letters from Michael Banner PhD. at the University of Colorado. Kurt told me that Dr. Banner wanted him to come to CU and major in mathematics. So you can see, he wasn't dumb. He also got two from Fort Collins, one from his younger brother Danny and one from Rachel. Like a fool, I had to make a sly remark.

"Who's Rachel? I'm jealous."

His answer was quick. "Just someone I knew once. You have nothing to be jealous about. We're just friends."

I knew he was lying. Whoever this Rachel is I felt he wanted her more than me.

Slowly I was putting a story to the man. He couldn't go back to school right away because of the anti-war atmosphere; he couldn't go home because of some argument with his older brother. I also knew I was growing fond of him and wanted him to stay all winter. He was preparing to leave.

Despite her apprehensions about Kurt, Mom continued to make lunches for him and Betty. Maybe Gladys had convinced her it was the Christian thing to do. One day after Kurt had his motorcycle running, he'd even rolled it out onto the street and back into the garage. I asked for a ride. He shook his head. "Not yet. We'd go around in a circle. I haven't got the fork on straight. I'll have to take it off and start over tomorrow."

"I have another letter for you."

"Who from?"

"Rachel."

"Put it in the trash."

"I will not." I carried the letter and his lunch in and put them on the kitchen table. He put his bike back in the garage and hurried inside. He went first to the bathroom and washed his hands, and then came out to the table.

"Okay, give me the letter." His voice was stern.

I turned the letter over and read the name on the back, "Rachel Johnson. Is she your wife?"

He didn't reach for the letter. Instead he sat down across the table from me. "Rachel is my brother's wife."

I handed him the letter. He tore it open and read it. I waited. It was a two-page, hand-written letter. When he had finished reading, he looked up.

"I met Rachel in college. I was a senior and she was just a freshman. We dated and fell in love. At least I did. I gave her a ring when I graduated and told her I didn't want to be married until I came back from the Marines" He looked down, "I was in Vietnam when I got the Dear John letter. She had married my brother."

"I'm sorry," I said.

"It's over as far as I'm concerned but read the letter."

I told him I didn't want to read the letter. He insisted. It was in some ways a love letter saying how much she missed him and worried about him, but then there were comments about how her husband, his brother, didn't understand her. It ended "With love, Rachel."

I handed the letter back. He shrugged, took the letter and tore it in half. "That's why I'm in no hurry to go back home. I've got to go back, but it's going to be hard."

I took his hand and led him to the couch in the living room. "Now sit down."

He sat at the far end of the couch and I sat down as close to him as I could. "It sounds like Rachel still has a thing for you. That can't work out if she is married to your brother, so don't think about her."

I put my hand on the side of his face and turned him toward me. "Look at me. Stop thinking about Rachel." I kissed him lightly on his lips. "I'm sure if you try, you will find someone else." His arms circled my shoulders, his kisses were warm. I pushed him gently away and stood up. He smirked. "I thought you'd do that."

"Move over. You're almost sitting on the arm of the couch." He moved over a little and sat with his arms along the back of the couch. I leaned forward and put my hands on his broad shoulders. I sat down sideways on his lap and nestled my head on his shoulder. "Now, let's see we were kissing like old friends."

This time his lips were hot and his hands were warm. They rubbed my neck and then slowly down to my breasts, like a gentle massage. I pushed his hands down to my lap and then I unbuttoned my blouse. I wanted him to know he would be loved again, someday. He showed me how much I missed being loved.

The next day when I came to his house we didn't make out or even kiss. We just talked. I told him about my father's death and why we moved to Hope. I told him how much I wanted to go back to college. He understood. He listened. He even listened when I told him about Sam.

Chapter 12
Kurt Finds Hope in Hope

Anna was an angel. No, make that Anna was a Saint. That was a big problem because I was Catholic, even though it had been awhile since I'd seen the inside of a church. There was another problem too— she was promised to Sam. It wasn't an engagement but it was close enough to make me shiver. My brother Danny had stolen my girl while I was off in Nam. I didn't want to do that to Sam.

Anna was the kind of girl a young man both desires and fears. She was so nice and wholesome that I would feel guilty if I made any sexual remarks. I felt guilty the first time I kissed her. I knew I wasn't good enough for her. She could do better, and she knew she could do better. Why she kissed me back, I will never know. Perhaps she was lonely.

After my cast was off, I tried to do everything. I didn't use that crutch one day and was so sore the next I had to use it to get to walk to the bathroom. After a while I made a point not to use it when I went to the café, but I hopped around on it a lot at the house. Pride was my enemy. I wanted to walk tall, to be someone Anna would be happy to see. From the start I knew I wouldn't get very far with her, and I didn't want to get very close either. A woman can be like a fire on a cold night. The closer you get, the closer you want to get, until you get burnt. Telling her about Rachel sparked a lot of memories.

I hadn't planned to be in Hope. In fact, I never planned to drift. That was my problem from the start. You see, I was going to be drafted the year I graduated from college. As soon as my deferment ran out my number was up. I foxed them. I enlisted in the Marines for three years. It was an impulsive move but I wanted to put my military obligation behind me and I needed to think I had some control how I did it. Boy, was I wrong. You see I had a girl. She was just a freshman at Colorado State University. In three years she would graduate and I would get out of the Marines. We even picked our wedding date. I sold my car to pay for an engagement ring. Man, I thought I was so smart.

Nothing worked as I had planned. They didn't send me to pilot training like they said. There were several aviation positions in the Marine Corps, but someone decided I was better suited to carry an M-16. They shipped me to Pendleton for my basic, and then on to Nam. I got a week's leave between the two assignments. I came home, Rachel skipped class and we had one wild week together.

The first six months I was in Nam. I got a letter every week. Then they stopped. I knew something was wrong. Three months later I got the Dear John.

I survived Vietnam, even got a Purple Heart. Hell, I was wounded three times; they should have given me at least one. It wasn't a war like you read about. It was just a series of battles, some big, some small. They said they would kill us all. They tried. They did kill some of us. We took pride in just being alive. I grew to hate it, and yet I get mad when someone who was never there talks about Vietnam.

After I got back home, I did go back to the school. I had a choice to take either math at UC or go to vet school at CSU. The campus in Boulder was different from Fort Collins. I ran into a few peace creeps. They marked me as military by my haircut, I guess. We exchanged a lot of words and I knew I couldn't go back to school, at least not there. I checked out Fort Collins. The campus wasn't as bad but it was too close to my family. I knew if I went to CSU I'd run into them; I'd run into Rachel for certain. I went back to the military and signed on as a civilian mechanic at the Air Force base up in Cheyenne. I lasted only one year and I had had enough of the military. I just wanted to be me. I had bought a motorcycle—a Honda CB750. I rode so fast I don't know why I didn't kill myself. At the end of summer I asked for three weeks leave. They turned down my request, so I quit and hit the road. I went everywhere. Up to the Black Hills. All over Colorado and Wyoming. Most of the time I camped out, but soon it started getting cold up in Montana. I turned west and planned to go on to the coast but I was running out of money. A moose in Idaho ended my trip. Now it looks like I will be stuck in Hope for the winter.

When I met Anna, she was like an angel sent from heaven. I tried to resist, but I fell instantly in love. She was a Mormon and I knew what baggage that would bring with it. Every time she brought up religion I'd counter with some comment about how many wives Brigham Young had. That didn't faze her at all; she had answers for everything. One night when I was up at the café for dinner, she offered me a copy of the Book of Mormon to read. I declined. She left the book on the table and told me to save it for later. That same day I got two books in the mail so later became much later. That week I was walking pretty well, and I was bored to death. Gladys came to see me one night and asked how I was doing. She reminded me that on the day I moved into the house she had set some rules. No smoking. No alcohol. No loud music or parties. That night she added another no-no.

"It is apparent that you and Anna are becoming more than just friends," she said.

I smiled at Gladys and wondered what Anna had told her. I kept my reply brief. "I like Anna."

Gladys nodded slowly as she spoke. "Anna is promised to another man. He is on a mission for the church. A gentleman wouldn't take advantage of his absence to woo another man's woman."

I controlled my temper well that night. I told her I knew about the Mormons sending their young men off on missions, and had seen more than one not work out when the man returned.

"People change," I told her. "I don't think you can plan another person's life."

"What religion are you?" Gladys asked me.

I told her I was a Catholic, a Christian and a scientist. She laughed. "You are also a Marine. Kurt, I didn't worry about you while you were recovering, but now that you are a healthy young man I do worry about you. Men your age can't help but be sexually attracted to Anna. She, in turn, is drawn to you. We can't change human nature but I am asking you to not pursue her. Her mother and I have plans for Anna. That young man on his mission is her best future. If you think about it, you will agree with me."

I told her there was nothing serious between us. We were just friends. Gladys picked up the Book of Mormon that Anna had given to me. "Perhaps you don't consider it serious, but I began to worry when she gave you this. Anna is not the kind of woman to just have a fling with someone."

"Neither am I," I told her. "Gladys, just relax. We have discussed religion several times. It is just something to talk about."

Gladys looked at me and asked directly, "What are your intentions?"

"They are the same as when I came to this house. I plan to fix my bike and ride out of town."

"What about Anna?"

She had me. I couldn't lie. I took a deep breath and put my right hand in hers. "If I am lucky, I'll get a kiss good-bye. I'm not in love with Anna. That could happen but I won't let it happen."

"Why?"

I felt my hand shake a little and I replied, "She told me she has a boy friend and he's off on his mission. I'd be a heel to steal his girl while he's away."

Gladys held my hand in hers and smiled. "That sounds too noble but I know Anna will do the right thing. I don't want you to get hurt. Let's keep this conversation just between the two of us. I want you two to continue to be friends. How are you fixed for money?"

Gladys is the kind of person you don't want to lie to. I told her I planned to apply for a credit card and start for home once I felt the bike was road-worthy.

"I don't believe a young person should go in debt to the bank. There is a night job down at the service station at the north end of town. Why don't you work there for a few weeks, save your money and then go home?"

"I could leave next week if the bike is ready."

"I don't think so. I've seen you walk down to the docks. One way fine, but on the way back you use the crutch." She shook her head. "A long ride on that bike could be fatal. Besides, have you noticed the weather lately? There is snow on all the passes already. You'd never make it to Colorado. I like you, Kurt, and Anna didn't pull you out of that mud just to have you get in another accident on the way home. I don't want you to leave until you're healthy enough for the trip and the roads are safe." She let go of my hands. "Take that job at the gas station. Keep up your walking exercise and come to my house for Thanksgiving dinner. We'll talk about leaving when you are sure that bike is ready for a long ride."

"Who do I see about the job?" I asked.

That afternoon I told Betty I was going to work at the gas station in the north end of town.

"Well, look out for Mad Freddy," she said.

"Who's Mad Freddy?"

"He was a logger. Didn't work for none of those big companies. He did it all himself. He fell logs, bucked them up and loaded them on his old flatbed truck. Made his living selling firewood to people in Sandpoint and for a few folks around here who were too lazy to cut their own. Trouble is, he never got no permit to cut wood. The Forest Rangers were always after him. One night in November, after a storm in which the rain turned to snow, he was up cutting trees on Lightning Creek. He got his truck stuck and had to walk all the way back to town to get someone to pull him out. None of the logging company truckers would do it 'cause they thought of him as stealing their logs. Well, when he got to town he walked the street, yelling for someone to help him. But no one would. Now this young fella, Rick was working the night shift at the gas station. Mad Freddy threatened to cut his head off with his ax if he didn't take the wrecker parked out behind the station and go pull him out. Rick knew Freddy wasn't playing with a full deck, so he agreed that after he was done working he would take the wrecker up Lightning Creek and see if he could pull Freddy's truck out. Freddy met Rick at the Soiled Dove Saloon, about midnight and the two of them set out for Lightning Creek."

"Did they get the truck out of the woods?" I asked.

"You bet'ya. The Forest Service pulled it out the next spring. They found the wrecker too, stuck in Lightning Creek. Never did find Rick or Mad Freddy."

I smiled. "Well, I'm not going there to drive a wrecker. I'll just sell gas."

"That's just what Rick would have said. Be careful, Kurt, they say Mad Freddy won't stop until he gets his truck back."

"What does this ghost logger look like?" I asked with a chuckle.

"Big man, high boots, black overalls and he always carries a double-headed ax. You watch out for him, Kurt. Mad Freddy is trouble."

Chapter 13
Anna: Thanksgiving

After Kurt took the job at the gas station, he still went for walks down to the docks in the mornings. Later in the afternoon, he'd walk to the gas station. The place also sold a few items like beer, magazines and candy. When I brought lunch to his house, he was still asleep. I banged on the door until he came and let me in.

"Sorry, Anna. The late shift doesn't end until midnight. Last night they had me clean up the place after it closed."

After that, I would set my alarm clock for midnight and watch for him through the telescope. The temperature was down in the teens at night. Kurt continued to work on his bike each day, and before Thanksgiving he was riding it to work and back. I worried because it might snow, and you can't ride a motorcycle in the snow. Then it dawned on me, the mountain passes in Montana had snow already. He couldn't go home.

I was elated when Gladys told me she had invited Kurt to Thanksgiving dinner. Mother was not so happy about it. But when she was fixing lunches for Kurt and Betty that day, she asked me if I thought he'd like pumpkin pie.

"His favorite pie is apple," I told her.

"And how do you know that?"

"It was what he ordered when we went to lunch in Sandpoint."

"You're getting to know this man too well." She looked toward the kitchen window. "I hear that motorcycle again. It must be fixed. When is he leaving?"

"I don't want him to leave," I said. Mother almost dropped the jar of peanut butter.

"Anna, his leg is recovered and that loud motorcycle is fixed. It's time he went home."

I nodded but countered, "There is snow on the passes in Montana. You can't ride a motorcycle in snow."

"Where is he from?"

"Colorado."

"East side or west side?"

"Fort Collins. That's east side. North of Denver."

Mom shook her head and mumbled, "The other side of the mountains. He could be here all winter."

My heart leaped at her comment. Kurt and I weren't technically lovers, at least not by any current physical standards. A kiss or two only meant you liked each other. Still, I grew excited every time I saw him, and I didn't want him to leave.

Thanksgiving was very different than I expected.

Hope was a small town, and I knew my Mother would not approve if she knew how I really felt about Kurt. He was a handsome young man. He was a little on the wild side. Not really so wild as Mother thought he was; just a free spirit. Although I was promised, I didn't have an engagement ring. The other men in town were so on the rough side. Not bad but good, hard-working men. They just lacked charisma. Kurt had it in spades. He called Gladys my beautiful sister, and me, hers.

He arrived just a little early. Of course, I had asked him to come early. He wore that big, black leather jacket. It made his shoulders look so broad, so strong. It was heavy, too. While Gladys and Mother finished fixing the dinner, we sat in the living room and talked.

He told me a story of Colorado. When he first got his new bike, he went on a ride alone up the Cache La Poudre River to Chambers Lake. He loved taking trips on back roads and he liked telling me about those trips. He was a good storyteller.

Mother came into the living room and listened to Kurt's story. She also asked some very direct questions. You see, Peter's death in Vietnam was still on her mind. She must have thought Kurt was on the run from the draft. Learning that he had been in the Marines and had served in Vietnam calmed some of her fears. He acted like a young, carefree man but he was really so old and so lonely. His clever stories were a cover for his fears. Now I sound like a grandmother, but back then I thought he was exciting, like a fresh breeze from the lake.

Everything happened in his story about going to Chambers Lake. It was so exciting. I felt myself leaning to one side or the other as he told of riding up the canyon and through the tunnel, where the canyon was so narrow there was no room for a road. I could see the snow-capped peaks reaching over 13,000 feet with my eyes wide open. But even more, I felt his stories were the only way he thought he could take me with him.

Gladys had purchased a big turkey. It was a wild bird and not a very fat one. She made the dressing from St. Maries wild rice. I'd never had that before and bet Kurt hadn't either. He ate a big helping of rice and called Gladys and my mother the two best cooks in all of Idaho. He certainly knew how to charm the ladies that day.

All through dinner Mother asked Kurt questions. He answered them courteously, although a few were rather personal. He told her he had graduated from college and then enlisted in the Marines to get his military obligation behind him. It hadn't turned out as he had planned. He wanted to be a pilot. The Marines put him in aviation, but as a mechanic, and then they changed that. He never told me what they changed it to. Mom asked what he planned to do after he returned home. Kurt said he'd likely go back to school. He had some GI bill funds he could use. He hadn't decided where he would do that. It had been almost four years since he left college, and it would be hard to readjust to student life. She asked only one question— about his family missing him this time of the year. His answer stopped any further questions in that direction. "The home I left isn't the one I came back to after Vietnam. Some things happened while I was gone that I couldn't accept. I'll get over it. In a way, being here in Hope has helped." My mother quickly switched her questions to how and when he planned to return to Colorado. That's when Kurt told her about checking daily with the Montana Highway Department to see if the passes were still snow-packed. It was obvious to me that Mother was asking when he planned to leave, but he didn't take offense.

After dinner we went back into the living room. Gladys and Mother cleaned up the dishes. Mother even brought us some pie. I think she wanted to make amends for all the questions she asked Kurt. He told me she was just being a mother protecting her naive daughter. We sat side by side on the couch, and when he finished his pie he turned to me and said, "That was so good I should kiss the cook."

"Mother did most of the cooking," I protested.

He did kiss me on the cheek. I was so surprised I almost dropped my plate. I looked up at the doorway certain I'd see Mother standing there. She wasn't, so I kissed him back. I couldn't just sit on the couch and kiss him. Who knows what Mother would have done? So I took our plates into the kitchen. Kurt was right behind me. He thanked both Mother and Gladys for the dinner and wished them the best for next year. I think he even said it in a Christian way. "God bless you both," or something like that. Then he announced he was leaving.

I went to get his coat, then called to the kitchen, "Mother, I'm going to walk Kurt down to the main street. Be back in a minute."

We walked down the road to a spot near the mailbox where I knew Mom and Gladys couldn't see us from the living room windows. He told me he had his bike fixed and offered to take me for a ride. I told him I couldn't. He put his hands on my shoulders and kissed me. It wasn't a peck on the cheek, it was a real kiss. I felt warm all over. A woman doesn't know what she feels about a man until she kisses him. If he were leaving town on that motorcycle the next morning, I would have asked him to take me with him. But he didn't. He stayed for another month.

After he came to dinner and Mother got to see him up close, she started acting really worried. She and Gladys talked openly about how to get Kurt to leave town. They also kept a watch on me like I was still in junior high. I know Mom didn't follow me when I took Betty her meal but I bet she was watching from the window and keeping track of the time. The weather didn't cooperate. There was no snow yet in Hope, but the temperatures stayed below freezing all week. I remember the first day in December there was a freezing drizzle. I sat by my window that night and watched for Kurt to come home. I was watching for his motorcycle but instead I saw him walking up the road in the freezing rain.

The next day over breakfast Mother announced her plan. She and Gladys could help Kurt return home. They plotted a trip down through Washington to Spokane, and then on to Ritzville. Truckers used the roads through Washington and Oregon to Boise, Idaho, because they didn't include any high passes. From Boise, he could ride across southern Idaho and down to Salt Lake City. From there he would be on his own. He'd just have to wait for Wyoming to be clear of snow, and then ride home. I suggested they discuss this option with him, but Mother told me to say nothing. She had to make arrangements for places for him to stop along the way. He was short on funds, but if they could find people to let him stay overnight at towns along the way, he would see it was to his advantage to do so.

Chapter 14
Kurt: Thanksgiving

Gladys was being too nice to me. I felt obligated to her for so much. She had given me a place to stay while I recovered from the accident, saved my bike from the junkyard, and even made lunches for me each day. Now she had invited me to Thanksgiving dinner at her house and arranged for me to get a job at the gas station. It wasn't that I was ungrateful, it was overwhelming. I'd be in debt to her forever. Then I had lied to her. I told her that Anna and I were just friends, and I intended to ride off as soon as I could. I hedged my bets as I had accepted both the invitation to dinner and went to work at the place at the end of town. It is always easy to postpone a decision. I had told myself to get a little cash, and then split.

The first day on the job was strange. Debbie Addison, owner of the gas station, stayed the whole shift, from four to midnight. She kept busy, and in so doing, kept me busy also. I bet we cleaned and dusted every counter in the small shop twice. Some places looked like they hadn't been cleaned in a month. She made it clear she didn't hire me to just sit and wait for someone and come to buy gas. I swept and then mopped the two bays, even though one had a car in it.

We had only a dozen gas customers after six that night but they were all fill-ups, truckers or travelers who planned to drive most of the night. It is a long way between open gas stations in North Idaho and Western Montana at night. We also kept a coffee pot on the hot plate behind the counter. Part of my job was to offer any customer who filled their tank a free cup of coffee.

We did have one walk-in after six—a Mexican guy in worn clothes and muddy boots.

"Debbie, that coffee sure smells good on a cold night like this one."

"Don't track in here with those dirty boots. We just mopped the floor," Debbie responded, in a voice too loud for the occasion. There were only the three of us in the shop at the time.

He backed out the door but held it open and waited.

Debbie turned to me. "Take Joe a cup of coffee. Be sure to put a lid on it. Don't want coffee spilt on this clean floor."

I filled a paper cup, pushed the lid down firm and carried it to the door. "Here you are Jose. Have a nice night."

"Gracias. Good night, Debbie."

When he departed Debbie told me his name was Joseph Trevino, but everyone in town called him Spanish Joe. "He's not the most popular man in town. He's dirty, makes a living finding junk along the highway and the shoreline of the lake. This time of the year when the lake level is low he goes poking his probe around on private property."

"His probe?" I asked.

"You know, one of those weird things that goes 'ding' when it detects a piece of metal."

"Oh, you mean a metal detector."

"Well, it ain't honest to find something along the shoreline of a cabin and keep it. You should take it to the person who owns the place; it most likely belongs to them." Debbie shook her head. "Take that mop and do behind that counter again."

I took the mop, dunked it into the bucket of hot water, squeezed it once and started to mop the area where I had just been standing. It was like being in the Marines— clean a clean spot just because the Sergeant couldn't think of something else to order you to do.

"Did Spanish Joe ever find anything of real value?"

"Why do you ask?"

I shrugged. "Well, you can't make a living finding change that someone lost out of their pocket when they went fishing."

"No, but you can find fishing rods that some kid dropped over the side of the boat and then sell them to tourists who come here to fish in the summer. He finds things that were lost years ago. This past fall he found an old boat out on the mud flats of the Pack River. It had a dozen bottles of whiskey under."

"Now, that's a prize." I backed up to the bucket and dunked the mop a few times.

"He got the fuzzy end of the lollipop on that one. The sheriff confiscated the liquor because it didn't have a state tax seal on the bottles."

I laughed. "I bet the sheriff and his deputies sampled the wares just to be sure it was good whiskey too."

"Last week, Joe came in trying to sell me a necklace he found. It was a silver chain with a cross on it. Strange cross. It didn't have a top piece. He said I could hang it by the cash register and sell it in a week. Of course he wants half of what I could sell it for."

I looked back at the counter. There was no chain. "Did you sell it already?"

"Of course not. Two reasons: he wanted fifty dollars for it and on the back the name Anna was engraved on it, so I'd have to sell it someone named Anna."

That night, as I walked home, I watched down the road for a logger carrying an ax. I didn't see one. I did stop at the Soiled Dove Saloon. It was closed but there was a dim light that allowed me to see a little inside. I squinted in an effort to see if there was a small, sexy woman sitting on one of the bar stools. I didn't see anyone. Vicky was not there that night.

The second night I worked, Debbie left minutes after I arrived. The shop was busy until about six and then it quieted down. Spanish Joe stopped by for a cup of coffee. I invited him in.

"Stomp your boots and come right over here. I can sweep that area if you leave any mud prints."

"Gracias, amigo."

"Name's Kurt. No problem. Debbie made me clean my boots when I came to work yesterday. She's a neat freak. It's nothing personal."

I filled a cup for him and set it on the counter.

"Debbie told me you are a treasure hunter. What could you find around here that would be worth anything?"

I found out that night how much Spanish Joe liked to tell about his exploits. If half of them were true, he'd be a rich man. He was as poor as any hobo who rode the rails heading west. I stopped to fill two cars with gas while he was there. At first I worried he might steal something from the shop while I was out pumping gas. As far as I could tell he only took the coffee. He reminded me what Betty had said about the ghosts in Hope. "They were lonely in life and now they are lonely in death." Spanish Joe was a prime candidate by Betty's criteria to someday haunt Hope.

He was there for an hour before he mentioned the chain and cross he had found. I pretended not to be interested. He took it from his coat pocket. It was wrapped in a dirty handkerchief. I took it and wiped it with a rag from under the counter.

"Looks nice. I bet it belonged to some fine lady. She must have lost it last summer when she was boating on the lake."

Spanish Joe waved both his hands over the necklace. "Oh, no! This is old. Really old." He nodded to me. "The woman who owned it is probably long gone from this life." He blessed himself. "Isn't it beautiful?"

I pushed back from the counter, like the necklace was a snake. "Betty tells me that around here the dead come back to Hope if they left something of value behind. Take it away."

"What does that old woman know? She lives just to tell stories to scare people. I know more about Hope that she does. Back when Hope was a stop on the NP, many rich people came here. It's a beautiful lake. Why, even Roosevelt stayed at Hotel Hope!"

In the next hour I had no other customers, so I listened to Spanish Joe tell one tale after another as possible origins of the necklace. They started with the very rich visitor from the old days in Hope, and progressed to the schoolgirls who came from Sandpoint last summer. With each story, the age and value of the silver chain and cross decreased. I paid only fifteen dollars for it.

Thanksgiving Day was cold and foggy. There was still frost on the road at ten in the morning when I walked up to Gladys' house. This gave her house a fresh, magical look. The quiet and the clean white look created a peace within me as I went up the driveway.

I felt embarrassed that I did not have a gift for Gladys. If they weren't Mormons, I'd have brought a bottle of Cabernet. I walked up onto the porch and Anna opened the door before I could knock.

"Hi! Happy Thanksgiving." She reached her arms around me and gave me a hug. I tried to turn my head in time to steal a kiss, but she spun back out of reach. "Come in and let me take your coat."

I took off my black leather jacket. She pulled it close in her arms. "I love the feel of leather." Taking my hand, she led me into the living room. "Our guest is here."

"Tell him to sit. The turkey is in the oven and the pies are cooling. I told him dinner wouldn't be until noon," Gladys called from the kitchen.

Anna called back, "I told him to come early so we could talk. He has such great stories."

She hung my jacket on a coat tree near the front door and hurried across the living room. "Have a seat. I'll be back in a moment."

I sat down in the largest of the chairs. It was set at an angle facing the television at the end of the room, but still allowing a clear view out the front window. It was like a dream. I had no right to be treated like this. These were nice people, and most of all she was a beautiful woman. I glanced around the room. On the wall, a photograph of a church with a tall, white steeple. Under it was a stand with the largest Bible I'd ever seen. I felt a tremor of fear up my back. What did I know of these people? What did they expect of me? I don't want to embarrass Anna.

She returned carrying two glasses. Anna was wearing a white blouse and a short, dark red skirt. The skirt was just barely knee length, and the fine lace around the neck of the blouse made it look to be very old, as did the white pearl buttons. She walked carefully as she crossed the room.

"Try this. It's punch. I made it myself."

I took a sip and said, "Simply delicious."

"Thank you," she whispered. "We don't drink beer, coffee or soda pop."

Anna then sat down on the couch at the end closest to my chair. I considered moving to the couch. Just as I rose to do so, Anna's mother entered the room.

"Stay seated, young man. You don't have to rise when I enter the room. Not at home anyway."

I rose anyway. "But a gentleman should always rise when a lady enters the room."

"You're a strange sort, Mr. Johnson. Where is your family from?"

I glanced over at Anna. Her cheeks turned slightly rosy. The inquisition was not of her making. I looked back at her mother. "I'm from Colorado. Family moved there from Virginia about twenty years ago. And before you ask, we are all Catholic. Except for me, they are good, practicing Catholics. I'm the rebel of the family."

I noticed her eyes were watching me closely. She didn't even blink before asking the next question. "Are you running from the draft?"

I chuckled and shook my head, "No, Ma'am. I did my duty. I didn't start running until I got back."

"Mother, I told you he was a Marine," Anna said.

Her mother looked only at me. "Why did you start running?"

I wanted to leave. I looked over at Anna and said, "I am lucky. A lot of guys came back in body bags. I don't know why I wasn't one of them, but I wasn't." I looked over at her mother. Her eyes softened a little.

"Oh, I see."

"No, you don't see. It's one thing to hear that someone has died in war; it's another to see it happen."

I glanced over at Anna then back at her mother. "There is another reason to run, but I don't want to speak of it today."

Anna shifted her position on the couch until she was facing her mother. "No more questions please, Mother." She turned and looked at me. "Kurt, tell us one of your stories about riding that motorcycle. Those are so much fun."

I waited to see if her mother would still ask another question. She didn't, so I began.

"In Colorado, just north of Fort Collins, is my home. The Cache La Poudre River cuts through the Front Range Mountains. It carved a narrow canyon from the divide down to the high plains. One morning I left home with a full tank and headed up the canyon."

I told of my first trip on my new motorcycle, up the canyon following the Cache La Poudre River to Chambers Lake. I tried to make the description of the steep canyon walls and the highway that went up over thirteen thousand feet more real that a slide show. The encounters with Bighorn sheep and elk came from another trip I took up to Rocky Mountain National Park, and I strived to make them as clear as the setting I placed them in. By the look in Anna's eyes I was having some success. I kept the story going for over an hour, in part to avoid another inquisition from Anna's mother and because both women seemed to be listening to me. Gladys even stuck her head in the room a few times and smiled. I had nothing to bring to this dinner but a story, so I made it the best story I ever told.

When we sat down for dinner, Anna's mother asked Anna to say the blessing. I was glad she didn't ask me. Roast turkey with wild rice dressing was the centerpiece of the meal. I felt embarrassed at the large serving Gladys put on my plate. I cleaned it up quickly, and I was just as quick with praise to the cook. When dessert was served, Anna made the Announcement before she took the first bite, "My mother makes the best apple pie in the world."

I took a bite and quickly affirmed Anna's declaration.

In return, Anna's mother fired another question.

"I'm surprised a man with your charm is not married?"

I looked across the table. Anna had closed her eyes tight. I looked over at her mother and then at Gladys. An impish thought rang in my head. Two beautiful sisters. I nodded slowly and then turned to Gladys. "She's right. I am wasting my life. Do you think a wanderer like me could find love with a beautiful woman like you or your sister?"

Gladys burst out laughing. She was joined by Anna. Anna's mother did not ask any more questions.

After dinner, Gladys rose and said. "Kurt, you are a one-man show. Go on into the living room and entertain Anna while we clean up the dishes." She turned to Anna and added, "Don't think you're getting out of the work just because you have a guest. I'm saving the pots and pans for you to do later."

Anna hurried into the other room and I was just a step behind. This time we both sat on the couch. Anna pulled her legs up under her and faced me. The short skirt rose just a little more than Mother would have approved of.

"Tell me another story."

I tried not to look at her legs. Thankfully, she had such a beautiful face. She reached down and pulled her skirt over her knees and then leaned toward me.

"Kurt, kiss me."

It was just a quick, soft kiss. She pulled her head back and whispered, "I hope my mother's questions didn't spoil it for you."

I let my hand fall lightly to her leg. I made small circles just below the hem of her skirt. She pushed my hand away. "We are still being carefully watched. Say something out loud or they will think we are making out."

I leaned back against the couch, telling myself not to be a fool. "If it starts snowing like this, I may never be able to leave this town."

Anna said in a whisper, "I'll pray for snow tonight."

"Be careful what you pray for, especially here in Hope." I glanced quickly at the doorway and two heads darted back. When I got ready to leave, Anna put on her coat too and told her mother she was just going to walk me down to the road. She took my hand as soon as we left the driveway. She led the way to a spot close to the uphill side of the road, just down from the mailbox. Then she turned to face me.

"When I watch for the mail, this spot can't be seen from the house. Not even from my room."

"Which room is that?"

She put her arms around my waist and gave me a hug. "The widow's watch."

I put my arms around her shoulders. In her boots she was almost my height. She pulled me closer. I glanced up and said, "I'll check it out some night."

She closed her eyes and titled her head back slightly. I kissed her lightly. Warmly. A series of quick but firm kisses. And then a long, hard kiss of passion. She pulled me ever closer. My boot slipped. My right leg gave way and we fell. Still she held tight and rolled over on top of me. How long we lay there I don't know. Passion has its own clock. When she pushed her head back from mine there were tears in her eyes. We struggled to our knees. Like a deer, she jumped to her feet and ran back up the road. I watched her until she turned to go up the driveway. She paused and blew me a kiss. It was the best Thanksgiving I ever had. Then I walked slowly down past Betty's house to my own.

I stopped and looked back. What of Betty? Why was she not invited to the Thanksgiving dinner? I scratched my head. There was a light on in her house. It was too cold to be sitting on the porch but she was there. I walked on, assuming Betty's ghost stories would not be as welcome as my adventures.

Chapter 15
Anna: Good-bye Kurt

Kurt worked a week at the gas station. The next Sunday he told me he was going to leave as soon as he got his first paycheck. That Monday, when I brought him his lunch, we were having freezing rain. I almost slipped just crossing the road to his house.

"See, you can't leave in this weather," I told him as I sat down at the kitchen table. "You will have to stay until spring."

"I can't do that. I have overstayed my welcome already."

He opened his lunch bag and then closed it.

"Don't like bologna today?" I asked.

"The sandwiches are great but I have something for you today."

He got up from the table and walked around behind me. I felt his hands on my neck. I thought he wanted a kiss so I tilted my head back. He had a silver chain with a cross on it. He said it was pure silver and he had it engraved with my name. I was to think of him whenever I wore it. I knew he lied; it was the same cross that Spanish Joe had found that fall. I wanted to tell him that I couldn't wear it; instead, I reached back and lifted my hair off the back of my neck so he could fasten the clasp. We did an upside down kiss. My hands reached up to pull him closer. His fingers traced their way down my back and then around to my breasts. After a long, strange kiss he stood up straight took my hand and led me to the couch. I told myself it was the couch, not the bed, so it would be all right. He unbuttoned my blouse but didn't try to take off my bra. We shared kisses and hugs that set my soul on fire.

Before I left that day, I tried to set things right with him. First, I thanked him for the crucifix, and then I told him about our belief in a risen Christ. I would wear the amulet under my blouse so my mother wouldn't get upset. He said he understood, and with gentle hands he buttoned my blouse closed over the tau cross.

I wore the amulet under my blouse the rest of that week. When I went to work, I'd put it out where it could be seen. All the men who came to the café noticed it. It was fun to see them pretending to look at the cross.

Gladys must have heard about it and told my mother. As expected, she voiced a strong protest, "We celebrate the risen Christ, and Catholics celebrate his death." I told my mother it was the Greek letter tau, but she said it was a tau cross. I showed her it had my name on the back, but Gladys must have told her the story of Spanish Joe finding the cross. She only laughed when I suggested Kurt had it engraved just for me. She was right, but I thought it was beautiful and I knew Kurt was leaving soon.

The following Sunday when I was at the café, Gladys stayed after her shift was over. I didn't think much of it, as we were often more busy on Sunday than other days, until Mother arrived. She took a seat at the table nearest the door and Gladys joined her there. They were waiting for Kurt. He arrived shortly and Gladys invited him to sit at their table. I brought him his coffee and asked Mother if she wanted something. She didn't. She waited until I left and then took some pieces of paper out of her purse and set them on the table. I waited on some other customers while she talked quietly with Kurt, then came back to the table and looked over her shoulder. On one page was a hand-drawn map; on the other was a list of names and phone numbers.

"What is this?" I asked.

Kurt looked up and replied calmly, "It's a way back to Colorado." He pushed his chair back from the table. "Not the trip I had planned, but still I'll give it careful consideration."

He put the two pieces of paper in his pocket, left a dollar on the table for the coffee and walked out the door.

That night I watched from my window to see him walk home from the gas station. I saw him turn on all the lights in the little house. He was packing to leave. I got dressed and went quietly down the stairs to the front door.

"Stay here," I heard my mother say in the dark of the living room. "It's too late."

I rushed to the front door and opened it. The sound of his motorcycle roared. I ran down the driveway in time to see his taillight going north out of town. That night I cried until morning.

Chapter 16
Kurt: Time to Depart

I had a surprise that Sunday when I stopped for coffee before going to work. Gladys and Anna's mother were waiting for me. They invited me to sit at their table, and after Anna brought me some coffee, her mother told me of her plan for me to return home. She gave me a map of a route she thought I could take, even in winter. She also had a list of places where I could stay along the way if the weather turned bad. They were all, she assured me, good Mormon families. I held my temper and thanked her for the list of friends. Actually, I knew something of the route she had chosen for me and it was not going to be easy. If I tried it, I just might need some friends along the way. It also occurred to me why she was doing this. She must have thought Anna and I were getting too close. Giving Anna the chain with the tau cross was the act that gave me away. I could blame Spanish Joe and the name engraved on the back of the cross, but the truth was I wanted to give her something before I left something else that said 'I love you.'

Anna's mother had covered all her bases. When I arrived at the gas station, Debbie had an envelope with my pay for the two weeks, including that night, ready for me. She told me to lock up when I left, shook my hand and wished me a safe trip back to Colorado. It was not very busy that night so I used the time to write Anna a letter. At midnight I locked up the station and walked down to my house. I couldn't help but stop to peek in the window of the Soiled Dove Saloon. Vicky wasn't at the bar, so I continued on home. I packed my things and cleaned up the house a little, then went to get my bike out of the garage. I noticed a dim light on in Betty's house, so I walked over and knocked on the door. It opened with a squeak and the small woman looked up at me.

"Sorry to wake you, Betty."

"You didn't wake me. I'm always up at midnight. That is when the most interesting things happen in Hope."

I held out the letter. "I want you to do me a favor. Give this to Anna tomorrow when she brings lunch. I am leaving tonight."

She took the letter and nodded her head. "You will return Kurt Johnson. You will return."

"No, I'm going home. Give the letter to Anna and please don't tell Gladys about this."

"I will tell her someday you will return."

I shook my head and turned to leave. She said it twice before I left the porch.

"You will return. You will return."

As quickly as I could, I loaded up the bike, started it and before it had warmed up rode north past Gladys' house, past Hotel Hope, past the gas station and out of town. The road was dry in most places. I went all the way to Spokane before the rain started. Cold rain and a dark night were the worst conditions for riding a motorcycle, but I was eager to put Hope far behind me.

It rained all the way to Pasco. I stopped twice for coffee and to warm up. The next day the rain had stopped but the wind was strong. I made it to Pendleton, Oregon that morning and stopped for breakfast.

I knew the road went up from there, so I asked about the pass. They told me the Meacham Hill was a sheet of ice. I went on anyway. It was a damn fool thing to do, but a man with little sleep makes poor decisions. For miles I rode about five miles per hour with my feet dragging on the snow packed road. I wore the heel off my left boot but I made it to La Grande and stopped for the night. The next day I slept in and didn't leave until after ten. That gave the sun and the sanders a chance to work the road south. I made it to Boise without any further trouble. There I stopped at a truck stop and asked about the road headed east. Truckers know the most about road conditions. They advised me it was snowing from Burley east, but the plows were out. The next day I rode on to Pocatello. While I was eating but over lunch a driver came over to my table and sat down. He said he'd passed me on the highway and asked where I was going. I told him I was headed home to Colorado. He offered to take me as far as Cheyenne. He was returning empty from a delivery in Portland. I'm sure glad I took him up on it. The wind was really blowing in Wyoming.

I wasn't much company, as I slept in the truck most of the next day. It turned out all right. The driver was a really nice guy. His name was Hank Deming. He had a small ranch outside Pine Bluff, almost on the state line with Nebraska. He raised dry-land wheat, ran a few cattle and drove a truck. From Cheyenne I rode down to Fort Collins. My dad and mom were glad to see me but after dinner I checked into a motel.

I was glad to be home, yet I felt terribly empty. With Rachel now a member of the family, I didn't want to keep close ties. She was a woman I could not resist and yet was bound to do so. A man does not covet his brother's wife. I thought of Anna, another woman I was not to want. I thought of going back in the Marines, but they were not interested in someone with a game leg.

I went over to Greeley and enrolled at Northern Colorado. For a while I did okay, but as soon as winter ended and the roads were clear, I wanted to head out again. It wasn't just riding a motorcycle, it was also traveling. The stockyards are in Greeley and at times the wind blows the wrong way. That's what I told my major professor. I just dropped out of school. It was the stockyards that brought Hank Deming to Greeley. He had delivered a truckload of Angus down from Nebraska and was headed for Montana to get another load. He asked me to come along. That's how I got started in the trucking business.

I called Hank my second guardian angel. He laughed at that tag but he taught me the trade.

We made trips along I-30, mostly between Ogden, Utah and Cheyenne, Wyoming, with a few excursions into Nebraska. It was over a year before he had a ticket to pick up a load in Pocatello, Idaho. The moment we crossed into Idaho I remembered Betty words – 'you will return.'

Part II

2005

Chapter 17
Kurt: Return to Hope

It was over thirty-five years later when I finally returned to North Idaho. I had just done a major overhaul on my Honda, and this was the first real vacation I had taken in years. I rode tall and fast. The front tire tracked into the left center position on the highway and wind whistled just a little in my helmet. The road made a long, sweeping curve to the left. I let up on the throttle and let the engine slow the bike. The road dipped closer to the shore of the lake. Up ahead a moose ambled up from the swampy area and stopped on the road.

My hand gripped the brake. The tires squealed as they dragged the bike to stop just ten yards from the giant deer. The moose turned his head sideways and stood firm, as if he regarded the motorcycle as a rival bull in his territory.

I quickly killed the engine and turned off the flashing headlight. The demon of a deer lowered his head, swung it from side to side and then ambled off the road down into the swamp. I watched the moose depart. The right antler extended a good three feet from the side of his head, while the left antler was almost a foot shorter. It looked as if it had been sawed off.

Slowly I pulled off my helmet and stared in disbelief. Thirty-five years ago I heard of a moose that got hit by a train and the conductor sawed off his antler to set him free. It makes no sense; that story is over a hundred years old and moose grow new antlers each year.

I looked down at the brushy swamp where the moose had gone. This was not the lake but the mudflats of the Pack River delta. For just a moment I closed my eyes. Thirty-five years ago I had almost met my death here. I glanced up the road but saw no angels waiting to rescue me this time. Angels and ghosts. This was indeed a strange place. I pushed my bike off the side of the road and rocked it onto the stand.

I got off the bike. It felt good to take the weight off my rear end and stretch my legs signs that I was a lot older now than the first time I had come this way. I put my right leg forward and stretched my calf muscles, keeping the leg straight so the knee brace was not twisted. I even did a little dance-like step along the shoulder of the road until I could feel the blood circulating normally in my legs. All the while I kept an eye on that moose as he walked. If I had a gun, I might have shot that monster. A logging truck rumbled by heading northwest. I looked out toward the mudflats as the truck rumbled passed. The moose had gone just a dozen yards off the road and now stood silently, his huge head to one side and a single red eye looking directly back at me. I backed up slowly to my bike.

"You win, moose."

The moose turned and marched off through the brush. I mounted my bike, backed it around until it was pointed in the opposite direction, started the engine, and the headlight began to flash once more. The Honda CB750 was a classic machine, one that shocked the motorcycle world when it came out back in 1969. It was a four-cylinder rocket that could easily reach 124 miles per hour, or cruise at highway speeds without the constant vibration like other cycles of its day. The new fairing and the flashing headlight were my latest additions but I'd also replaced the four chrome exhaust pipes.

Looking back at the swampy area I muttered, "Okay, ghost moose, Morgan, or whatever they called you, you win. Spread the word among the other ghosts. Kurt is back in town."

I shook my head and mumbled, "You're getting old. You rode right past Hope and didn't even notice it. Maybe the lake swallowed up the town. If it is worth coming this far, it's worth taking a second look."

I gave a one-finger salute to the brushy area where the monster had departed, checked in my mirror for traffic and pulled out onto the highway. A few minutes and as many miles down the road, I saw the sign on the left side: Hope. I crossed the road and started up the side road that went steeply uphill. This was the Hope I remembered. Signs announcing West Main and then Highland Avenue came into view. I kept to West Main, passed a few old, brick buildings to where century old wooden houses looked down from Highland Avenue. Like old painted ladies, they watched me enter Hope. Across the road from Hotel Hope, the most distinguished structure in town, I parked my bike. In a town like Hope the ghost of the past is everywhere but especially in that old hotel. The clean, white building with its grand, white picket rail on the veranda across the second floor was a welcoming beacon.

I took off my helmet, leaned over and pulled my right pant leg smoothly over the knee brace, then walked across the street. The lower floor of the building was divided between an antique shop, a small café and the Soiled Dove Saloon. I walked into the latter establishment, half expecting to see Old Pot-Belly Bill behind the bar, but instead there was a woman in a lacy white blouse.

"Hi! We aren't open yet."

Bottles of whiskey, gin, brandy, vodka and other assorted liquors lined the shelves of the pair of rich wooden structures built into the wall like open hutches. She could deal me any poison I wished. Above the top row of bottles were three tall, ornately framed mirrors spaced across the wall.

I stepped sideways to look directly into the center mirror. There was no curvaceous female image looking back at me. Where is Vicky? Oh, I remember, I chuckled to myself. She only comes here at midnight. Hell, by now Vicky would have given up late-night rendezvous. No, if she were a ghost she wouldn't grow any older, she'd be just as enchanting as she was thirty-five years ago. I closed my eyes and tried to remember what she looked like, but instead of Vicky, another woman's face came into focus— Anna. Vicky and Anna. There were never two women more different. Who would I rather find, now that I was back in Hope?

I opened my eyes and grinned at the woman behind the bar. "Just looking. I never drink this early in the day myself. What I need now is breakfast."

"Try next door but don't forget to come back later."

I approach the bar. "Is the hotel open? I need a place to stay."

"No borders but we open late. Stop by for a drink tonight."

I grinned. "Any suggestions on where to stay? There used to be some cabins they rented down near the lake."

"Not anymore. Say, are you here with that motorcycle group of vets?"

I nodded. "I plan to join up with them tomorrow. I wanted to stay in Hope tonight."

"You can try the resort in East Hope, or what I'd do is go over to Red Fir Resort. Nice cabins, real quiet this time of the year. Tell Nick that Karen sent you, and he'll give you a good deal."

I left the bar and went into the café next door. The place looked familiar but it wasn't the same as it was back in the fall of 1969. The waitress was young and cute, but she wasn't Anna. She wore tight, hip-hugging jeans and a T-shirt with a bulldog on the front. Anna would never dress like that. She did wear short skirts, however even in winter.

The special that morning was a chili omelet with hash browns. I ordered that with coffee. For just a second I closed my eyes, and Anna slowly pushed the cobwebs from the back of my memory and stepped forward. She was tall, about my height. That was tall for a girl back then. Light blonde hair, not bleached or tinted, just lighter than brown. Blue eyes, not so blue as those of Gladys; that woman had eyes the color of a bluebird back in Colorado. Anna's eyes were different. They were a lighter shade, but they showed so much of what she was thinking. Nice figure, too. She was no

Sophia Loren but she had boobs, hips and a nice little curve in between. My hands reached out across the table and clasped together. She stepped back and there was that smile. Anna was more than human, she was an angel. She had saved my life and then restored my will to live; a princess in a lost little town, but she was not mine. I took a deep breath and opened my eyes. I better not do that again. In Colorado the years had blurred the memory of Anna, but here in Hope they were bright as day. This is today. I am back and I just want to see her again, that's all.

Hip-hugger brought the coffee and a few minutes later she returned with the main course.

"Here's the breakfast. Need a warm up?"

I jerked my head up and pulled my arms back quickly. She filled my cup back up to the brim.

"Thanks," I said with a wink.

She blushed and hurried off behind the counter.

I shook my head. Now, I shouldn't have done that. When will I ever learn not to flirt with young girls? Hell, I'm an old man now. I glanced around at the other patrons. They must think I'm some kind of pervert an old man on a big motorcycle, flirting with a girl young enough to be my grandchild, if I had any grandchildren.

I took a large bite of the omelet. The hot chili burned the roof of my mouth. I quickly took a sip of water, swallowed and then emptied the glass of ice water. Hip-hugger must have been watching, for she quickly returned with a fresh glass of ice water. When she set it on the table she said, "Watch out for that chili, it's hot."

I nodded and winked again. Got to stop that. She smiled and went to check on the other tables.

I carefully added some sugar to the coffee. If that girl was Anna and some old biker had been flirting with her, what would I have done?

I finished breakfast, pushed back the chair from the table, stood up and checked my pant leg to see if it was buckled at the knee brace. It wasn't, so I paid the bill and went back outside. I left my bike parked where it was and walked down West Main as far as Lake Street. This short piece of asphalt went straight uphill. I stopped and looked at the houses in both directions. They looked somewhat familiar. The house that should have been where Gladys lived was different. I'd been invited to the house only once, but I'd looked up at it at night many times. I glanced at the downhill side of the road. The little house that had been my home for a few months looked badly in need of paint. I glanced a little farther down the road. There on the porch sat an old woman in a rocking chair. She waved for me to come closer.

A little fear walked with me. It grew heavier when I stepped up onto the porch.

"You have returned. I knew you would." She nodded to her left and then to her right.

I glanced in both directions but saw no one.

"She is waiting for you."

I smiled. Did she mean Anna or Vicky? I took a half step backward. "I bet everyone I knew here has long gone. Say, is that Gladys' house up on the hill. It doesn't look right."

Betty laughed, looked to her left and laughed again. For just a second I heard a second laugh.

"Gladys has left us. Anna married and moved away. Vicky will be here with the new moon. She will be anxious to see you again."

Once more she looked around as if there were others on the porch with us. I dared not look around or even wait to listen. I left.

Discouraged and frightened, I walked back to my bike. To prove to myself I was not really afraid of returning to Hope, I rode around town until I felt I knew it again. They had moved the highway down along the lake. It used to go right through both Hope and East Hope. The bridge was a necessary part of the improvement. I blamed the faster road for my riding past Hope earlier that morning. I just couldn't resist the challenge of a fast, winding road with little or no traffic. Some of the old cabins down near the lake were gone. The resort at the southeast end of town was now a large, modern enterprise, the kind of place I hated in Colorado. They were businesses that didn't take kindly to bikers, either. I got directions to the Red Fir Resort and rode south out of town. Having not found Gladys, I had some planning to do before making my next move.

Chapter 18
Anna Pours Ashes in the River

"Mother! Was that Father?"

The wind whipped the fan of ashes out behind the boat. The curl of the wake from the Good Faith swallowed the dark gray patch of ashes as soon as it reached the water. My hands shook as I cracked the urn on the steel rail of the boat and tossed the broken pieces into the boat's wake.

"Yes. Your father has left us now."

"But Mom?"

"It's what he wanted. The last request he made of me." She pointed back at the spot and softly said, "Now, you had better stay there. I don't want people telling stories of how they saw you out fishing on the lake".

"Mom! Why now?"

I turned and made my way slowly up to the captain's chair and sat down. The Good Faith was one of the luxury models of the South Bay line of pontoon boats. The twin outboard motors pushed the craft upriver into the wind. Sam had purchased it the year he retired, the year before he told me he had cancer. Lara, my oldest daughter, was at the helm. Despite voicing her objection, she had kept the craft on a steady path up the river. She would be thirty next year; she was old enough to understand her father's wish.

I put out my right hand. "Slow down. We have all day."

"This isn't what I thought we were going to do."

Anna smiled, "I told you I wanted to take one last cruise before I put the boat up for the winter."

Lara countered, "Well, you told me you wanted to talk. A woman-to-woman talk."

I looked around. The sun was shining on the north shore, but clouds were pushing around the side of Bald Mountain to the north. I opened the storage compartment in the bunker in front of my chair and took out a map and a pair of binoculars. The Good Faith was built to handle a dozen passengers; with just two, it would ride high in the water on its three large pontoons.

"Lara, I know what you and Jim have in mind for me now that Sam has died, but I am not ready for that now. Give me some time to adjust to life alone. Let's take a quiet cruise on the lake and talk. Being your mother, I get to speak first. You listen and then I promise I will listen to you."

Lara throttled back on the engines and steered the boat more toward the middle of the river. It was hard to say where Lake Pend Oreille ended and the river of the same name began. Those living in Sandpoint used the long bridge as the dividing line; others used Contest Point, claiming this was where the deep lake ended and the shallower Pend Oreille River began.

"You're taking control, which means I won't get any time to speak at all," Lara complained.

I looked across the river at the town of Sandpoint then east toward the long bridge. "I'm taking control? Recently I've wondered if I were ever in control of my life. I was a tennis ball being batted back and forth by two people, each with their own objectives. I objected at times but I never rebelled."

"Mother, don't be so melodramatic."

"I just need to talk to someone. Let's go east into the lake."

"To Hope?" Lara asked with a grin.

"Yes, why not? I like that end of the lake. It's so quiet. It is also fitting to go back to where it all began."

Lara laughed as we motored east past Murphy Bay. "The whole lake is quiet. Nothing like in July with all the water-skiers zipping by."

I glanced over at Lara. We had had so many conflicts when she was younger. What she didn't realize was most conflicts could be traced to her father. Hearing a splash near the dock below Swan's Landing, we both turned.

Lara shook her head. "Father always said 'Never swim in the lake before June or after September.'"

I watched as two boys climbed quickly back onto the dock. The phrase 'Father always said' was a warning. Just as Sam had insisted my mother move close to us when she grew older, my daughter and her husband were now planning my retirement. Well, I am not that old. I want to be in charge of own life for a few years. First my mother, then Sam, and now my own daughter. Why do they all want to plan my life? What would Lara think if I told her that I went swimming in the river this morning?

I glanced back down the river. "This is my home. I lived here for five years, the last two taking care of your father. Take it slow as you go under the bridge."

"But that's the point. This year you'll be alone. You need family."

I pointed at the approaching bridge.

Lara nodded. "I know. The river is deepest between the center two supports." She tossed her hair and glanced up as two semi-trucks rumbled by. Neither driver looked down and she did not wave.

After we passed under the long bridge, I looked back. It was harder to see the traffic on the bridge for the second structure, the original highway bridge, blocked the view. This old bridge had been left as a part of a bicycle path that extended to Sagle. The deep rumble of a motorcycle could be heard echoing off the cement railing of the bridge. I quickly stood up, hoping for a better look. It was a big, black bike with a lone rider. I raised the binoculars. The sound of a second rider came to me just as I focused on the first, followed by a third, a fourth. There were eight in all. The lead cycle had an American flag mounted on the back. Just behind him was a motorcycle with the brilliant red flag of the

Marine Corps. I lowered the binoculars and pulled down the bottom of my sweater over the top of my slacks.

Lara smiled and pointed at me. "Say, is that a new outfit?"

"Yes. I finally lost ten pounds and have kept them off for a month, so I celebrated by buying this. It looked great in the store but the pants are too low on the hips and the sweater not long enough." I glanced down at the tight belt line. Now, if only I could lose another twenty pounds. The wind had blown open the jacket. I put my hand on my midsection I knew the new, white fleece sweater fit snugly. Yes, I needed to lose those other twenty pounds, but it was nice to hear my daughter say it looked great. I allowed one last look at the passing cycles before sitting down.

"Well, Mom, It's the new style. A little bare midriff is not a crime. Did you see anyone you know on those motorcycles?"

"Of course not." I sat and turned toward Lara with a grin. "I heard they were coming. An army unit is returning from Iraq next week. These people are mostly Vietnam vets and are going to form a motorcade to welcome the troops home."

"Mom, let's not talk about the war today. You know how Dad felt about our going into Iraq. How far is it to Hope?"

I leaned back in my chair and looked east. How far is back to Hope? That depends on how you measured things— just a few miles of open water or a lifetime. I could not see the town of Hope from the Good Faith. Gold Peak blocked the way. I scanned the hills to the north. "The year your grandfather died, we moved to Hope to live with Aunt Gladys."

"I heard that story a hundred times."

I lowered the binoculars to my lap. "I didn't know at the time but I think God sent me there to test me. I don't know if I failed the test."

Lara tuned the boat north as she approached the railroad bridge.

"Don't say it Mom. I know the third support from the west has the deepest water."

She steered directly between the two supports and then shoved the throttle ahead. The bow of the Good Faith raised a little and the boat jumped up in speed. She turned and smiled. "Grandma told me she had to move to save money."

"Yes, that was true. Dad died, I dropped out of college, and we moved in with Gladys to save money and wait for Sam to return."

"So what was this test?"

"Every time you go to a new place or meet someone for the first time, you are tested. What will you do? How will you treat them?"

"I bet Gladys was a real test for you. Was she as wild as Grandma said?"

"I thought she was a grand lady, a wonderful woman. She cared for people. Every day she would fix meals for her Aunt Betty, who lived in a miner's cabin down below Gladys' house. I don't think Betty was really her aunt. Betty was an old woman with several major faults. She smoked and she told stories. The first day I met Betty she warned me I might see a ghost or two while I stayed there. The next day when I took her a dinner Gladys had fixed, Betty told me a ghost story that had me staying awake half the night. Oh, I'm sorry, I am drifting off. You wanted to hear about Gladys."

"Hey, I like ghost stories. Tell me the story."

"The story was of a woman who drowned in the lake and then came back once every year on the day she had drowned. Betty told me stories to frighten me, and even today ghost stories frighten me. The very next day I put on my bathing suit and went down to the lake. It was cold and this was in the summer. Some guys at the docks kidded me by saying if I started to drown they would give me mouth-to-mouth resuscitation. Just to show them, I swam out as far as I dared before turning around and coming back.

"Now, here is the weird part. That night I dreamed I went swimming in the lake and met Vicky. She kept urging me to swim farther and farther out from the shore. I awoke cold and shaking. I told Gladys of my dream the next morning. It was so real. Gladys told me not to listen to Betty's wild stories, but I still did."

Lara shook her head. "She was trying to frighten you out of swimming in the lake. I would have rebelled too."

"We do have some traits in common. Did you like your father?"

"Of course, I loved him."

Anna nodded. "Yes we both loved him. My story won't change that. Sam Chapman, like his father before him, was a man who planned his life and the lives of everyone around him."

"It was a good life, Mom."

"Yes, Sam did everything well. What I hid from you was the many problems he created that I had to fix. You're getting me sidetracked. I want to tell you about that winter I spent in Hope. That's a good place to start."

I took a deep breath. "And if I have the nerve, I'll tell you about Kurt."

Chapter 19
Kurt Begins His Search

At the Red Fir Resort I took one look at the steep gravely road that led from the office to the cabins by the lake, and considered finding another place. Instead, I parked my bike under the carport next to the office. The manager was watching me through the window and he met me at the door.

"Welcome to Red Fir. Will you be staying long?"

I tried to sound positive. "I just need a place to sleep for this weekend. Karen over at the Hotel Hope said you would have a cabin open."

"That we do. Is it just you?" the old man behind the counter asked. He was slight of build and bent over a little. In an extra large, black sweatshirt with a bear on the front he looked like a child dressed up in his father's shirt. Pinned on the left side above the bear was a nametag with the inscription "Just Ask Nick."

He nodded his head twice. "I see you got a motorcycle. I wouldn't ride it down the road to the cabins. No sir. Just leave it where it is. I'll keep an eye on it. Besides, it might rain tonight."

He handed me a brochure of the little resort and a key to cabin number two. "Don't pay any attention to those prices on the back; they are for the summer season. The cabins are fifty dollars a night this time of the year."

I gave a passing smile at the T-shirt on display with four bears dressed like fishermen. *What am I doing here, I don't fish?*

I walked down to the cabin and looked inside. A few minutes later I returned to sign in and carry my small travel bag down the hill. The cabin was an A-frame, with a living-dining area that looked out over a large wooden porch, a small kitchen, a bath and a bedroom on the main floor. Upstairs in the loft was the sleeping area. Liking privacy, I put my bedroll in the loft.

Ten minutes later I carried a mug of hot coffee out onto the deck. The cabins at Red Fir all faced north and all had large wooden decks where guests could look out at Ellisport Bay. Since the Corps of Engineers had begun lowering the lake, the proprietor had hauled all but the smallest of his boats out of the lake. I watched the young couple staying in the cabin next to mine as they loaded up their fishing gear.

I waved as they trod by my deck on their way to the dock. "Good luck."

The woman who wore tight-fitting blue jeans and a Washington State University scarlet and gray sweatshirt waved back. "We're just going over to the Trestle Creek area. It's a good fishing spot."

I smiled. There was a boat launch just east of Trestle Creek; my guess was the area would be fished out this late in the season. The young man beamed as he walked past carrying two poles and a tackle box.

I nodded. Youth. They waste those precious years. Instead of fishing they should be back in the sack making whoopee. When they are old like me, they will regret those wasted opportunities.

I stood up straight and looked across the bay to East Hope. Why are there a Hope and East Hope? Combined they hardly make one town. My eyes tried to focus on the white, square building high up on the hill in Hope. The Hotel Hope. That is where I should be. It's locked this year. Maybe if no one was around, I could break in just to see for myself. There are a few things I'd like to know before I die. Does the ghost of Vicky still haunt the hotel or was that just a drunken dream. If Betty was right, she wouldn't be there until the full moon, so today I won't waste my time looking for her. How do I find Anna?

I laughed and shouted to the lake, "Kurt, you are a dreamer. After all these years you're still interested in Anna."

I walked back to the small picnic table and sat down. *Gladys had been my only hope for contact, and now Betty says she has died. I should check on that.* I took a long sip of coffee as I raised my head and looked toward the little rows of houses above the railroad. "There is always hope in Hope."

I put my coffee down and waved to the small boat as it made an S-turn to get out of the dock area. Once it was gone I walked down the hill to the dock. Thanks to the tall fir trees and the A-frame-style cabins, the deck was in the shadows. The sun felt good, and I stopped just short of the long, inverted L-shaped, wooden dock. There was a fire-pit dug into the hillside. It looked like a piece of a three-foot diameter culvert turned on its side. Firewood was stacked in a long row going up the hill. I went back to the cabin and got some lighter fluid intended for starting the charcoals for a barbecue. In a few minutes, I had a warm crackling fire. As the smoke drifted uphill and into the trees I watched it. *When it's all over, will I just drift away like smoke on a hillside? Yes, I bet I will.*

I sat on a stump just upwind of the fire, with my right leg out straight, and looked across the fire out to the lake. Other than the little fishing boat that had just left, there was only one other craft in the water— a jet ski heading west.

"Now, that's the way to go."

My eyes followed the fast-moving craft until it was out of sight. The hotel was still there. It ain't open but it's there. I looked up at the sky. Too early for a bar to be open, but maybe tonight. I focused on the hotel across the bay. "I told Anna I wasn't going to drink there anymore but that was over thirty-five years ago. Then she went off and married her missionary. I'm not obligated to that statement. I should never have said it. Still, that was some dream I had that night."

The clouds parted and the sun washed over the deck. I raised my head to feel the warmth on my face. Why does the warmth of sunshine on a cool day make me think of Anna after all these years? For several minutes I just sat there letting the sun warm up my body and my spirit.

"Hope! It's your fault. I had no troubles until I came here."

I stepped to the side and dumped the last of my cold coffee onto the gravel. "Hell, Anna wasn't a ghost; she was a real, live woman. By now she is long gone. But I came this far and I've got to at least try to find her. She believed in miracles, maybe I should too."

I marched up the hill and past my cabin. I entered the back door of the resort's little store. Nick, who was seated behind the counter, stood up.

"What can I do for you, Mr. Johnson?"

I leaned on the counter. "Do you have a local phone book?"

Nick turned slowly, limped back into the office behind the counter and returned with a black book labeled Sandpoint And Surrounding Area. I spread it open and flipped through the pages. There were a few Morgans. I fanned to the end of the listings and checked Williams. There were more of them. It would be awkward to ask about Anna. By now she would be a grandmother. I could ask about Gladys and find out when she died. With luck someone might mention her niece.

"Can I help?" Nick asked. "I know many of those who live here, even some of the summer people?"

I smiled but didn't look up, "Do you know Gladys Williams?"

"Sure do. We'll never forget Gladys. She lived in Hope in Captain Karl's house. If you come to see her, you've come too late."

"Sounds like the one. She lived up on either Lake Street or West Main. I can't remember the address." I chuckled. "Of course that was thirty-five years ago."

"It's probably the same woman. Died in that fire. Let me see." He stopped and scratched his baldhead. "Five...no, four years ago. Yes sir, it will be four years this December. Did you know her well?"

I bit my lower lip. Dead? That's what Betty said. This isn't going to get me anywhere. I looked up. "Haven't seen her in thirty-five years. She did me a favor back then. I told her if I ever stopped back this way, I'd say hello."

"It could be the same woman. Gladys was always helping someone. She was always kind to Betty and a few others who came back to Hope." He paused, "There was a fire in her house. She tried to put it out and died of smoke inhalation. We all miss her."

I rubbed my chin with the fist of my left hand. I guess I'll have to try these telephone numbers and hope I get lucky.

Nick leaned forward and spoke softly, "Gladys had hundreds of friends in Hope. She's buried in the cemetery off Round Top Road. Do you know where that is?"

"I can find it," I replied.

"Tell her I said hello when you stop by. You won't have any trouble finding the grave. Her niece, a fine-looking woman, often brings fresh flowers to her grave."

I fought hard to suppress a grin. "She has a niece! Do you know her name?"

"Anna."

"Last name?"

"It was Morgan once. She got married years ago but somehow I never got to know her husband. They moved to Spokane. So did Alice Marie, Anna's mother. Anna would come back to visit Gladys every summer but I don't recall her husband or her mother ever coming with her."

I thanked him and turned to leave by the front door.

"Mister Johnson!" Nick called out.

I held the door and looked back.

"If I remember correctly, someone told me that Gladys' niece moved to Sandpoint after her husband retired. I bet if you stopped at the LDS church in Sandpoint, they could tell you where she lives."

I nodded and waved as I walked around the front of the building. What a piece of luck! Who needs miracles? The old man told me what I wanted to know and I didn't have to ask any awkward questions. Gladys is dead, Anna's mother is in Spokane, but Anna lives in Sandpoint. Who cares? It is Anna I want to see. I wonder what she looks like today.

I revved the smooth, four-cylinder engine twice before dropping it in gear. The narrow, paved asphalt road wound its way around Ellisport Bay. I would stop in Sandpoint and find where the LDS gather.

Chapter 20
Anna Recalls Living in Hope

Lara turned the Good Faith to the east, set the helm and pulled back on the throttle until the nose of the boat settled into the water. "Mother, it will take all morning to reach Hope at this speed. Should I set it faster?"

"No, I don't want to be bouncing around," I replied. "I told you it would be an all day affair. We'll stop at East Hope and eat at the floating restaurant."

Lara sat back in her captain's chair. "Do you think it's open?"

"If it's not, we can go up to the Hotel Hope. They serve lunch."

"Hotel Hope? That's too far to walk; besides, I heard it has closed for the season."

I shook my head. "They never opened the hotel this summer but the restaurant is open for lunch and the bar is open in the evening. This is just between us girls."

Lara grinned. "Okay, Mom, but I want to talk you out of staying in Sagle alone this winter. Don't take all day to tell me this story."

"This story had a lot to do with my state of mind. I feel like I've been kept in the dark all these years and someone just turned on the lights. Everything is too bright. It can't be this clear. Don't roll your eyes like that; this is your mother talking. I promise you, I'll give you plenty of time this weekend to present your case. Get me a water bottle before I start."

With a fresh water bottle in my hand and reluctant audience of one, I began my story.

"I had just turned twenty the year my father died. Mother was devastated, so I dropped out of summer school down at the U and returned home."

"Hey, Mom! I've heard that story a hundred times. You moved to Hope to live with Aunt Gladys, to save money. Today, you would have gotten a student loan and gone back to college," Lara commented.

"Nineteen sixty-nine was not today," Anna replied. "And, as I learned much later we were not that short of money. It was all a conspiracy to keep poor, innocent little Anna from going astray."

"Now, Mom that's being too dramatic. Just tell me what happened."

"After Grandma died, I went through her things. Dad had an ample life insurance policy. There was no need for me to drop out of college. Our house was paid for and she made a good profit when she sold it. No, the reason we moved to Hope was to keep me from going back to the university. It was not until Sam died that I learned the rest of the reason. Well, Mom's little scheme almost didn't work. She didn't count on Gladys' generosity."

I took a drink from my water bottle and began again. "Gladys also kept watch on some homes which belonged to people who only came to Hope in the summer season. Some were snowbirds that traveled in their big Airstreams to Arizona each winter; others only went as far as Sandpoint or Spokane for the winter. Gladys would check on the houses whenever they were away. Those who lived in Spokane for the winter wanted to keep the water and electricity connected, in case they wanted to return some weekend. She also used to check on her neighbors who were old and living alone. One of these was a woman named Betty Nietzy. Gladys called the woman Aunt Betty. The first time I met her she asked me if I had ever seen a ghost. I told her I believed in the Holy Ghost, the spirit of God."

"'You must be religious,' she said. 'They teach about heaven and hell, so religious people often think of the dead as saints or some totally lost souls. Well, people aren't just good or bad while they are alive so maybe they aren't just one or the other after they die.'"

"She had a horrible smile, yellow teeth from smoking cigarettes. From the start she wanted to frighten me. Betty was old and she had very strange looking eyes, a mixture of green and black. The first day she closed her eyes tight and whispered, 'You may see a ghost or two while you are in Hope. They return for many different reasons. Some come back to tell loved ones something they failed to tell them when they were alive. Others come back to right a wrong done years ago. But most come back because they are simply lonely.'"

"It was weird. Her voice was much deeper than normal, like she was a puppet and someone else was speaking. Then she opened her eyes, those deep dark green eyes never looked directly at me as she spoke, 'They were lonely in life and now they are lonely in death. They wander between the two worlds looking for someone or something. Do not fear them but treat them kindly.'"

"Oh, what a witch," Lara shook her head. "Welcome to Hope. How old was this woman?"

"If Betty really was Gladys' Aunt she must have been at least seventy, but she looked a lot older. That's what happens when you don't take good care of your health. When I arrived, Gladys gave me the job of checking on Betty, at least once each day. It was a difficult walk down there in the winter because they didn't plow that street. Actually, I came to enjoy that walk when another tenant moved into one of the houses Gladys was watching that winter. Do you remember her house before the fire, when it had that octagonal room we called the widow's watch? That's where I stayed."

"Did you used to look out at the lake through that telescope that Gladys kept in the closet?"

"How did you know about that?"

Lara laughed. "Remember when you and Dad went to Canada and left me with Gladys for a week. Well, Gladys set up the telescope and we looked at the cabins across the Ellisport Bay. She didn't introduce me to this Betty. She did take me to the Soiled Dove Saloon, not to drink but just to look. She told me not to tell you or you would be upset."

"I certainly would have been. You were only fourteen."

Lara stood up and looked at the docks along the shore. "Now, let's talk about you staying alone up here this winter."

I shook my head. "Right now I can't go to Spokane. I'm not ready for that yet. Let me tell you my story and you will see why I need some time alone."

"Not another ghost story."

"No, this is the story of someone who was very much alive. He crashed his motorcycle in the Pack River Flats. Gladys and I saw the accident and we rescued him. Gladys being the good Christian woman she was, arranged for him to stay in Hope while he recovered. He stayed for two months, and while he was there we fell in love."

"Mom! What were you thinking?"

"I was young and I was lonely. There were men in Hope. Most worked for the lumber companies and a few for the Forest Service. But this man was different. He came to Hope with no intentions of stopping but he stayed for the winter. His name was Kurt."

Lara let go of the boat's steering wheel and waved her hands in the air like swatting flies. "A biker! Mom, you have better taste than that. Why?"

I waited until Lara finished her dramatics before I continued.

"Gladys and I drove to Sandpoint and brought Kurt back to Hope. He stayed in the little house below the road. I would bring a lunch to him every day, just as I did for Betty. He was alone, and now I see we were both in Hope against our will, each wanting to be somewhere else. At first I felt sorry for him, and that helped me forget about my own problems. But that soon changed. I helped him relearn to walk and I even tried to help him fix that motorcycle. It was a big blue Honda. I didn't understand what that bike meant to him. It was his freedom machine. I wanted one because I saw how it made him feel free. He did teach me to ride it before he left town."

"Well, I'm glad he left." Lara shook her shoulders like she was shaking something off.

"I cried that night. I cried all night. He left without even saying good-bye. At least that is what I thought. I didn't learn until last year he had left a letter for me."

I could feel the tears form quickly in my eyes. "He left because he loved me and knew he wasn't good enough for me. It was the middle of winter. He rode off on a motorcycle and was never heard from again."

"Mom, now I really think you should come to live with us. I don't want you living alone up here and being depressed." Lara spread her arms out from her body. "That's what is wrong up here. When it's warm and the sun is shining, it's fabulous. When it's cold and rainy, it's depressing. Admit it. You were depressed that winter. Your father had died, Sam had left and you felt depressed. Why else could you have fallen for a guy who rides a motorcycle? I hope you two didn't do anything ... anything you regret now."

I took out a handkerchief and wiped my eyes. "Okay, Miss Smarty, blame me, blame Hope, but remember I could have gone back to school that year. We had the money."

I blew my nose and then gave her my best in-charge look. "Today I am glad Mother made us move to Hope. If I hadn't been there Kurt would have died. I saved him and I healed him; now I wish I could find him."

"Why?" Lara shouted.

"I know what happened to me." I smiled. "I married and raised a good family— three beautiful girls. I want to know what happened to Kurt."

Chapter 21
Kurt Goes to Sandpoint

I rode through Sandpoint and its maze of one-way streets. After a while, I stopped at the old Mobil Station. They didn't sell Hondas anymore but they had a map of the town and a telephone book. The Church of Jesus Christ of Latter-Day Saints was located north of town, out by the airport and the fairgrounds. The usual tall, white steeple identified it. There were a dozen cars in the parking lot but I just drove on past. At the corner I stopped and looked back. I needed a good story before I started knocking on any doors. A strange fear came over me—not that Anna wouldn't remember me, but that she would. She had never written, never made any attempt to contact me. Here she would be surrounded by her family. Mormons had large families, and they had even larger extended families because of strong social activities in their church. All these were things I could have had, but had rejected. I rode on to Boyer Avenue and headed south. At Main Street I headed east to the main part of town. There were a dozen motorcycles parked just up the street at the Quality Inn. I knew if I joined up with them today, I would never finish my search for Anna. I turned south, then east again and parked at the public parking. For a while I just walked around Sandpoint's downtown. It had become a tourist area, but it still had some local color. The art galleries carried the usual Western prints but also the work of some local artists. The sporting goods store had some very impressive elk racks mounted on the wall behind the gun rack. The selection of canoes, kayaks and other man-propelled watercraft was pretty extensive. With a lake on one side, a river on the other and a sizeable stream running through downtown, water sports were expected. I even strolled along the docks at the mouth of Sand Creek and admired the boats.

Just before noon, I walked into Connie's lounge. The hostess escorted me to a booth near the front windows. The walls of Connie's were brick, but they were clean red bricks that gave the place a little class. The booths and tables were well-stained Ponderosa pine with dark-green seat covers. The windows were colored glass, keeping those in the street from a clear view the tables but allowing those sitting there to see the traffic on Cedar Street.

The hostess, in tight-fitting black slacks and a white silky blouse, put a menu on the table and asked, "What can I bring you to drink?"

"Ice tea."

"High test or regular?"

I shook my head. "Just ice tea."

She departed and I glanced around the room. The two nearest tables were empty but the three along the back wall were filled. At the center one an older woman sat, folding and unfolding her napkin. She never looked up at the two younger women who sat across the table from her. They leaned forward to hear what she was saying. Only a few words came clearly from the conservation. "Recovering ... Pray for him ... The doctors said." The rest was too hushed for me to grasp it.

A waitress came to my table with a menu and a glass of ice tea. "The special today is ham and cheese on rye. It comes with either fries or a salad. Soup of the day is tomato basil."

I looked over the menu and ordered the City Beach Dip, a roast beef on French roll with au jus. Just before the waitress brought my meal the trio at the table by the wall got up to leave. The waitress turned and called after them, "Tell Charlie to get well soon. I'm saving a piece of huckleberry pie for him."

After the three women had left, she brought my lunch to the table and said, "Her husband is eighty-four years old and still rides a four-wheeler. Ran into a tree last weekend. At that age a broken leg is serious. Damn fool. I hope she sells that thing before he gets out of the hospital." She shook her head. "She won't. I just know she won't."

I nodded. "A broken leg is serious at any age."

I sat up straight and glanced out the window as the three women were crossing Cedar Street. The hospital was just two blocks away, if I remembered correctly.

When I finished my lunch and I walked over to the hospital. I didn't go in but just looked from the outside and tried to remember where my room had been. The building was much larger than I remembered. A confusing set of signs sent me walking around it. I discovered this new wing on the hospital was larger than the old building. Finally, in the northeast corner I recognized the parking lot I had hobbled across to get to the station wagon. This was now the administration wing of the hospital. Like at a college campus, the highest paid people often had offices in the oldest building. A garden to the north was likely intended as a waiting area for those who had come to see someone in the hospital. I walked through it slowly, thinking about the past.

I could have died back then. Fate, God or whatever had sent that moose across the road at the worst possible time. Hell, I was told the moose wasn't even hurt. I would have died except for Anna. Why Anna? How dare I come back to see her? She was engaged, or at least promised to another man, when I met her. I should leave it at that. By now she had a dozen kids and twice that many grandkids; after all she was Mormon. What right had I to want to see her again?

I turned and walked back through town to where I had parked my Honda. It felt good to stretch my legs and it gave me time to gather my courage. It was a short ride out toward the airport to the LDS church. With a wooded area to the south and north ands the mountain in the background, it was a grand setting. There were two cars parked near one door. I parked my bike next to a red

Ford. I mentally rehearsed my little speech. I was from Colorado and had met Gladys Williams some thirty-five years ago but had just yesterday heard that she had died. That would do for starters. I knew where she was buried, but I would ask anyway and hope they would mention her niece.

I had only taken two steps from my bike when the double doors opened and two men came out. They both walked directly up to me. One extended his hand, "Good afternoon. How can we help you?"

He was a few inches taller than me but about the same age.

My stomach muscles contracted in a knot. What if this is Anna's husband?

"I, ah. I, ah was just passing through." I tried to look straight at the man and hoped my hands were not shaking. "I stopped in Hope to look up an old friend, Gladys Williams."

The man stepped forward and put a firm hand on my shoulder. "Gladys Williams passed on a few years ago."

I stood still and didn't pull back as I replied, "When there was no one at the house in Hope, I feared that might have happened. She was pretty old."

"God decides when our time here is to end."

He removed his hand and I felt a little more comfortable. My time should have ended thirty-five years ago. Did God decide it wasn't my time, or was it just luck?

The man went on to tell about her funeral and mentioned the grave in Hope. He also invited me to services that Sunday.

"You must come. Many of Gladys' friends will be there. Her niece, Anna Chapman, will be there. In fact, her family is coming up from Spokane this weekend. They all would love to meet you."

I didn't have to act surprised. I only hoped I didn't act too excited. Chapman? Now that was a name I'd have to check out in the phone book.

"Thank you, but I'm afraid you misunderstand. I knew Gladys thirty-five years ago and I'm not LDS."

"Not too late to change that." He reached in his suit coat pocket and took out a business card. "Where are you staying?"

"I'm just passing through. I will go back to Hope and visit Gladys' grave before I leave. Would you recommend a florist in town?"

"Part of that vet group that's going to Post Falls?" the younger of the two men asked.

I nodded, "Yes, I'll join up with them here in Sandpoint tomorrow."

Both men shook my hand before they departed. I turned the business card over and wrote Anna Chapman and the time of the service on Sunday on the back of the card. It was a fast ride back down Boyer to highway 2 to find a phone book. There were only two Chapman's listed. I rode by both addresses. The first was a little house in the west end of town. No one answered the doorbell and the lawn was tall grass and weeds. The second one was across the river in Sagle. It was a big house set back from the road. I stopped in the driveway.

A big station wagon with Washington license plates was parked in the driveway. The man had said Anna's daughter was visiting her this weekend. That could make things a little awkward. He hadn't mentioned Anna's husband. The phone book had listed the address under S. J. Chapman. What would I say if a man answered the door?

I motored quietly down the driveway and parked my old Honda. The birds in the trees stopped chirping. The breeze from the river disappeared. A dark shadow covered the house, the driveway and the surrounding trees. It grew darker as I walked up to the front door. I took off my helmet and held it under my left arm. I bent over, straightened my pant leg, and then stood erect and pushed the doorbell. A light chiming from inside was followed by silence. I felt I had entered into a cave. There was no contact with the world around me. This was suddenly its own strange world. In a minute a tall man would open the door and demand to know who I was and why I had come.

I stood tall and zipped my jacket up to my neck. Still, there was no sound from inside. I shifted my weight from one foot to the other. Silence closed tighter. I extended my hand to the bell again but stopped just before touching it. The breeze pushed around the side of the house like a guard dog. I jumped and turned to face it. Above, the treetops bowed toward the road. I backed away from the door and looked up. Dark gray clouds were passing quickly overhead. I turned and walked briskly to my bike.

The rain greeted me just as I pulled out of the driveway and onto the road. At the highway I headed north across the long bridge. The shower was short lived, and it hardly settled the dust on the road. With a feeling of relief, I set my bearing on a route to the florist.

It was hard to get the florist to wrap the flowers so I could carry them on the bike. The wind from riding at any speed whipped around the bike and the windscreen. The bouquet and the small vase barely survived the ride back to Hope.

Chapter 22
Anna Tells About Kurt

I suddenly had doubts about how much I could tell my daughter about Kurt. She adored her father, and having died this past summer this conversation served to enhance her memories of him. Lara was looking ahead down the lake; I turned my gaze back at Hawkins Point, and then traced the shoreline to the highway bridge over the railroad tracks. A man on a Jet Ski came into view. He must have spotted Lara for he turned from his path and came closer. He was wearing a black wet suit. Lara waved and he waved back, then he cut behind us and jumped over the wake before heading west again.

"Doesn't that look fun?" I asked.

"It looks cold to me," Lara replied.

"Cold if you fall in, but it's exciting too. A person needs some excitement in her life." I looked back at the disappearing Jet Ski. "Don't you wish you could take off on a Jet Ski and go anywhere on the lake? No destination in mind, just take off."

"Well, I'm glad you like speed because I am going to speed this up or we'll be too late to eat at the floating restaurant. You just keep talking. How long did this motorcycle guy stay in Hope?"

I watched the highway bridge pass by; it wasn't there back in 1969. From here east the highway would be closer to the shore than the railroad. Even from here I could tell most of the houses were closed up for the season.

"He stayed until December."

Lara rocked back in her chair. "December! It didn't take that long for his leg to heal, did it?" She raised one finger. "My, what could have made him stay so long?"

"I was just going to tell you about that." The old Waldron house could be seen through the branches of the pine trees between it and the lake. Higher on the hill was Gladys' house. It didn't look so grand without that widow's watch; the fire had destroyed the front half of the second floor. Gladys probably had gone up there to try to put the fire out, and been overcome with smoke.

"Hey, Mom, are you home?"

I turned back toward my daughter. "Just thinking. I had to go check on Betty every day so I'd stop by and visit Kurt. Usually this was in the morning before I went to work at the café. The Waldron house was just down the road from Betty's house. He must have been lonely because Betty once told me he would stop by and talk every afternoon."

"Mom, I don't care about Betty. Tell me about Kurt," Lara complained.

"I don't know what to say. I don't want you being judgmental."

"Judgmental? I bet Grandma didn't like it when you got interested in this guy. He rode a motorcycle. What else? Did he drink?" Lara asked.

"Why do you ask?"

"I was just trying to guess where this little story of yours is going."

I tried to smile. "He talked of drinking. You see, Gladys had warned him about not drinking if he was going to stay at the Waldron house, and we were going to help him. I never saw any evidence that he had liquor down at his house. Let me tell you what he was like."

Lara looked ahead on the lake pretending, she was still listening.

"At first, all Kurt was concerned about was getting better. He would hobble around on just one crutch when he should have been using two. When he should have been resting in bed, he was down in the garage trying to clean up his motorcycle. Mom fixed the meals at our house since Gladys and I both were working. She fixed a lunch for Betty that included enough for her to have something left over to eat that night before she went to bed. I'd take the meal to her and then stop to visit with Kurt. I told Mom he only ate two meals a day—a breakfast of cereal and milk and a dinner of sandwiches and soup. She too felt sorry for him, so the next day she fixed a special lunch, much bigger than the one she fixed for Betty. He was surprised and embarrassed when I brought it to him. "

"'Look,' he said. 'I can't take charity. You all are doing too much for me.'"

"I told him, 'No. You look. Mom wants you to get better and move on, so eat and stop talking about charity.' I sat down and took a sandwich out of the paper bag. 'See, it's just bologna and cheese.' I took a bite and held the bag out to him. He took a sandwich out and began to unwrap it."

"I noticed you have taken your bike apart. Will it run again?"

"He took a large bite of his sandwich before answering. 'I'm still cleaning it up. The engine doesn't look bad but the front fork is cracked and the rear wheel is way out of line. And, he held up a long chain, 'I've got a broken chain.'"

"'Maybe I can borrow Gladys' pickup and drive to Sandpoint and get you a new chain.'"

"'Do they have a Honda dealer there?'"

"I shrugged, 'There was an ad in the paper last week with Hondas for sale at Bill's Mobil.'"

"He finished half the sandwich in a few bites. 'Newspaper? Could I see the paper?' He smiled. 'Unless of course you using it for something important like lining the bottom of a bird cage.'"

"We don't have a bird. We also have a phone if you need to call someone. Your family must be worried sick about you.'"

"Worried? Maybe. Sick? No. Is there a mailing address for down here?'"

"I couldn't help but smile at how fast he ate that sandwich. I told him the address would be the same as ours since Gladys practically ran those houses year round. The next day I brought him some letter paper and stamps. He insisted on paying for the stamps. That week he wrote two letters, one to a Rudy Johnson and the other to a Michael Banner. They both lived in Colorado; Rudy in Loveland and Michael in Fort Collins."

The Good Faith turned into the breeze and the boat rocked a bit. With only two of us in the craft it road high in the water. Lara was looking forward to the docks by the resort.

"Don't stop, Mom. Okay, so he's down at this house and you go down to visit him. Just you and Kurt in that house alone. When did it get to be more than just visits?"

I looked away. She is being judgmental. Well, I can't leave the story here or who knows what she will think.

"We just slowly got to know each other. As I tried to explain at the start, I felt depressed. My father had died, Sam was gone and didn't write much at all, and my friends were all at college having fun. Kurt was all I had and he needed me. Once a week I would clean Betty's house. One day Kurt saw me doing that and said, 'When you're through over, there stop down at my place.' I did. I carried the vacuum, the mop and a pail down to his house."

"You cleaned his house?"

"Let me tell the story." I took a sip from my water bottle and then recapped it. "Despite hopping around on one leg, Kurt had kept his house remarkably clean. He said he had learned that in the Marines. Clean the barracks every Friday, or no liberty. I did mop his kitchen and bathroom floors. He had a vacuum but since he didn't go out of the house much that first two weeks he didn't track in much dirt. It was sunny the day he finally tried to walk down by the lake. I had finished cleaning Betty's house so I walked with him. He got along well with one crutch the second week he was there. Men hate to have you help them."

We had passed Hope and were off East Hope; now the trees hid the Waldron house from my view. "It was the first time he told me anything about himself. He thanked me for letting him have the newspapers. There was some news about the Vietnam War and he said he had been there."

"This is the second time I broke this leg. In Nam I tripped in the jungle, broke my leg and rolled down a hill." He laughed. 'No big deal but it got me a ticket home."

Lara nodded and looked over at me. "So he was in combat?"

"He never said he was in combat. He'd change the subject whenever I asked what he did in the Marines."

"So he wasn't combat?"

"I've talked with some men who came back from Iraq. The ones who saw real combat don't talk about it much." I bit my lower lip. "I think, yes, I'm sure he was in combat. I have no idea what he did."

Lara slowed the Good Faith as they approached the resort. "Keep talking. I want to know more about this Kurt. Was he just bumming around after coming back from Vietnam? A lot of them did, you know. Most were on drugs."

"That's what Mom was worried about too. No, I don't believe Kurt was ever on drugs. He was at times so soft spoken I thought something bad had happened to him over there. Something bad had happened all right, but it wasn't just the war in Vietnam. I got a clue when he starting receiving mail." I reached over and took Lara's arm. "Hey, slow down. The dock is just over there. You'll run into it."

She throttled back and shook her head. "Mom, I know how to drive this boat. Remember, Dad taught me."

The boat slowed, I stood up and looked up at the highway. I heard the rumble of a motorcycle and looked back toward Hope, but saw only a logging truck. It must be a diesel engine. By now I should recognize the difference. It's important when you ride a motorcycle.

My daughter stepped off the boat and tied the front end to the dock. "You will finish the story?"

Feeling I had neglected my duty to the boat's captain, I dropped the two dock bumpers over the dockside and secured the aft end of the Good Faith. "I'll finish this story over lunch. I hope I have time to tell you about the conspiracy. If not, I'll tell you tonight."

"But Jim will be here tonight," Lara said.

"I'd rather tell the story to just you; it's something Jim would not understand. I hope you do, or will at least listen to me."

"Mom, don't be so melodramatic."

Chapter 23
Kurt: Hope Cemetery

I rode much slower than usual on the way back to Hope. It was strange, for at first I missed the thrill of speed. I began noticing more things along the side of the road and realized I had not really seen the country. I had only seen the road. That thought frightened me a little. Near the Hidden Lakes Golf Course I braked and pulled to the shoulder of the road. The feeling I had back at Anna's house had returned. Who was I to come see her? On the road with my bike beneath me, I had an identity. Stop the bike and get off, and who am I?

A cow moose and calf silently crossed the road and went down the hill toward Pack River. I don't belong here. Those moose belong here; I'm the outsider. I checked the road before I pulled out and raced up to speed. Moose are just too big. If you hit one on a bike, it could kill you; not hitting one almost killed me. Even if I am afraid of living, hitting a moose is not the way to end it.

By the time I reached Hope, I was thinking again how I owed my life to Anna and to Gladys. Now Gladys was dead but I knew where Anna lived. If only it was the right Anna.

I slowed to twenty as I entered Hope. Again, as I approached Lake Street, I looked up the hill. That house was in the right spot but it just didn't look like Gladys' house. I stopped at the next fork in the road. East Main went on into East Hope. The road to the left was signed Grandview Avenue. I rode along slowly until I saw yet another fork in the road. The left branch called Round Top Road was steep. There was no sign on the right branch. I raced the engine, released the clutch and spurted up Round Top Road. When it leveled out a little I pulled to a complete stop and looked around. Down to my right, the upper level of the graveyard was an open area; the lower half had some big, old pine trees. I motored down carefully on what were little more than car tracks that seemed to divide the graveyard into two plots of about the same size. I found a level spot and parked my Honda in the grass. I untied the bouquet of flowers. It wasn't damaged by the wind. Carefully I carried it as I wandered around the lower half of the area. There were few bold gravestones and many more plain flat markers in the earth. It didn't look like anyone had been here in weeks. I don't want to be buried but I don't like the idea of cremation either. What if I just rode off the Going-to-the-Sun highway at night? Forget it, Kurt; you came here to find Gladys.

All small-town graveyards have a system of grave locations that makes sense to the local population, but are completely baffling to a stranger. Narrow lines of concrete that showed just above the surface divided the place into what appeared to be family plots. I found some graves with markers dated 1908, and others so old I could not read the dates. In a plot near the top of the area I found some more recent dates.

I walked up the hill to a spot where I could view the entire little graveyard. Knowing that she had died in the past few years would be of little help. I had no idea of the family plots, or if Gladys was even buried in an area owned by her side of the family. Damn, I wished Anna were here. She'd know where Gladys' grave is.

I looked down at my bouquet of flowers. That's it. Old Nick had said that Gladys' niece often brought flowers to the grave. I set my sights on an arrangement of small yellow flowers tied together with a big, blue bow. As I came closer, I became more confident it would be the right spot. Gladys had the bluest eyes I'd ever seen; the blue ribbon was a fitting marker for her grave. I looked down at my floral arrangement of red and white flowers and smiled. Then I took the blue ribbon off the old flowers and tied it around the fresh bouquet. I pulled the dried yellow flowers out of the basket, set them at the foot of the grave and put my bouquet in its place. Then I knelt and read the headstone:

Gladys Williams
July 4, 1909 ~ December 10, 2003

I said a silent prayer, then rose to my feet and picked up the old dried flowers. I looked over at the nearby graves and selected one to receive the dried flowers. It was just down the hill from Gladys' grave. I leaned the flowers against the gravestone before I read the name engraved there:

Elizabeth Nietzy
December 10, 1850 ~ December 13, 1950

I stepped back and closed my eyes. Nietzy? Where had I heard that name before? Elizabeth Nietzy? What if not Elizabeth, but Betty? I know Betty. No, this woman died in 1950 and I met Betty in 1969. I stood upright and looked around at the nearby gravestones. All in this area were recent, that is, the last twenty years. I walked to the lower part of the graveyard and systematically began to read the names and dates. Slowly I worked my way back up the hill. I didn't plan it but I found myself looking for Vicky Anna O'Sullivan. I never found a grave with the name O'Sullivan. The man at that resort said Gladys had died in a fire. That would explain why I didn't recognize the house; it had been remodeled. The big octagonal-shaped room on the second floor, Anna's bedroom, was gone now. I started to look for another grave with the same last date. I soon gave that mission up and filed the idea of asking more about Gladys' death of Anna, if I ever found her.

I returned to Gladys' grave, knelt and said another prayer. This was the most I'd prayed in years. Rising, I walked down the side of the graveyard to a spot where I had a good view of the lake. I was surprised I hadn't noticed any graves of the Chinese workers who had built the railroad. They had built the Great Northern Railroad and the Northern Pacific, so they must have lived here in Hope. Betty had told me once they also worked the mines at Gold Creek and south along the lake. If so, some would have died in Hope. They all could not have left on that ghost train at midnight in the story Betty had told me.

Her words came back to me as I walked silently past the gravesites. 'The Chinese, they built the railroad you know. Well, they were paid very little and much of what they did get they sent back to relatives in China. When they died, they wanted their bones to be shipped back to China, but most died too poor for that to happen. One of the dishonest railroad men in Hope, named Matthew, offered to ship their bones to Seattle in the freight cars for a very reasonable price. Well, the elders of the camp took him up on his offer. They paid him his money and then they dug up ten of the graves of their countrymen who had died the last year. They had to put the bones in wooden boxes and bring the boxes to the railroad yards at midnight. The guy would load the boxes on the freight car just ahead of the caboose. Just a few miles out of town the train goes out across the Pack River Flats. Here that guy tossed the boxes off the train on the lake side of the tracks.'

I shuttered at the thought that there may be some truth in this tale.

'Now, Kurt, you can hear the trains coming through town at night even if they didn't blow their whistle, but they always do. But if you ever hear a steam engine chugging to a stop in Hope about midnight, come down to the lake here and watch. The dead in the lake will hear the train whistle, come out of the lake and walk down to the station and wait for the train to stop. When it does, they will be loaded back on the train and it will chug away to the west. Of course, it only happens on the night of a full moon.'

I grinned as I walked back up the hill to my motorcycle. Who knows? The moon was almost full last night. Maybe while I'm here in Hope I'll meet a dead Chinaman. On the other hand, I'd rather meet Vicky at Hope Hotel.

Chapter 24
Anna: Lunch in East Hope

Lara docked the Good Faith at the resort. We walked the long boardwalk to the floating restaurant and were seated at a table inside. The waitress, there was only one that day, gave us menus and told us what items were available for lunch. Lara ordered a BLT with a cup of hot chocolate. I was about to order the same when I heard the distinct sound of a motorcycle. Not any motorcycle, but Kurt's big Honda. I glanced up the hill toward Hope. No, it couldn't be him. He'd probably given up riding years ago. Beside he wouldn't be here. I looked down at the menu and ordered the most expensive entree on the lunch page.

"The Crab Louie sounds good, and a glass of ice tea." I turned the menu over and studied the wine list. If Kurt were here he would order that, and a glass of wine too.

Lara handed her menu back to the waitress. When the waitress departed, Lara leaned forward and whispered, "You ordered ice tea."

"Have you ever had wine?"

"Now, Mom, of course not."

"Really?"

"Okay, once. More than once, but that's all I'll say."

I could see the highway from our table. The traffic was an equal mixture of semi-trucks and cars. No motorcycles. Still I kept track, and just before I finished my salad I saw a motorcycle rumble by, then another. I watched until the second rider was out of sight and wondered where Kurt was this fall afternoon.

Lara finished her sandwich and the waitress came with the bill.

"Could you bring me some more ice tea?" I looked across the table at Lara. "I need it to continue this story."

Once the waitress departed, Lara grinned and asked, "Now tell me what really happened between you and Kurt."

I looked up at the highway in the direction the motorcycles had gone.

"All my life I have been like a puppet on strings. There are so many things I didn't do because I never knew how much I was being restrained. I don't know who I really am."

"Mom, go on with the story and I'll find out who you really are."

"Kurt and I quickly became friends, nothing serious, just friends. He was terribly bored. He couldn't go far with a cast on his leg. Some days he would try to hobble down to the lake. When it rained he was completely housebound. I'd bring him lunch and the paper every day and I'd always stop and talk for a while. The paper was always a day or two old, but he didn't care. I asked him if he wanted to come up to our house and watch television some time but he declined. The television in his house didn't get but two channels. He did listen to the radio a lot. In November, he was scheduled to go back to the hospital and get his cast taken off. I volunteered to drive him there."

The waitress brought a fresh glass of ice tea to the table and looked at Lara. She shook her head and looked anxiously across the table at me. "Go on, Mom, get to the good part."

After the waitress left, I took a sip of tea and decided to tell less of this story to my daughter.

"When we got ready to go back to Sandpoint, Kurt put a pair of jeans in the cab of the truck and some parts from his motorcycle in the bed of the truck. I started the truck and backed up to Lake Street, turned around headed west on Main. I knew my mother was watching from the window. Kurt must have thought the same thing because he waved out the side window. When we got to Sandpoint, we went first to the hospital. He fretted about leaving the parts to his bike in the back of the pickup, but I assured him Sandpoint was a safe town. The doctor came in and talked to Kurt before he cut the case off his leg. He examined the leg again and had him flex his feet and bend his knees. He told Kurt to be careful about putting his full weight on the leg for a while and insisted Kurt take one of the crutches with him."

I had to smile as I remember Kurt telling me to leave the room so he could get dressed.

"It was almost noon but we went to the Mobil station before lunch. Kurt looked different in long pants. He acted different too. I knew he was in pain but he held his head high. Most of the parts Kurt needed had to be ordered. We left the Mobil station and went to a restaurant just a few blocks from the hospital. We talked about silly things, like what it would be like if we could fly. Not in airplanes, but with wings, like birds. People wouldn't need roads or bridges, if they could fly. It was foolish yet relaxing, and I just felt so grand being there with him."

Lara put her elbows on the table and folded her hands together. "So, Mom, you weren't falling for this guy, were you?"

I nodded. "Yes, I was. At first he had been just a relief, someone to worry about instead of thinking about myself. That afternoon he changed. I bet we spent two hours at that table."

Lara looked over her shoulder toward the waitress across the room. "Talking about people flying? I bet the other customers thought you were a couple of nuts."

"Kurt said riding a motorcycle was the closest thing he'd done to being free like a bird. He was right. He even taught me to ride."

"You rode his motorcycle?" Lara gasped. She pulled her chair up a little closer to the table, "Is that all there was to the Kurt story?"

I finished the glass of ice tea before I continued. "Kurt changed once he had his cast off. That night I saw him sitting at the bar in the Soiled Dove Saloon. I wanted to go in and tell him to go home, but instead I ran back to Gladys' house. I can't tell you the rest of that story." I pushed my glass toward the center of the table.

Lara pushed her chair back, stood up with a disappointed look and said, "So, your hero Marine turned to drinking. You should have expected that."

"I expected it but I didn't accept it." I opened my purse and took out some money to pay the bill and left a big tip under the ice tea glass. "I said a prayer for him and went home."

Lara glanced at her watch. "My look what time it is. We'd better be starting back."

As we walked down the boardwalk I added a little to the story. I didn't want Lara to think Kurt was an alcoholic.

"The next day he came to the café about dinner time. He told me he'd gone to the Soiled Dove Saloon the night before and had one too many. He never went back. Kurt stayed in Hope until December. Gladys even invited him to Thanksgiving dinner. He was a nice man. He wrote me a letter before he left for Colorado. I didn't get it until last summer."

Lara turned her hands palm out. "Now that doesn't make sense."

I nodded. "It was a love letter. Now that I have read it, I want to know what happened to Kurt after he left Hope."

"What was that, thirty-five years ago? He's probably married by now and has kids, maybe even kids who have kids. Forget this guy. Look, Jim and I want you to move down to Spokane where you will be closer to us and your own grandkids."

"I plan to stay in my house in Sagle this winter. I need the rest. You don't know how stressful it was this last year taking care of Sam. I'll visit Spokane often but I don't want to live with you and Jim. My mother lived with your father and me for fifteen years, and it almost ended our marriage. I won't do that to you. Besides, unlike my mother, I am very much able to take care of myself."

Lara raised her hands. "Wait. Did you tell Dad about Kurt?"

I managed a smile. "No, I never told your father about Kurt, but he knew. You see, he had that letter."

Lara took my arm. "Mom, I think you are hiding something from me. This isn't fair. You got me curious about Kurt and now I want to hear the whole story."

Chapter 25
Kurt Recalls Vicky

When I left the graveyard, I rode slowly down the narrow road that wound around the hillside until I came back to Hotel Hope. There was a sign on the Soiled Dove Saloon saying they would open at four. I turned around and rode east on Main, crossed Strong Creek and rode up Big Hill Road just for the fun of it. On a bike at moderate speed, the roads in Hope and East Hope were a dream; for a full-size car or a pickup truck, they were dangerously narrow. On the downhill I simply geared down and let the engine rumble as it slowed the bike. The people who lived along those roads may not have appreciated it, but many of the houses looked empty. I tooled through East Hope on Lookout Boulevard. Twice I stopped and looked down at the lake and the new resort and the floating restaurant. At Snell's Hill Street, I again dropped the bike into a lower gear and rode down to Wellington Place. Here I turned east again on what was the old road to Clark Fork. A few miles out of town I took a side road and stopped at the railroad tracks. Not seeing or hearing any trains, ghost or real, I crossed the tracks and came to the highway and jetted across it. I sped up a bit as I followed the asphalt road through the David Thompson Wildlife Preserve, and on to the Red Fir Resort.

After parking my Honda beside the office I started down the trail to my cabin. The entrance to the cabin was on the bay side of the A-frame. When I rounded the corner, there was Nick sitting on the deck waiting for me.

"Hey," the old man called. "How did you do? Find Gladys?"

"Oh, yes, I even brought some flowers for her grave."

"Now that was a nice thing to do. How about her niece?"

I smiled. "I tried. She wasn't home. From talking to some people with the LDS, I think this Anna is the woman I met when I was here thirty-five years ago."

Nick motioned for me to come closer. He leaned forward and said, "If you knew her before, you've got to make more than one try to say hello."

I shook my head. "After thirty-five years, I doubt she would remember me."

"This here is Saturday; you said you'd be staying until Monday. What are you going to do now?"

I pointed over across the bay. "Tonight I'm going over to the Soiled Dove Saloon and have a drink."

"Now, if this Anna is Mormon, you won't find her in a Saloon." He chuckled. "Of course you might just meet someone else. Done that more than once in my day. Too bad the hotel ain't open. It's a long ride back here."

I stepped back from the table where Nick was sitting. "Hang on. I'll be back in a minute." I went inside and filled the coffee pot. In the cabinet above the sink I found two mugs. A few minutes later I returned to the table on the deck with two cups of brew.

Nick nodded. "Thank you. Got any additives?"

"Sorry, no sugar or milk in the place." I sat at the big wooden table across from Nick.

The old man shook his head. "I didn't mean that."

I watched as Nick took a small flask from his inside jacket pocket and added a little whiskey to his cup. He held the flask toward me.

"Thanks, but I'm limiting my input of alcohol to beer nowadays." I leaned on one elbow and pointed out across the water. "Back in the winter of nineteen sixty-nine, I stayed in a small house just down from the hotel. You can just see the top of the roof from here. It was straight down the hill from Gladys' house. She was the one who convinced me to stay there. I had broken my leg and needed to wait for it to heal before I could ride on."

The old man took a deep sip of his coffee and smiled. "Is this when you met Anna?"

"No, this is about when I met a girl named Vicky. One night, it must have been in November, after I had that damn cast off my leg, I hobbled up to the Soiled Dove Saloon for a drink to celebrate. Gladys didn't want me drinking or smoking in the house where I was staying. The people who owned that house were tea drinkers."

I paused and took a sip of coffee and watched the steam rise. "I had a few rounds of whiskey. Not many. I was watching my money pretty closely. It was just about closing time."

I looked across the bay to the hotel, a white fortress on the hill. I was a fool, a young fool, back then. It is all so clear, as if it just happened.

"Well are you going to tell me about meeting Vicky, or just sit there?"

"I met Vicky about midnight. The bar was deserted, except for the two of us. I bought her a drink. We talked a little. It was bar talk, when every comment seems to have more than one meaning. My memory gets a little clouded about what happened next."

Nick looked across the table at me, his eyes studying mine. When I didn't say anything more he began. "You recall going upstairs with this Vicky, but the hotel was closed that winter. You recall a wild passionate night but you haven't seen her since."

I raised both hands off the table. "You know this story? The next morning when I awoke, I was back in my own bed in the little house. It's all so weird. I had never been in the upstairs of that place, but I was sure I had spent the night up there with Vicky. I asked about town but no one knew where Vicky lived. Some laughed and said it was just another Vicky story, whatever that is supposed to mean."

I looked over at the smiling old man at the table.

"Did you ever tell Betty this story?" he asked.

"No, don't think I did. You know this Vicky?"

Nick nodded. "Vicky is a ghost that haunts Hope. Story is she drowned years ago but returns once in a while. Us old folks would understand, but this new generation will think you are nuts." He smiled at his cup. "Stick to the drinking story. Everyone will understand it. Whiskey can take you away from all your troubles. I learned that out in the Pacific." He shook his head and added, "It still haunts me. Whiskey is no solution. It always dumps you back into the real world. There've been many a night I don't remember how I ever got home."

I looked across the bay at the Hotel Hope. How did I get home that night?

Chapter 26
Anna and Kurt

The breeze tussled my hair as I walked down to the Good Faith. I glanced up at the gray clouds slowly sailing in the sky above. Lara walked just a step ahead, unlatched the gate, stepped on board and looked back. "Should I put up the canopy?"

"Might as well do it now," I said as I untied the boat. When I stepped on board the Good Faith drifted away from the dock, aided by a slight breeze.

Lara quickly got the canopy locked in place and hurried to her captain's chair. She started the engine and drove forward into Ellisport Bay before making a large circle and heading west. I settled into my captain's chair and snapped my jacket. "Before I start back with my story about Kurt, tell me why you and Jim are so concerned about me living here alone?"

"A little. It's not a health thing; we both know you can take care of yourself. It's the opposite. Jim is afraid that some guy will see you as a wealthy pigeon. He actually said an attractive pigeon."

"He did, did he?" I laughed. "Tell him to reserve his judgment until I lose another twenty pounds."

"Don't set your standard too high. The last time we were here, Jim noticed several men stopped to talk to you after church. He told me we should get you to move down to Spokane where we can keep an eye on you. For your own protection, of course."

"Maybe I shouldn't tell you the rest of the story."

"You had better or I'll think of something worse," Lara said aloud.

I laughed and looked across the bay. Most of the houses on that side of the bay looked closed, with no boats at the docks except for one, The Red Fir Resort. They were always the last to close for the winter. I opened the compartment in front of me and took out the binoculars again. Yes, I could see two people on one of the decks and lights on in the cabin just to the west. Two old men sitting around telling lies while the womenfolk fix dinner. If that is retirement, I'd hate it.

I lowered the binoculars and restarted my story.

"Kurt and I made a second trip to Sandpoint to get the parts for his motorcycle. We had been having a running discussion about religion. He acted like he had never been inside a church or had any idea why someone would go to church. It was all an act. When I gave him a copy of the Book of Mormon, he jerked his hands back like he was afraid to touch it. He joked, 'Now, I better stay clear of this.'"

I chuckled. "He knew more about the Mormon faith then he let on. I worried he had heard bad things about us."

Lara added, "Lots of people are like that. What happened while in Sandpoint?"

"We stopped at the Mobil station to get the parts for his motorcycle, then we went shopping. He was a terrible shopper. He just looked at things, and then picked up a pair of pants and a sweater. He never bothered to try anything on. We shopped at a corner used bookstore. He picked up a copy of a Louis L'Amour book, and then a strange book by Isaac Asimov, *The Human Brain*. I was shocked. As it turned out, he had graduated from college with a mixed major of math and biology. We went to the movies but I don't remember what we saw."

"Did he try anything?" Lara asked.

"Of course not."

"If he didn't try anything, why don't you remember the movie?"

"It was a Western. They are all alike. Anyway, after that trip he had the parts for his motorcycle and some books to read. That motorcycle was his escape from the world. Kurt was in some ways like a boy who had run away from home. He graduated from college, served in Vietnam, and while he was there his girl married someone else. I think the girl was the last straw that had sent him drifting. He used to make comments about my short skirts. 'Anna, you look like you are dressed for a banker's office.'"

"Mom, I think you are censoring the story too much. It happened a long time ago. Get to the issue. You must have been more than friends. How much more? Did the two of you..." Lara tossed her head toward her mother. "You know, go all the way."

I looked down for a moment and then back at my daughter, my thirty-year-old daughter. "We had a few stolen moments, just kissing and such. I bet Betty noticed how long I stayed when I stopped to see Kurt. I bet she told Gladys."

"Did you or didn't you?"

"Of course not. We didn't do anything more than kiss and hug."

"So how long did this go on?" Lara asked.

"He managed to get his motorcycle running before Christmas and left when there was a break in the weather. Before he left, he taught me to ride."

"You're changing the subject. Tell me about those passionate moments at his house. Did he have nice hands?"

"Look, it wasn't just a physical attraction. I had someone to talk to. He listened. He took me for short rides. It was exciting."

"Making out and riding a motorcycle are two different things. One is fun and the other is dangerous. Well, in a way they are both dangerous."

"Let me tell you about learning to ride and maybe you will want to try it too."

Lara raised her chin slightly. "Mom, I have the feeling that you are leaving out the best part of this story. Relax, I won't tell anyone as it happened over thirty years ago. It happened before you married Dad."

I looked across the bay. "I wonder what happened to Kurt after he left Hope. I want to see him again. Just see him."

Chapter 27
Kurt Remembers Anna

I went back inside and got the coffee pot and the pair of binoculars off the counter, and carried them out to the table. The sun had made its way under the clouds and created a pattern of light and dark blotches on the water. Across Ellisport Bay a pontoon boat motored slowly away from the resort.

I pointed to it as it began to pick up speed. "I'd love to have a boat this time of the year. Not many others out in the lake." I glanced over at Old Nick. "Of course I'd want one of those Jet Skis. That thing is too slow."

I raised the binoculars to my eyes. I could see only two people in the boat. The nearest one sat with her legs crossed—always a good sign from a woman. The other sat leaning forward a little. Her long hair trailed out a little behind her head. Two women. I wondered what prompted them to go out on the lake alone. It was cool in the shade and the boat was going fast enough to provide a bit of wind for the two passengers. I shifted the focus to the name on the pontoon Good Faith. What an odd name? Good Time would be a better name for a party boat. I turned my attention back to the women. The nearest one opened the compartment in front of her and took out a pair of binoculars. She turned and looked my way. The binoculars rested in her lap. I quickly lowered mine to the table. I felt an urge to go ahead and make eye contact. From this distance what could hurt? Looking at a woman through binoculars wasn't making eye contact; it was something else. Even as she turned and looked my way, I did not pick up the binoculars. Nick tapped his coffee cup on the table. I jerked my head that way.

"Son, you just drifted off into dreamland. What did you see on that boat? Two bikinis?"

"In this weather? No, just two women out for a ride on the lake. Their husbands must be at a football game or out hunting."

Nick lifted his empty cup. "Can I trouble you for another cup of that hot stuff?"

I picked up the pot and filled both cups. Nick carefully doctored his coffee, then looked up at me. "I bet Gladys was fit to be tied when she heard about you boozing it up. Did she kick you out of that house?"

"No. I guess she never heard what happened."

The old man smiled. "Hope is a small town. A very small town. If you got drunk at the Soiled Dove Saloon, she would have heard about it." He took a sip from his cup and leaned forward a little. "Nineteen sixty-nine, if I remember correctly, was the year her sister-in-law came to live with her." He turned his head slightly. "Seems to me she had a daughter."

I nodded. "That was Anna. You are too smart for me, old man."

He grinned. "I was a friend of Gladys but a better friend of Betty's. In nineteen sixty-nine I was back in Montana, but Betty told me about you. Now tell me about this Anna. I never got to meet her."

"Anna was an angel. No, Anna was a saint." I looked down at the coffee. Saints don't drink coffee a reminder of how religion was always an issue whenever I thought of Anna. I raised my head. "That was the big problem back then. Now, there is a bigger problem— she's married."

I took a deep drink of coffee. It was warm, not hot. Anna drank hot chocolate, not coffee. Hell, I could learn to do that. Could I learn not to say hell?

I looked out at the boat heading west across the bay. "I was in an accident. Broke my leg and damaged the bike. Gladys saw the accident and took it upon herself to help me get back on my feet.

Anna and her mother were staying with Gladys that winter. Anna got the job of checking up on me when I was down at the little house, waiting for my leg to heal. I called her my angel but she didn't like that tag."

I leaned forward and squinted out at the lake. The boat was leaving the bay now and was entering open water. It rocked a little more. It sped up some, likely to compensate for the choppy water. I thought I noticed one of the women look back across the water. I waved. The boat continued on its journey and I continued my story.

"Anna was the kind of girl who a young man both desires and fears. She was so nice and wholesome that you felt guilty if you made any sexual remarks. I felt guilty the first time I kissed her. I knew I wasn't good enough for her. She could do better and she knew she could do better. Why she kissed me back, I will never know. Perhaps she felt sorry for me. Perhaps she was lonely."

I put the cup down on the table. "After my cast was off, I tried to do everything for myself. I didn't use my crutch one day, and was so sore the next I had to use it to get to the bathroom. After a while I made a point not to use it when I went to the café, but I hopped around on it a lot at the house. Pride was my enemy. I wanted to walk tall, to be someone Anna would be happy to see. From the start I knew I wouldn't get very far with her and I didn't want to get very close either. A woman can be like a fire on a cold night. The closer you get the closer you want to get, until you get burned. It happened just that way for me."

"You from Colorado back then?" Nick asked. "Me, I've been everywhere. I just drift."

"Me too. I didn't plan to drift. That was my problem from the start. You see, I was going to be drafted the year I graduated from college. As soon as my deferment ran out my number was up. But I foxed them. I enlisted in the Marines for three years. It was an impulsive move but I wanted to put my military obligation behind me. I needed to think I had some control of how I did it. Boy, was

I wrong. You see, I had a girl. She was just a freshman at Colorado State University. In three years she would graduate and I would get out of the Marines. We even picked our wedding date. I sold my car to pay for an engagement ring. Man, I thought I was so smart."

My right hand formed a tight fist. "Nothing worked as I planned. They didn't send me to pilot training like they said. There were several aviation MOS but according to my tests I was better suited to carry an M-16. They shipped me to Camp Pendleton for basic training, then to MCRD San Diego for specialized training before shipping me off to Nam. I got two week's leave before going to Nam. I came home, Rachel skipped class and we had one wild time together."

My fingers relaxed and I watched them join as if in prayer. "The first six months I was in Nam, I got a letter every week. Then they stopped. I knew something was wrong. Three months later I got a Dear John letter."

I raised my right hand and turned my palm toward Nick. There were still two thin, white lines across the palm, two scars left by the broken glass. "In one letter I had lost my girl, and the relationship with my brother was forever shattered. I survived Vietnam. I was proud to be a Marine. Ho Chi Minh said he would kill us all. He sent the NAV down to do just that. If you left Nam alive, it was a victory. I was wounded but I returned home."

"After I got home, I did go back to the school. But things were different. I bought a motorcycle— a Honda CB750. I went everywhere. Up to the Black Hills. A moose in Idaho ended my trip just outside Hope."

I tried to smile. "So Anna was like an angel from heaven. I fell instantly in love, but she was a Mormon. So, in the end, I had to move on. Gladys was sharp; she spotted the problem before either of us did. She told me straight out the best thing I could do was go home." I finished my coffee.

Nick shook his head. "Say, how well did you get to know Betty?"

"Oh, kind of well. She was a strange old lady. I don't mean anything bad, but still strange. She always had a story about Hope— discovery of gold, building the railroad, the commercial fishing in the lake. Did you know they even built boats in Hope back when they were steam-powered? Sorry, you live around here and you know all that. It was new to me. Interesting and yet I grew bored. After a while I didn't stop at her house very often."

"An old woman can't compete with a young one, not even if she has a stack of stories to tell."

I grinned. "You got that right." The pontoon boat was completely out of sight. "If you think you can hang onto the back of my bike, let's go over to Hope for dinner."

Nick stood up slowly, taking one leg out from under the table at a time. "No, thanks. I don't think I can ride on the back of that bike, but there is another reason. I've got a date with a sassy old lady. As a special treat I'm taking her to dinner."

"At your age? I'm impressed."

Nick beamed. "One last question. Did you tell Betty you were leaving Hope?"

I closed my eyes for just a moment. "I did more than that. I wrote a letter to Anna and left it with Betty. She said she would take care of it. Today I can't remember what I said in that letter. Hell, whatever I said wasn't enough. She never wrote to me. Now I ask you, what am I doing here?"

Nick smiled. "There is always Hope. Remember that, son. There is always Hope."

Chapter 28
Anna Remembers Kurt

As we passed Warren Island, I offered to take my turn at the helm. After a meal Lara was always a bit sleepy. I motored closer to the shore for a good, last look at Hope. Several semi-trucks rumbled by on the road near the shore. The change in exhaust tones signaled their progress as the road wound higher up the slope. I looked and listened but didn't see or hear any motorcycles. At Trestle Creek, I turned west to Hawkins' Point and Sunnyside. I always liked the name Sunnyside; it invoked a positive view of life, as did Hope. Sunnyside was both the name of the mountain that formed the peninsula and the small community on the south shore. The clouds moved eastward, but the shadow cast by Blue Mountain high above Sandpoint extended into the lake to greet the Good Faith.

Lara snapped her jacket tight around her. "Okay, Mom, I'll take over now."

"It's all right. I enjoy doing this. You get a rest."

"Yes, but you stopped talking. Now let me drive and you talk. There must be something about this man that you haven't told me. Why would you want to go see what happened to a motorcycle rider? Just how close did you two get that winter?"

Lara stood up and stepped behind my chair. She had, by age ten, adopted her father's assertive character. I reluctantly got up and moved to the chair she had left. There is no way I could live in the house where my daughter is the queen. Another bundle of clouds drifted across the lake to block the sun, and I zipped up my jacket. Without the sunshine the breeze was cold. I looked off across the lake toward Sandpoint.

"You say 'motorcycle rider' like it was something immoral. I know some very nice people who ride. Did you hear about that group of vets who form a motorcade for the troops when they return from Iraq?"

"Sure, it gives the old, retired misfits something to do. Motorcycles are dangerous. They have a death wish."

"It is dangerous and that is a part of it. It is also enjoyable and in a strange way relaxing."

Lara laughed. "Sure, Mom. Like you're an expert. Let's get back to Kurt."

I raised my chin a little. What would she say if I told her I've wanted a motorcycle ever since Kurt taught me to ride? Of course I had to wait until Sam left to buy one. She will find out soon enough, so I might as well tell her.

"Riding is an adventure. Kurt told me stories of trips he took on his bike. They were his escape times. He needed them. Everyone needs to relax and, for a short time, escape from the cares of the world. Remember, he had been to war and had his heart broken."

"Now, Mom, you don't know that. Besides, everyone falls in love when they are in college. It's just the time and place for romance. If you can't find a friend of the opposite sex at that age, you are a case. Besides, did you ever meet a guy who didn't have at least one sad story of the girl who got away?"

"Point taken. Now, let's go back to motorcycles. Kurt got his bike running just about the time it snowed. I'd stop by Betty's house and Kurt would be there, standing out in the road and looking at the sky. I just knew he was praying for the sun to melt the snow away. I told him one day to pray for rain not sunshine, as he'd have a better chance. I was right the second week in December; the rain melted all the snow on the roads. In a few shady spots it was just slush. Kurt got his bike out that day and rode up and down the streets in town. He even took me for a ride on the back. We went down by the lake on the road to the docks.

There was little traffic there. No one went fishing that much in December."

Just thinking of that first ride did something to me. I sat up straight and put my hands in front of me.

"He persuaded me to try riding the bike myself. It had an electric starter like a car. Not a key, but a button on the handlebars. The throttle was on the right side and the clutch was on the left. He put the cycle in first gear and climbed on behind me. It worked just like he said."

Anna held onto the steel bar above the bunker and looked sideways at Lara.

"I just rode up to the docks and stopped. He helped me turn it around and then we rode back down to the highway. After a few trips he let me go by myself."

"Did you ever shift gears?" Lara asked.

"Yes. Before we had to stop that day, I was riding up the road, turning around by myself and riding back to where Kurt was standing. It was fun. We rode back to his house, put the bike in the garage and went inside to warm up. I was excited. We both were. Hugging led to kissing and kissing led to…"

"Petting, and that always leads to a romp in bed. Mom how could you?"

"I didn't. We didn't. Lara, don't even think that about me."

"Why are you yelling at me? You're the one who was doing whatever with the motorcycle clown."

"All we did was make out for a little while, then I went home, changed my clothes and went to work." I turned to Lara and measured my words carefully, "What is it you can't handle— that your mother was once a twenty-year-old woman and liked this man, or that he rode a motorcycle?"

Lara shook her head. "Okay, Mom, you were young once. Making out with a guy is no big deal, but you skipped a little detail. How far did you go?"

"I told you he had nice hands. That's all I'll tell you about that part. We were close. He understood. He didn't get on my case for wishing I were back in college. No guilt trip from him. He listened and he understood. And we shared things like him teaching me to ride his bike. That was not only exciting, but it was nice of him to teach me. The bike meant a lot to him. He had just fixed it and he let me ride it. I dare you to ride a motorcycle, a really big highway bike. You'd see how exciting it was."

"Well, Mom, just to let you know, you aren't the only tomboy in the family. Jim and I rode four-wheelers this summer. I didn't tell you because I thought it would freak you out. Dad always said four-wheelers and dirt bikes were examples of money poorly spent. You know, like the Walkers. They are always complaining about the price of gas, but they have a big four-wheel drive pickup and every mechanical toy there is."

I folded my arms and looked ahead. There was that phrase 'Dad always said' again. I never realized until he died what a dominant force he was in the family.

"Why didn't Kurt leave if his motorcycle was fixed?" Lara asked, with a superior smile on her face.

"He wanted to go; I was the one who wanted him to stay. He worked the night shift— four to closing— at the gas station. There he'd talk with the highway patrol when they stopped by. He had a toll-free number for the Montana Highway Department. He'd call every day while at work. All the passes in Montana were snow-packed, and he was stuck on the west side of the Rocky Mountains. I told Mom about this. Just like you, she thought he'd be gone as soon as he got that motorcycle running. She is the one who sent Kurt home. I think it was the tau cross that made her do it. The first week Kurt worked at the gas station he gave me a present. It was a silver chain with a cross on it. The cross was shaped like the Greek letter tau. I told Kurt we celebrate the risen Christ, while Catholics celebrate his death. As I look back, that wasn't a very nice thing to say."

"But it's true," Lara said.

"Kurt insisted I keep it because he had my name inscribed on the back. So I did."

"Wait a minute. How did he do that?"

"He must have bought it from Spanish Joe, but that's another story. What is important is he gave it to me. I wore it under my blouse at home, but wore it on the outside when I was working at the café. Someone must have seen it and told Mother. She told me to take it off. She also got Kurt to leave."

"Go on with the story," Lara prompted, as she turned the helm and headed southeast to pass Sandpoint on the port side.

"Kurt was a handsome young man. He was a little on the wild side but not really as wild as Mother thought he was. Just a free spirit." I looked up as we cruised under the railroad trestle.

Lara turned the Good Faith south and headed for the third arch from the left on the highway bridge. "If it was just a flirtatious relationship, why are you so interested in him now? You both went your separate ways."

I stood up and scanned the bridge as we approached. "After Mother discovered the cross, she and Gladys openly talked about how to get Kurt to leave town. They also kept a watch on me like I was still in junior high. I know Mom didn't follow me when I took Betty her meal, but I bet she was watching from the window and keeping track of the time. They plotted a route for him down through Washington to Spokane, and then on to Ritzville. The truckers used the roads through Washington and Oregon to Boise, Idaho, because they didn't include any high passes. From Boise he could ride across southern Idaho and down to Salt Lake City. From there he would be on his own. He'd just have to wait for Wyoming to be clear of snow and ride home. I suggested they discuss this option with him but Mother told me to say nothing. She had to make arrangements for places for him to stop along the way. He was short on funds but if they could find people to let him stay overnight in towns along the way, he would see it was to his advantage to do so. Another conspiracy. I never thought my mother was such a manipulator."

Lara swung the Good Faith to the left and slowed as she approached the dock below the house. "All mothers are manipulators. Did he leave?"

"Yes. Mother came to the café when Kurt stopped for dinner before going to work at the gas station. She gave him a map and a list of contacts. He left the next morning."

Lara cut the engines and waited for the Good Faith to come to a complete stop. Then, just as it started to drift sideways, she shoved it in reverse and did a slight S-turn to line it up with the dock. I looked over my shoulder back out at the center of the river. *See, Sam, you aren't the only one who can dock this boat in reverse.*

Chapter 29
Kurt Makes Plans

After Nick left, I went back inside, put the coffee pot and my cup on the counter and sat down on the sofa in the main room. The resort had a dish and almost fifty channels. I scanned a few and then found the reference channel. Letting it scroll by took several minutes. There were continuous sports channels, a dozen movie channels and the usual big six. On the Turner Classic movie channel was *Once Upon a Time in the West*.

I changed quickly to that channel. The show had started. This was one of my favorite movies; I'd seen it so many time I hit the mute button and leaned back deeply into the sofa.

This was a man's story of the rough West when the railroad was being built. It made me wonder what Hope was like when the railroad was under construction. Two images kept imposing themselves over the beautiful Jill character— Anna and Vicky. Vicky was more in character with the story but Anna had that impressive physical presence. A man dreams of finding a woman like Jill, but in reality neither Vicky nor Anna fits the role.

I watched two more men get shot in the movie and wanted so desperately to just be able to end a conflict that way. In *Once Upon a Time in the West* there were many male characters. All were bad or at least had major flaws. There was but one woman. She was no better than the worst of the men. Still, my eyes focused sharply at every scene she was in. In a dress that came from the neck to the shoes, she was inviting. In scenes where the neckline of the dress was much lower, she was irresistible.

Thoughts of that last week in Hope battled with the images in the scene. The conflict was the same— would he leave or stay?

Each night of that last week, Anna would creep into my dreams. We'd make love and then I would ride off into a blinding snowstorm.

The movie ended with the woman having those inviting breasts and one man left standing. The rest of the men were all dead. It never said if he rode on or stayed. I would have stayed, but that was a movie. In real life I had ridden on.

I snapped off the television and rose to my feet. A needle of pain pricked my right leg in six different places. The old injuries had healed but the inflammation associated with arthritis was setting in. I looked across the bay where the lights of town were turning on. There was always Hope. I'd have dinner, stop at the Soiled Dove Saloon for a drink and then plan tomorrow. I will go see Anna before I leave for Colorado, but tonight I need someone like Vicky.

Chapter 30
Anna: Dinner at Swan's Landing

The telephone was ringing when we entered the house. I hurried to the phone in the kitchen.

"Hello."

"Where have you two been? I've been calling for hours."

"Now, Jim, relax. We just went for a little cruise on the lake." I motioned to Lara.

"Can I speak to Lara?"

"Here she is." I handed the phone to my anxious daughter.

Lara walked into the dining room, nodding her head as she went. I went back out to the dock to see if the Good Faith was tied up securely. Sam had always checked the boat when one of the girls had docked it. Now, here I was checking, just as Sam would have done. I stood up straight and looked out at the river. "Sam, stop watching me. I can do things myself."

I went back to the dock and sat down. Finally Lara walked out and joined me.

"Hey, Mom, Jim will be late." She walked to the end of the dock.

"He sounded upset. Is something wrong?"

"Yeah, I didn't answer my cell phone." She grinned. "He said he called a dozen times. He really worries about me."

"Lara, I raised you to take care of yourself. You can tell him I made you turn off the phone."

"Jim also said he's bringing a friend with him, Phillip James McGary III. He said we shouldn't fix anything for dinner; he wants to take us all to dinner at Swan's Landing. He says they have the best steaks. You aren't upset, are you?"

I got up and started back toward the house. "Upset? Why should I be? I didn't want to cook dinner tonight anyway. I'll call and make reservations. Isn't it strange to identify a man we don't know with such a formal name as Philip James McGary III?"

Lara hurried ahead of me. "You will understand when you meet him. He's quite a character. Mom, you aren't upset at the change in plans, are you? Jim just takes over sometimes."

"Like your father always did. Lara, you married a man just like Sam."

Lara opened the door to the kitchen and waited while I called to make dinner reservations. Then we went to the living room. Lara sat down in a chair near the fireplace.

"Okay, Mom, we have time now. Tell me about that conspiracy."

I sat down in the love seat facing her, spread my hands out on my knees and began.

"I admit Kurt and I were becoming more than friends. He'd stop at the café late in the afternoon for a sandwich and coffee before going to work. I'd give him a kiss when he got up to leave. If no one else was in the café at the time, it was more than just a kiss." I pulled my arms in close to my body. *Some days we went in the pantry to the kitchen and closed the door and to kiss but I can't tell Lara about that.*

"Mom, who were you fooling?"

"I never saw anyone watching us but I bet the cook knew what we were doing. Hope is a small town. Mother was smart. She may not have needed to see us. One day she came down to the café at noon. She saw I was wearing the chain and cross Kurt gave me. She was very upset. She yelled, 'Anna, take that off this minute. I told you not to wear it.' Everyone turned and looked. I took it off and put it in the change pocket of my apron. Mother didn't order anything; she just sat at the first table by the front door. Gladys stopped waiting on customers and went to talk to her. I was so embarrassed and the two of them just sat there. Gladys didn't leave when her shift was over. It was almost three hours later when Kurt came in. To his credit he stopped and spoke courteously to both Mother and Gladys. They asked him to join them at their table. Kurt always orders coffee but I was afraid to bring it to him. Gladys took over. She got up from the table and took Kurt's order like she was still on shift. Mother didn't wait until his coffee arrived— she started right in. I couldn't hear all of what she was saying but when she opened her purse and put a map and a sheet of paper on the table, I knew that she was up to. Kurt didn't say much. When Gladys brought his coffee to the table she sat down and weighed in on the plan. I saw Kurt take the map and the sheet of notepaper, fold them neatly and put them in the inside pocket of his black leather jacket. Mother had a smile of satisfaction on her face when Kurt got up to leave the café that day. I hurried to the door when he was leaving. 'You're not leaving without saying good-bye, are you?' I asked, as I blocked the door. He gave me a kiss and a wink and said, 'Good-bye, Anna.' That was the last I saw of Kurt. I cried every night for a week. He never really said good-bye, or so I thought."

Lara shook her finger. "Either he said good-bye or he didn't. Anyway, I don't see any conspiracy here. Grandma gave him a way to leave and he took it."

I sat back in the love seat and looked toward the fireplace. "Sam began to write more often. When I didn't hear from Kurt for a month, I made it a routine to write Sam every week. Through those letters we grew closer than we were before he left on his mission."

"Did you ever tell Dad about this Kurt?" Lara asked.

"I didn't, but he knew."

"How do you know he knew? Did Grandma tell him?"

"It was all part of the conspiracy. I didn't understand until years later. I should have put it all together, but I just missed the clues. Remember when you were sixteen and your Grandmother rented a boat on Lake Coeur d'Alene for your birthday party?"

"Oh, that was cool," Lara, said with a whistle.

"It was also expensive and was well supervised."

"That didn't stop some of the boys." Lara grinned. "It was dark by the time the boat got back to the dock."

"Your grandmother paid for the whole thing and invited Sam's father to be one of the chaperones. I think now she was picking out a husband for you and wanted his advice."

"Oh, Mom, that's ridiculous."

I leaned to the side and put my fists in my lap. "No, she told me after the party. She explained I must take an active part in finding a proper husband for you. It didn't dawn on me but this was just what she had done for me years earlier. She had manipulated me by controlling my environment— moving to Hope."

Lara squirmed in her chair. "Did she ever tell you why she did this?"

"I mentioned it to Sam. Now, remember you and Jim had been married for some time. It was thirty years after I married your father. He waited until then to tell me."

"Tell what, Mom?"

"He said his father told him if he gave me an engagement ring before he went off on his mission, it would be a waste. With my father having died, I was depressed and needed comforting. When I went back to college and started dating other guys, they would be more than anxious to comfort me and he'd get a Dear John."

Lara looked down. "So?"

"So! Mother played the poor widow and moved me to Hope where she thought there was no chance I'd met anybody."

"Now, Mom, you're being melodramatic again."

"Am I? Sam told me his father wrote him and said my mother had a plan, and if it worked, his girlfriend would be waiting anxiously for him to return. He actually told him there was no one in Hope, Idaho, who would have a chance at cutting in on his girl. He waited thirty years to tell me that."

"But, Mom, it's still not much of a conspiracy. Except for Grandma."

I raised my fists. "He knew. All those years, Sam knew and said nothing."

"Now, don't criticize Dad. He was off on a mission when it all happened. He couldn't have done anything."

I stopped rocking. "Maybe not then, but he knew and he waited. This man who was always so confident, who planned everything to the last detail, simply waited. It was not until he was in the hospital and knew he was going to die, before he finally told me."

I pushed my palms together like hands in prayer. "Kurt wrote me a letter before he left Hope. Sam's father gave it to Sam when he got home from his mission, over two years later. No one ever said anything about the letter to me. They all knew Mother, Gladys and Sam's family. And Sam waited until he was on his deathbed to tell me."

Lara got up and walked quickly to the love seat. She sat down beside me and put her arm around my shoulders. "Now, Mom, maybe he was embarrassed. You know, afraid to find out what you were doing while he was off on his mission. Maybe he was so excited to be back with you he just tossed it and found it later." She laughed. "Then years later, like when you were moving or something, he could find it and say, 'Hey, Honey, I got a letter for you from an old boyfriend. It came thirty years ago.'" Lara relaxed and put her hands in her lap, mimicking my position. "Okay, what did the letter say?"

"The letter is private but I will tell you this. It was unopened. Sam had that letter for over thirty years and never opened it. He never told me about the letter. Mister Confident was afraid to show me the letter and was afraid to read it. No one, all these years ever spoke of Kurt, not even Gladys."

"No big conspiracy. They all assumed Sam gave you the letter and what it said was none of their business. It was between you and Sam."

I stood up. "I feel like I was treated like a child. None of them trusted me to make my own decision. I was a pawn in a game to get Sam a suitable wife."

"Now, Mom, you're being overdramatic."

"Kurt was from Colorado. I want to go down there and find him. Don't jump to conclusions; I know this all happened thirty-five years ago. I just want to see him. I want to know he didn't ride off the road in a snowstorm. I plan a trip to Colorado."

"But Mom, something could happen to you."

"This is the United States; a woman can travel safely to Colorado."

"Yes, but should a woman your age travel alone?"

"I'm not that old. Lara, I want you on my side. Promise you will not tell anyone why I am going to Colorado. I'll take my new cell phone with me so you can call if you get too worried. I don't want Jim and half the ward calling and to check on me."

Lara put out her arms as she stood up. "But Mom, you have never been to Colorado. Everyone will ask why you are going there. Besides, how will you ever find him?"

"I know he graduated from Colorado State University. I did some checking through them; universities keep track of alumni. And I used the people search on the internet. I have some good leads. I think I know where to find Kurt. When I do go to Colorado, I don't want anyone else to know. This is just between you and me."

"Are you going to fly? Good. That takes only a few hours. Maybe you can be back the same day."

I motioned to my daughter to follow me and walked back into the kitchen.

"When are you going? When you go, don't keep it a secret from me. I can drive you to the airport and I won't tell Jim."

I opened the door leading into the garage, snapped on the light and stepped down the two stairs. There, beside Sam's big SUV, was a shiny red motorcycle. "It's a Honda ST1300. ST is for sport touring. I got it this summer. So far I've only been as far as Missoula and back."

"No, Mom. I can't let you do this."

"If you try to stop me, I'll just leave the cell phone at home and tell you about the trip when I get back. Who knows what would have happened if I had read that letter when Kurt left. I may have taken my mother's old station wagon and headed for Colorado. Mom made Kurt get on his bike and ride away, off to Colorado. Now I am going to do the same thing. I am going to get on this bike some morning and ride to Colorado. I may even take the same route he took. Not a word about this to anyone. I'll phone you every night. Is it a deal?"

"Let me read the letter first."

"I'll leave it here for you to read, after I leave. Is it a deal?"

"No, Mom. You can't ride a motorcycle to Colorado alone. I just won't let you do that. You could run into snow in Montana."

"Bad weather was the same problem Kurt faced when Mom sent him away. I'm not young or as good a rider as Kurt, so either I leave next week or I must wait until next spring."

Chapter 31
Kurt in Hotel Hope

I watched the news and then switched to the weather channel; local weather was clearing and cooler. The national weather channel showed that the showers passing through North Idaho were the tip of a larger system sliding down the east side of the Rocky Mountains. This fast-moving storm would be followed by colder temperatures. A high-pressure system was building over the Northwest, and it would force the next few Pacific storms north into Canada.

I hoped this meant good weather for my return trip to Colorado. By Monday, the storm in Montana will have drifted into Wyoming. It will be nice to ride east with snow on the mountains and clear roads. By the time I turn south, the storm will be over Nebraska. Crossing the Continental Divide on a motorcycle was problematic any time of the year. I thought it was better to follow a storm system then to be out in front of one. By leaving on Monday I planned to be home by Friday.

I switched back to a Spokane station for more local news. They were running a report on the projected economic prosperity for the Christmas season, followed by ads for clothing and jewelry. My thoughts turned to the cross I had given Anna. I could close my eyes and see it as if it were yesterday. The little T-shaped cross dangled at the end of the necklace, just away from the line of pearl buttons. When she moved it swung back and forth across the two mounds beneath her nylon blouse. I reached out carefully and lifted the cross in my fingers. She leaned closer and whispered, "I told my mother that it was the Greek letter tau but she said it was a tau cross. I know why you chose it; my name is on the back."

My fingers brushed against the pearl buttons and I turned the cross over. "Would you believe I had it engraved just for you?" I let the back of my fingers rest where they were as I looked up at her face. "A beautiful gift for a beautiful woman."

"Thank you, but I know the truth. Spanish Joe found this chain and cross in the lake. Gladys and I helped him clean it up." She glanced over at the door to the dining room and then back to me. "Kurt, kiss me!"

I clapped my hands together with a smack. The sting in my hands brought me back to the present. I was not young and in love, not any more. I would need a much more refined approach when I saw Anna this time. Hell! She'd have a husband and family behind her. I wouldn't count for much anymore. Still, I wanted to see her. As for romance, my best bet was Vicky.

The flashing headlights reflected off the dark asphalt as I rode from the Red Fir Lodge to the main highway. I turned left, picked up speed and headed for Hope. It was dark enough I worried about deer on the road or, worse yet, a moose. At East Hope I slowed and watched for Centennial, the old road that crossed the railroad tracks. As luck would have it, a long freight train beat me to the double-tracks crossing. As I waited, I considered heading to Sandpoint for a steak dinner but the end of the train passed. I checked for a train coming the other way. Seeing none, I rode up the hill. On Wellington I rode on until it merged with West Main. Here I slowed as I motored past the house Betty lived in. There were no lights on in the place. Parking across the road from Hotel Hope, I locked my helmet to the bike and walked over to the café.

The waitress was a woman with some gray in her hair and a twinkle in her eye. She wore jeans and a snug-fitting sweatshirt with a wolf head on the top and the word BEWARE under it.

I winked and asked, "Is it safe to eat here?"

She put her fists on her hips and replied, "It's safe to look, but don't think about petting the wolf."

I laughed. She put a menu and a glass of water on the table. I noticed she had three rings on the fingers of her left hand, one definitely a wedding ring.

"The special tonight is steak and shrimp with wild rice. What would you like to drink?" She tilted her head toward the open door between the café and the Soiled Dove Saloon, "The bar is open if you're interested in something to take the chill out of your bones on a night like this."

"Never drink on an empty stomach."

The Wolf Woman walked away. For her age she had a good figure, but married women have always been off-limits. Rachel had been the hardest to accept. Now, what in the hell was I doing going to see Anna? She was married. I read the menu but nothing perked my interest. When Wolf Woman returned, I ordered the special and a beer.

"We have a wide selection. You aren't going to make me recite them all, are you?"

I glanced at the wolf and then up at her face. "Is there a local brew?"

"Laughing Dog."

"Bring me a Dog."

"They have more than one kind," Wolf Woman said.

"You choose, just as long as it's not canine pee."

Everyone in the café roared at that remark. Wolf Woman's laugh was the loudest.

I winked. "Don't bring the beer until after I've had something to eat."

I looked around at the other tables as I waited. There were three older couples, each sitting at their own table. Five members of the younger generation, three boys and two girls, all crowded around a table meant for four. One of the girls had blonde hair but dark eyebrows, which made her eyes look large and inviting.

I thought of Anna. Her hair was blonde or very light brown. Thirty-five years ago I had kissed her good-bye in this room and walked out the door. I hadn't planned on leaving then, despite the urging of Anna's mother. In fact, when I walked to the gas station I was thinking it was a good sign. If Mom was worried, then I must be really making progress with Anna. It certainly felt that way when we kissed the day before. Later that night when things were dull down at the gas station, I studied the map. Everything looked flat on the map. There were a few spots I knew would be real challenges on a motorcycle in winter. Southern Wyoming was the biggest one, southern Idaho was another, but I didn't know about the roads through eastern Washington and eastern Oregon. The list of homes where I would be welcome to stay took me just to Boise; after that I would be on my own.

When I arrived at work the owner had an envelope of cash for me – my pay included working until closing tonight. I was out of a job. About eleven, the blue and white Ranchero pulled up past the pumps. I hopped over the counter, landing carefully on my good leg and hurried to the door. It was Gladys, not Anna, who got out of the small pickup truck.

"Need gas?" I called from the doorway.

"Not tonight." She buttoned her coat close about herself and walked carefully to the door.

I held the door open while she entered. She walked to the counter and leaned on it with her left arm. I hurried around the other side. "What do you need?"

Her blue eyes never look so bright. "Kurt, it is time for you to leave town."

I felt defiant. "Not now. There is snow on the passes."

Gladys spoke calmly, "I like you Kurt. Anna likes you too much. Remember she saved your life. You would have died in that swamp if she hadn't waded out in the water and dragged you out from under those logs."

"Just running away isn't my way of showing gratitude."

Gladys smiled. "You're in love with Anna, aren't you?"

I remembered licking my lips. It was hard not to say, 'That's between us.' Instead, I nodded my head. I was in love all right, but it was hard to say. Four years ago I told a woman how much I loved her, and she didn't waste any time finding someone else once I was out of sight. Anna wouldn't be like that. She was different.

"Kurt, Anna has a boyfriend. He is away on his mission. When he returns, he will certainly ask Anna to marry him. He has a lot to offer her, a lot more than you can ever offer her. You see, they both are believers and you are not."

I leaned on my right leg. It still hurt but I didn't care. "Why not let Anna decide her own future?"

"If we could wait a year, I know she would make the best decision. Right now I am afraid the two of you will do something that might bind you together for the rest of your lives." She raised her hand, "Don't interrupt. I am not saying you have been having sex. But I am saying physical attraction is something neither of you can deal with logically. No one can, at your age. God made it that way. I'm asking you to leave because I like both of you and I feel responsible. Anna is not alone. She has her mother, and she has brothers and a sister. In addition to a large family, she has the church. You are an outlaw, a free spirit. I don't know why but you are estranged from your family. That is not the way we live. You would not adapt to her world even if you tried, and she would always want to return no matter how far away you took her. Kurt, it is time for you to leave."

That night I listened to the weather forecast and plotted my trip home. I would start out on the route as Anna's mother had mapped it. I tore up the list of people I could contact along the way. The last two hours at work I wrote a letter to Anna. It wasn't a long letter but it was to the point.

The table shook a little when Wolf Woman put the plate down. "Hey, wake up. The food's here."

I leaned back, rubbed my eyes and then took a deep breath. "If it tastes as good as it smells, it's the best."

"We only serve the best."

As she left the table my mind returned to the letter. Anna had never replied. It had ended but then why was I here?

The shrimp was good, and since they may cool off quickly I ate them first. Wolf Woman brought the beer to my table, a bottle and a cold glass. I took a drink from the bottle and winked at her. "Good stuff."

Wolf Woman paused at the table and gave me a smile. "Where are you from?"

"Colorado."

"What brings you to Hope?"

I looked up. I wasn't going to tell her I was looking for a woman. Instead, I nodded toward the door to the Soiled Dove Saloon. "A man once told me about this place. Said he stayed at Hotel Hope. Everyone could use a little hope, so I stopped by on my way home. I wish it was open so I could at least take a look."

"Hotel isn't open. Hasn't been for years." She pointed to the open door. "Now the Soiled Dove Saloon... it's worth a visit."

"I plan to do just that."

The meal was good and most of the patrons had left by the time I paid the bill. I left Wolf Woman a five-dollar tip and walked next door.

There were only two men sitting at the bar and two tables occupied. I sat down on a vacant barstool near the center of the long wooden bar. A bald-headed man in a white apron sauntered over.

"How was the Laughing Dog?"

"Good beer. How about another? Don't bother with the glass," I replied.

I drank the beer and tried to remember what it was like the first time I was here. Perception changes with time and with age. Back then, this was a fascinating place. I was drinking Whiskey the night I met Vicky. Maybe that was what made her so beguiling. Using the mirrors behind the bar I studied and judged the only two women in the bar. One was cute but hanging onto her boyfriend's arm; the other was older, more reserved and sat at a table with two men.

As I finished my beer I heard the door behind me close. A moment later she bumped my elbow. I glanced up at the mirror and watched Wolf Woman take a seat in the barstool.

"Can I buy you a drink?" I asked.

"You already have," she said, and put the five-dollar bill on the bar. "Mike. Canadian Club Sherry."

I sat back from the bar a little, turned my head slightly and looked at the rings on her left hand. What was a married woman her age doing drinking in a bar alone on a Saturday night? I didn't want to be rude, yet I didn't want to stay around until an irate husband showed up.

"Did you come all the way from Colorado on a motorcycle just to see Hope, or are you one of those biker vets?"

I smiled and could not help but let my gaze move to the wolf, then slowly up to her face. "I'm a biker and a vet, but tomorrow will be the first time I'll ride with a group. They are meeting in Sandpoint; I stopped here because I wanted to see the hotel. Too bad it's closed."

She pointed across her body at me with her right hand. "It's closed but Mike here has the key. Now don't jump to conclusions."

I raised both hands off the bar. "I never make a pass at a married woman. It would be nice to see what the place is like, but I have a place to stay tonight." I finished the beer bottle, and then put the empty on the bar. "I'm about ready to go."

The bartender set the glass of ice and whiskey down carefully on the bar in front of Wolf Woman. It was so full she had to lean over and take her first sip with it sitting there. She raised her head and pointed to the bartender. "Mike, you are the best. How do you do it without spilling the stuff?"

"Magic," Mike replied. He looked at me. "Need another?"

"No, thanks. I was just leaving."

She put her left hand on my arm. "Stay until I finish this and I'll give you a quick tour of the finest hotel in North Idaho."

I looked at Mike. "Now, you look like a knowledgeable man. Tell me? Is it safe to go upstairs with this woman?" I pointed to the ring on her left hand. "I've done some foolish things but that looks like a wedding ring to me."

Mike laughed. "Sure does. If you two are up there longer than ten minutes, I'm coming up after you."

Wolf Woman lifted her glass carefully and took a long swallow. She set the glass down on the bar and turned to me. "What's your name?"

"Kurt. Kurt Johnson."

"Kurt, I'm Darlene Whiteman." She nodded toward the bartender. "This is my husband Mike. Everybody calls me Dolly. Mike here is the best man in the world and if we stay too long he will come up after us." She picked up her drink and jumped to the floor. "Let's go."

Chapter 32
Anna: Dinner at Swan's Landing

It was well after eight when Jim Stanford and Phillip James McGary III walked into The Landing.

"So, this is Swan's Landing," Phillip said in a booming voice.

Everyone turned to look at the six-foot-six giant with the fiery red beard. Lara's face turned a shade pinker and she stole a look at me.

"Be thankful he didn't wear a kilt," I whispered to her.

We were seated at a table near the tall windows on the riverside of the room. I sat across from Lara with Jim on my right and Phillip James McGary III on my left. He was, I guessed, about my age, fifty-something, and lying about it. He must have led an active life, for despite his weight he looked fit. He also looked hairy, which I found attracted me. His red beard came down to almost the middle of his barrel chest. The white turtleneck sweater would have been better on a younger, trimmer man. It was stretched so taut on his massive biceps I wondered how he managed to get it on. He took a long moment to appraise the cocktail waitress before ordering.

"What is your best Scotch?"

She raised her finger to her chin as she replied, "Balmenach, Caol Lla, "

He interrupted her, "Do Americans always alphabetize everything?" He shook his head in disbelief. "Don't you have any Laphroaig?"

"I'm sorry, sir, but we do have Highland Park. The owner orders that one for himself."

He glanced over at me with a devilish smile. "Tell him he has good taste. Highland Park comes from the isle of Orkney. Very rich with a dark color and excellent, smooth taste. I insist you bring a glass for everyone."

"No, thank you," I said.

"Come on, give it a try," he patted my hand. "I promise it will improve your view of the world."

"Just water for me tonight," I said, as I tried to pull my hand out from under his huge paw. Sam was a tall man and his hands were much bigger than mine, but they had long, graceful fingers. This man's hand was as wide as long, like the paw of a bear. I turned in my chair and looked at the light blue eyes above the hairy mask. "I don't drink alcohol. It's against my religious beliefs." I was sure my voice carried thought the entire dining area. He had strange eyes; they didn't blink or show any reaction to my outburst, they just looked straight ahead like headlights on a car. To my relief, both Jim and Lara quickly added they also wanted only water.

He released my hand. The red beard wiggled as he spoke, "Make that hot tea for me tonight."

We each ordered steak for dinner; Phillip ordered his rare. While we waited for the steaks, he told us of his plans to build a golf course resort west of Spokane. He needed an international airport nearby, as it would draw people from all over the world. The Scots had invented the game and it was time they showed these Americans how it was properly done. I had eaten at the Landing often, but tonight I felt like everyone was listening and watching us.

An older couple sitting at the next table ordered a dinner steak for two. It looked like a large tenderloin topped with a mushroom sauce. Phillip must have noticed I wasn't giving him my full attention, for he leaned in the direction I was looking and said, "That damn thing is cooked to death."

The old man at the table turned and gave him a stern look, shrugged and turned back to eat his steak.

"I think I just got the evil eye," the Scotsman whispered to me. "Am I being too loud?"

"Yes, you're being a bore." I replied.

He sat back in his chair and patted my hand again, lightly this time. "I'll behave. The last thing I want to do is upset a charming lady like yourself." He leaned forward and lowered his voice. His breath had a pungent smell, a mixture of strong English tea and smoke. "Jim told me you will be spending the winter alone, by the lake. "

I tried not to breathe. Why don't smokers ever notice the smell?

He raised his eyebrows and continued. "Now, that doesn't sound like much fun to me. What do you plan to do this winter to keep the blues away?"

Before I could answer, he looked around the table and said, "I'll only be in Spokane for a few more days, if I get this land deal settled, then I plan a quick trip to the Eastern Mediterranean."

Both Lara and Jim leaned forward to catch his next few words.

"It can get cold and rainy in the highlands, so I spend my winters on the old Roman Lake. You know, we Celts sailed the world before anyone else knew there was more to the world than what could be seen from the shore. I have a yacht, aptly named Utopia. It's docked at Andros, away from the crowded city, and my crew of seven is very discrete and loyal. Have you ever been to Greece?"

I shook my head and wondered when this night would end.

"Doesn't sailing the Mediterranean sound more exciting than watching the snow fall in North Idaho?"

He stopped talking and I realized that last remark was aimed at me. "I'll pass on the Mediterranean. I confine my sailing to Lake Pend Oreille. In fact, that is what Jim came up for this weekend.

He's going to put the Good Faith up in dry dock for the winter. Aren't you, Jim?"

"On my schedule for tomorrow afternoon." He glanced over at Lara.

I looked over at the red bearded man. "Before you build your golf course, you should check out the one over by Hope. They say it's world class."

"World class?" he raised both his eyebrows. "Then I must see it. Perhaps when Jim is putting your boat up we can slip away to…" he paused and raised his voice, "to Hope?"

I shook my head and was saved from further comment by the arrival of the food. A hush settled around the table but I quickly broke it. "Lara, would you offer the blessing?"

She looked surprised at my request as we usually just bow our head for a moment in silence when out for dinner. She bowed her head and in a whisper offered a quick prayer. It was, in truth, a double blessing. It ended Phillip's domination of the conversation and it brought a moment of peace to me. In fact, I could hear some of the conversation at the tables nearby where people were talking in normal tones.

The old man at the nearby table was telling his friend, a woman of perhaps equal age about someone whom he met today. I could only see the back of the woman's head. She was small but she sat very straight in her chair.

"It was a big, old motorcycle but it looked brand new. He must have spent a lot of money fixing it up. He said he'd ridden all over the West. I kind of felt sorry for him. He told me he met you the last time he was in Hope, but that was long ago."

Her voice was soft but deep for a woman, especially an old woman.

"What was his name?"

Red Beard to my left swallowed a too-large bite of meat, coughed and then said in his deep voice, "Motorcycles are a cheap thrill. The man must be using it as a substitute for sex. It will give him a thrill but it's not the same." He looked around the table and grinned. "Never accept a substitute when you can get the real thing." He took a deep drink of his strong-smelling tea, exhaled, and then licked his lips.

I tried to ignore him and missed what the man at the next table said. I only caught the woman's reply.

"I told you, Nick, you meet some very interesting people in Hope."

I took a sip from my water glass. Phillip was waiting for a comment on his opinion about sex and motorcycles, and so was Lara.

"Riding a motorcycle sounds like fun to me. It's perhaps the closest thing to flying a person can do." I looked around the table to see who I had shocked most.

The red beard twitched. "Do you mean riding a motorcycle is more fun than sex? I have never ridden a motorcycle but I can assure you, you are wrong."

I ignored his remark and leaned toward the other table. Because of the Scotsman, I missed the name of the man on the motorcycle; I didn't want to miss the last of his story.

"He told me why he came back to Hope, but I didn't believe it for a minute. He said he's looking for someone, a woman he met there years ago."

I turned to listen to the woman's reply, as did the rest of those at our table.

"People return to Hope for many different reasons. Some come back to tell a loved one something; others come back to right a wrong. But most come back because they are simply lonely. I've seen many strange things happen, especially around midnight in Hope."

A deep voice beside me repeated the words, "Midnight in Hope."

I jumped in my chair at his interruption.

The Scotsman persisted. "Anna, is that right? Do strange things happen at midnight in Hope?"

I gave up trying to listen to the low voices at the next table and looked across the table at Lara. "We were there this afternoon. Nothing strange happened."

There was a glint in Lara's eyes and she delivered her reply. "Nothing this afternoon, but a midnight in Hope is a very different thing. I heard a story, several in fact, that strange things do indeed happen at midnight in Hope."

The red beard twitched as the Scotsman shifted his attention and my daughter relished having center stage.

"On the night of a full moon, a strangely attractive woman visits Hotel Hope at midnight and no man there is safe. Some will tell of a wild adventure the next morning; others simply never return. No. No. Don't even think of going to Hope at midnight— especially not tonight— for there will be a full moon in the sky."

She had the Scotsman's attention and for several minutes he played along, asking questions with double meanings. Lara, from childhood, has been skilled at weaving tales, but tonight she amazed even me. A few of the ghost stories I had told her that afternoon found their way into her performance. He was hooked and I was left to finish my dinner in peace. When the waitress cleared the dishes, she left the dessert menu.

I declined. "I am too full for dessert and it's getting late." I turned toward Phillip and added, "It's a long drive back to Spokane."

Jim cleared his throat. "Anna, I offered Phillip the opportunity to stay overnight. You have such a big house."

I tried to look at Jim, but I could feel my eyes straining to look the other way at the laughing giant with the red beard. I held my head still, facing Jim.

"Very kind of you to offer, Jim, but I noticed a hotel down by the lake. I'm sure they will have a vacant room this time of the year."

I could tell Jim was on the spot. He had said this man was a big client. Not offering for him to stay at my house would sidetrack any deal in the works. I relaxed and turned my head to the left.

"I have a guest room." I tried hard to make my smile seem sincere. "I only wish Jim had told me earlier so I could straighten it up a bit."

"Now, Mom, your house is always clean and neat," Lara, countered.

As we were leaving The Landing, ten motorcycles rumbled into the circle-shaped parking lot. They parked in two lines filling the remaining parking spaces. Lara and Jim walked with Phillip back to his Cadillac; I turned and walked toward the group of cyclists. All wore black leather; most all had a military emblem on the back of their jackets. I approached the one with MARINES in gold letters and the Marine Corps Emblem on the back. He took off his helmet, revealing his baldhead and cold, blue eyes.

"Excuse me," I said. "I see you were a Marine, but what does that insignia on your sleeve mean?"

He pulled his leg over his cycle, stood up straight and said with a wink, "Di bo Chet."

I nodded and continued to smile. He was an old, over-weight man trying to stand tall like he did when he was younger. He still had that swagger. I pointed at the emblem. "I knew a man who had a tattoo with that on it. He never told me what it meant."

His shoulders pushed back a little. Another man came to stand beside him. "First Battalion, Ninth Marines. We were the walking dead."

The man beside him, a much slimmer guy with long, gray hair tied in a red bandana, put forth his hand. "Name's Adrian. Who was this guy with the tattoo? I just might know him."

His handshake was tight and rough. "Kurt Johnson," I said meekly, wishing the man would let go.

Adrian shook his head then turned to the two men standing behind him. "You know a Kurt Johnson?"

The older of the two with the long, gray hair smiled. "Not sure, but a guy named Kurt called me from Colorado last week. He said he'd join us tomorrow. We're going down to Post Falls to welcome back some men from Iraq."

My fingers closed tight. I looked toward the gray-haired smile. "He was from Colorado. Do you know him?"

He nodded. "I ran into a grunt named Kurt in Sturgis a few years back. I was really surprised when he gave me a call. That man is a real loner. It will be good for him to ride with us."

I heard my daughter call my name. I turned and waved to her. "Be there in a moment." I looked back at the man with long, gray hair. "Did you know him in Vietnam?"

He shook his gray head. "No, he must have shipped out before I got there. But he was a Marine."

"Thank you," I said and turned to leave. The group parted and I heard two comments.

"Lucky Kurt."

"Now, that's the kind of lady you get if you lead a clean life."

We had ridden the short distance to the Landing in the Scotsman's rented white Cadillac. We returned the same way. Jim sat up front with the giant while Lara and I sat in back. Lara squeezed my hand and whispered, "Jim will not hear the end of this tonight."

The Scotsman parked his big Cadillac next to Lara's station wagon in the driveway. Once inside the house, Jim went to the task of starting a fire in the fireplace. Lara and I sat and listened to the Scotsman's tale of the terrible rains that had fallen in his country two years ago. A stream in one of his golf courses left its bank and carved a new channel through holes six and seven. "To restore the course to the its original state took all winter. We completely missed the first half of the season that next summer."

When the wood was burning, Jim joined Lara on the love seat. She leaned her head on his shoulder.

"I'm keeping you up. Not good behavior for a guest." The giant stood up and looked down at me. "Would you show me to my room?"

I led the way upstairs and pointed out that the bathroom was the first door on the right. Beyond were two other doors, both open. He started in that direction but stopped and turned around when I did not follow.

"Lara and Jim will have the room at the end of the hall. I'll leave the hall light on for you." I quickly walked past the open door of the master bedroom to a smaller door at the very end of the hall, and opened it. The guest room was the room over the garage and as such the walls slanted inward. There was plenty of headroom in the center, but the Scotsman put his hand out to the sides as he walked in. "A nice, big bed near the window. I thank you for your kindness to a stranger."

I said, "You're most welcome."

I walked out of the room and down the hall. He followed and I could hear his footsteps pause at the opened door to my bedroom. I continued on down the stairs. He was a few steps behind and he went from the stairs to the front door. In a few minutes he returned, carrying a large, soft-sided suitcase in a brilliant plaid. He held it up high before going upstairs. "Every clan has its own colors. These are mine."

I smiled as I watched him go up the stairs and down the hall. Then I turned and looked across the room at my son-in-law. "You owe me an explanation, and it had better be a good one."

Chapter 33
Kurt Tours Hotel Hope

Dolly took the key from Jim and walked back to the door of what used to be the lobby. I followed and she showed me a glass case with some Chinese artifacts collected long ago near the hotel.

"The Chinese built the railroad that made the town of Hope. Oh, in its day there was a lumber mill and even a boat builder in town. We had everything once— mining, timber, fishing and a railroad station. Those little pipes are for opium. There was a small room under the hotel the China boys used as a den. Actually, there are three separate cellars under this building."

Dolly walked to the door that led to a short stairway.

"Notice how quiet it is as soon as you close that door. This is the second hotel Joseph M. Jeannot built. The first was wood, but it burned down in 1886. This building was built in three sections each with its own basement. One of them served as a meat cellar. There was also a tunnel to the railroad depot. You see, Jeannot used the Chinese as miners when the railroad was completed. He also let his China boys smoke opium down there. As long as no one saw, who cared? Let's go upstairs."

Dolly walked just a step ahead of me up the stairs. "Since the first hotel burned down, Joe had the second built of cement and brick. Look up there. Pretty fancy."

I stopped and looked at the balcony area. The walls were a clean white, accented by the woodwork along the lower half. Higher up on the wall, in a wooden frame, was a portrait of George Washington. A long lounge sat against one wall with a chair nearby. It all looked so familiar, like I was seeing it for the second time.

"This is one of two settee areas on the second floor. In its day, this hotel was a rest stop for Teddy Roosevelt and later, Bing Crosby. Now that about covers the range of our country."

I smiled. "It does if you include me."

"I thought you said you wanted a tour. Now don't tell me you've been up here before."

I looked around. "I don't think so. I don't remember this area. Let's take a look at one of the rooms."

Dolly stopped at the first tall, dark wooden door. "There are only twelve rooms left as hotel rooms; two were remodeled as bathrooms and the others are used for different purposes. Do you remember the room number?"

The number on the door was eighteen, but that meant nothing to me. I noticed the large bed and the dark carpet. A chill ran up my spine. I remembered a room like this. The two small tables with ornate lamps on them I didn't recall. I walked over to the double windows and peered out at the veranda. Yes, I remembered this clearly. "If it wasn't this room, it was one very much like it."

Dolly put her hands on her hips, took a long look at the big bed, then glanced over at me. "I assume you weren't alone."

I shrugged and tried to smile. "You won't believe this story, but I met a woman at the bar and followed her up here. I don't know which room it was. I had been drinking. The strange thing is the hotel was supposed to be closed that winter."

Dolly laughed. "Don't tell me. Let me guess. The woman's name was Vicky."

I nodded.

"Mister, you have got to talk to Mike when we get back downstairs. Let me show you one other room."

Molly took me down the hall to the room she said Bing Crosby had stayed in. It didn't look much different than the first room except for more the expensive painting on the wall, and it was closer to the bathroom.

When we returned to the Soiled Dove Saloon, all the lights but two were out and Mike was sitting on a barstool. "I was just about to come up after you two."

"Sit down, Kurt," Molly said. She went around behind the bar and poured two fresh drinks. One she set in front of Mike, the other in front of me. "It's story time. Kurt met a woman named Vicky here in the Soiled Dove Saloon and he's going to tell us about it."

Mike picked up his drink and took a sip. "Hell, yes. I want to hear this."

I pushed the drink away. "I've had my limit— two beers— but I'll share my story. You won't believe it. Some days I don't believe it either."

Mike nodded. "No one believed me when I told them I met Vicky." He raised his right hand with four fingers held high. "Since I've been tending bar here, I've heard four Vicky stories. You'll be number five. You tell me your story and I'll share mine."

I sat down. Molly took a sip from the drink she had prepared for Mike and leaned on the bar.

"It was back in 1969. I'm not sure if it was in November or late October. It was before Thanksgiving anyway."

I pointed to my right. "I was sitting down there near the center of the bar sipping a whiskey. I had more than I should have, which could explain why I have a hard time remembering the details. I know I was drinking for a while. It was late, the last call before closing and I ordered another whiskey."

I went on, slowly recounting how I first saw Vicky in the mirror. She sat down at the bar and asked me to buy her a drink. The bartender had left the room so I let her have my last round. Neither Jim nor Dolly asked any questions as I told the story, even the part about following Vicky up to her room.

I finished with, "I have no idea how I got home that night but I woke up in my own bed. You see, I was staying in the Waldron house just down the road."

"Your guardian angel must have taken you home," Molly said.

"I never thought of that. Perhaps she did."

Mike finished his whiskey and set the glass on the bar. "I'm not going to tell you all the Vicky sightings I've heard about; just my own."

He turned in the chair and leaned his left elbow on the bar. "In 1963, I had me a new Chevy—cherry red and hot as can be. One night me and some friends drove up here from Coeur d'Alene. We went camping at Beyond Hope. You know where that is? Anyway, we had more than enough beer to drink, but somehow we drank them all. The local store at the point was closed so I drove back to Hope to buy more beer. I got confused on the road and ended up down by the lake. When I tried to turn around I got my car stuck on the lakeside of the road. As you probably can guess, I shouldn't have been driving."

He smiled and shook his head. "Like you, my story gets a little fuzzy. After spinning my wheels a few times I got out of the car. I had one wheel off the road in the dirt. I should have been able to drive slowly out but after spinning my wheels I had dug a hole. Well, this woman came up to me. I swear, she came right out of the lake. Damn good-looking woman. Dark hair, nice pair of headlights and big eyes like a cat, only green. I asked her to give me a push. And to my surprise she said she would if I told her a good story."

Mike shook his head. "Telling a story was the last thing I wanted to do. She gave me a look that said she knew what I was looking at, and it wasn't her eyes. She said, 'My name is Vicky. What's yours?' She took a long drink from a whiskey bottle and held it out to me. I took a swig and real quick made up a story about just buying my new car and coming up here to fish."

Mike reached up with his right hand and rubbed the back of his neck. "That night I initiated the back seat of my new car. That woman was something else. Wild. Cat-like. Warm and cold at the same time."

"That's what a drunk remembers of sex—fantasy," Molly declared.

Mike put his hand back on the bar. "I took this job in 1985 after my leg got too sore to drive a logging truck any more. They ain't automatic, those rigs, and it was a hard climb up to the cab. Just by chance, I was telling this story here one night and a man was listening intently. Then, after everyone else had left, he told me his Vicky story."

Molly put both her hands down flat on the bar with a slap. "Which proves that you all have the same sexual fantasy—a beautiful woman, a bottle of whiskey and a romp in the hay."

Mike nodded. "But Molly, my dear, how do you explain the women being so much alike, the name Vicky and midnight hour?"

Molly raised her hands with a smile. "Simple. The drinking and the late hour go together. As for the name Vicky, it could be any other name and the story would be the same."

Mike turned his head slightly and looked at Molly. "I put all the stories together and found a pattern. There is always a full moon. I forgot to mention that, but the reason I could see the hole where my wheel was stuck was the bright moonlight." He looked at me. "Was your encounter with Vicky on a night with a full moon?"

I took a drink of my coffee. "I don't recall if it was a full moon, but it was a moon-lit sky that night."

Mike raised his hand. "There was always a full moon and the month was October. It was October when Vicky and her boat disappeared. It was the next October when the first Vicky sighting was made. And if my collection of stories is correct, she only comes back to Hope when there is a full moon in October."

"There's a full moon every October. In fact there will be a full moon tonight," Molly said. "Let's just stay here and see if this Vicky shows up."

I checked my watch. "It's just after ten. We'd have to wait until midnight."

Molly clapped her hands. "I'll fix a fresh pot of coffee and I won't have another drink tonight. You two keep up the whiskey and see if it sparks a Vicky sighting." She looked across at me. "You said you were drinking whiskey when you met this woman. Well, let's try it again."

I protested but she filled two glasses with ice and whiskey and set them on the bar.

"I can't do this; I'll never make it back to the Red Fir."

Molly held up the key to the hotel. "You must stay. You want to find out if Vicky is real, don't you?"

Mike put up both hands. "Now. You've got to stay. Molly, bless her heart, will tell me a story she thinks I want to hear tomorrow. I need a real witness—a man."

"Oh yeah, Kurt," Molly laughed. "You have to stay. You're a man and Betty has always said Vicky was only seen by men, lonely men."

Chapter 34
Anna – Phillip: Midnight in Hope

I watched the Scotsman disappear up the stairs, and then I sat down on the chair nearest the fireplace, crossed my arms and looked over at my son-in-law. "Where did you find that buffoon?"

"Now, Mom," Jim said meekly, "he's a little on the rough side, but he's real."

"What do you mean by real? A real womanizer?"

Jim put his arm around Lara's shoulders. "He is worth millions. His family has developed international resorts around the world. This could mean a lot to us."

Lara raised her head off Jim's shoulder. "Come on, Mom, where's your Christian charity?"

I looked up at the ceiling. "I have four bedrooms in this house but none has a lock on the door."

Lara popped up straight. "Now, Mom, I can't believe you just said that."

Jim raised his right hand and pointed at the ceiling. "He wouldn't do anything to jeopardize this deal. It is going to be called The McGary Castle. We're talking over a hundred million dollars just for the land. Can you imagine a resort built like a castle in Eastern Washington with not one, but two world-class golf courses? It will attract people from all over the world."

"How long have you known this man?" I asked.

"I met him years ago when I was on my mission in Scotland. He seemed like a nice enough guy, and boy was he rich. He gave me the grand tour of a McGary golf course and resort. It was fabulous. He's touring the US looking for spots for new golf courses. He remembered me and looked me up. I've been traveling with him all week," Jim replied rapidly before slowing and lowering his hand and his voice. "Up until today he's been a perfect gentleman. Now, let me tell you about McGary Castle. He needs eight hundred acres for the golf course and resort. The farm is just under twelve hundred, but the access road splits it with one thousand acres on the west and two hundred on the east."

"Jim! Are you talking about the Chapman farm?"

"Yes. He wants to buy the farm. Think about it. Ten million dollars for the land and we would still hold two hundred acres just outside the resort. When he builds McGary Castle, we will have a paved road fronting the two hundred acres. We could subdivide and sell off the land for home sites. This is the big chance for us."

I sat back, my arms across my chest and my hands gripped tight. How can he do this to me? "The Chapman farm is in a trust, and I am the administrator of that trust fund. It is certainly not worth a hundred million dollars."

"But, Mom," Lara interrupted, "it's a trust for the family and Jim knows all about real estate. You should be thanking him."

"I'll thank him to keep me better informed. I never asked him to sell the farm. I certainly never asked him to bring this buffoon into my house. What did you tell him? My mother-in-law can be charmed into selling the farm? Just mention a trip to the Mediterranean in your yacht as a down payment."

Jim looked down at his feet. "Okay, Anna, I overstepped my role. I should have talked this over with you. It all happened so fast. He really liked the location when I took him out to the farm."

He shifted his feet back a little and looked up at me. "I told him you lost your husband recently and needed to just get away for a while. What I meant was you would be willing to sell the farm; he took it as something else. I didn't want to say anything that might put the deal in jeopardy. He's rich and unattached. If you wanted to get away to the Mediterranean this winter that is none of my business. I've been with him for a week now and he's been a perfect gentleman."

I sat down at the end of the love seat by the fireplace. "A perfect gentleman?"

Jim leaned forward with both elbows on his knees. "Okay, he has some faults. Anna, this man uses Scotch for mouthwash." He shrugged. "I bet he takes a drink with breakfast. The fact that he didn't have any at dinner tonight is a clear sign of consideration for your feelings. I couldn't hear what you two were whispering about during dinner, but it seemed you were having a good time. Now admit it, Anna, you like him. Don't you?"

My whispered voice hit a high note. "What? What were we whispering about? James Stanford don't you insinuate I had anything to do with his wolfish behavior."

Jim put his hands together and nodded. "I meant nothing of the kind. But I did hear you say midnight in Hope sounded romantic. Now, before you blow a fuse, consider this. He is an older man, a man of the world. He would not be easily infatuated with a young woman, even a provocatively dressed one. I know. I've been with him the last week."

I just stared at him. "What are you getting at?"

Jim's fingers intertwined and he leaned forward. "Forget his wanting to buy the farm; he knows he has to deal with me on the price. He acted the way he did because of you. Anna, you are a very good-looking, mature woman. A man his age would naturally be attracted to you. Sexually attracted. Add a little hint of midnight in Hope and you have seeded his dreams for tonight."

"For your information, Mister Stanford, it was the couple at the table next to ours who mentioned a meeting at midnight in Hope. The red-bearded idiot said it sounded strange and I said it sounded romantic. And if that is what turned him on, he's not as mature as a man half his age should be." I glared at Lara. "And you just heaped fuel on the fire with your ghost stories."

Lara stood up and glared back at me. "Oh, sure, Mom. You looked to me like you enjoyed his attention until he started to listen to me. Let's talk about the farm in the morning. I'm tired."

I shook my finger at Jim. "Before you make any deal, I need to be informed about the details. I am the administrator of the Chapman Trust and I am in no hurry to make any deal."

Jim sat back in the love seat. "I'll get up early and start breakfast. Let's talk about it then. Later tomorrow afternoon, I can talk to Phillip alone."

Lara put her hand on my arm. "Don't worry, Mom. Jim won't sell the farm if you don't approve of the deal. Good night."

Lara and Jim departed to the room on the second floor on the riverside of the house. When I went up I noticed the door at the end of the hall was open and the light was on. I went to my bedroom. After shutting the door I looked for something to place in front of it. A tap on the door almost caused me to fall fell backwards on my bed. The door opened halfway.

"Sorry, I didn't mean to frighten you." The red-bearded giant smiled down at me sitting on the side of my bed. He lifted his right hand and popped open his cell phone. "It's seven in Scotland and I have some business calls to make. So I won't disturb you, I'll just go downstairs to make the calls." He took a step backwards and pulled the door shut.

*   *   *

Phillip James McGary III chuckled to himself as he walked down the stairs.

He thought he really startled her. What would she have done if he had waited until she was dressed for bed, he wondered. He shook his head. No, Phillip, you can't put a million-dollar project in jeopardy. Besides, with her daughter and son-in-law down the hall she would make a big fuss.

He tried his cell phone and got a weak signal. To test if it was the metal roof on the house or the distance to a cell tower, he went to the front door, unlocked it and stepped outside. Just beyond the roofline the signal was fine. The office in Scotland answered on the third ring. His father wasn't in yet so he talked with one of the senior managers and made his pitch. This would be a joint venture between our companies. He could get the land cheap by giving the owners a little money up front and stock in the resort management company. He would not offer any stock in the golf course itself. For several minutes he laid out his plan and tried to counter all the objections raised. Finally, his father arrived and took the phone. "No. No more developments in America. We have other projects in the works."

"You can't say no. Listen to me; I've worked hard on this. Hear me out."

Phillip shrugged. Some people tell me I'm too strong-willed, but that is a family trait. His father was still way ahead of him. Twenty minutes later Phillip was left with only this advice. "Relax, have some fun over there for a week and then come home. Give up your dream of building over there. We have work to do here."

He didn't say good-bye; he just snapped the phone shut. He looked up at the trees and complained. "Defeated again by my own father. I'll show him. I'll find a way to finance this project myself. He'll see." He turned to go back in the house. "Relax and have some fun? Not if I go back in there."

Phillip reached into his pocket and took out his keys to the Cadillac. "Midnight in Hope; that's where the action is."

The Cadillac had a GPS system. He set it with directions to Hope, Idaho, and backed up the driveway. In minutes he was crossing the long bridge to Sandpoint and his mind was already making a midnight rendezvous. He laughed to himself. Fools look to tomorrow while wise men use the night. Well, Dad, here is how Phillip James McGary III has a little fun.

He leaned to his right and checked the GPS screen at the intersection of Highway 95 and 200. He drove east on 200 and picked up speed. The headlights were on low beam but with the bright moonlight he could see over a mile ahead. He tromped on the gas until the speedometer reached a hundred miles per hour. If they want to build world-class automobiles they should put the kilometers in bold numbers and miles in smaller ones.

After a few miles the terrain became more hilly. He responded by pressing harder on the gas pedal. He took the next curve in the road too fast and drifted far into the left lane. Damn heavy car doesn't corner very well. Phillip braked for the sharp curve in the road ahead. Just as it skid around, the road snaked along the shore of a swampy area. He slowed the car and went carefully around the next long curve.

"What the hell is that?"

Two large headlights appeared up ahead. They flashed twice. Phillip jammed on the brakes and moved to the right side of the road. Once the truck passed, the big car moved to the left as if it knew driving on the left side of the road was the proper way to go. He shook his head and turned back to the right until one wheel was kicking up gravel in the shoulder. With a sigh he slowed the car.

After it crossed a short bridge, the road came down close to the lake again. Phillip checked the houses on the right but none had any lights on. The railroad was on the left, with no house on that side except far up the hill. When he came to a gas station, he pulled off the road. The sign said East Hope. He checked the GPS. Yes, he had driven past the white dot labeled Hope, but it was right next to the one labeled East Hope.

Phillip turned the Cadillac around, put the lights on high beams and headed back on the road he had just traveled. This time he drove very slowly, checking out each road and each structure he passed.

* * *

The surface of the lake was so still it looked like a slab of granite in the moonlight. The water was so clear the light from the huge harvest moon could be clearly seen more than twenty feet beneath the surface. At ten feet down a few bright stars came into view in the sky above. Every star in the heaven could be seen looking up from twelve inches beneath the surface. Here, the attraction of the moon took over and she floated higher. The lights in the heavens appeared closest just before her head broke the surface.

There was no wake as she swam slowly from the deep to the shore. Before her on the steep slope of Mount Eagen, in neat parallel lines like books on shelves, she could see the old homes that made up the town of Hope. She turned her head slowly and looked to the northwest where on the second ledge above the lake, was a white structure much larger than the others— Hotel Hope. It was also the only building with a light on. The windows of the Soiled Dove Saloon were like big, cream-colored squares. The reflected moonlight was enough for her to see the other houses clearly. The little village was quiet. The moisture formed a small mist of fog as it exited from her clothing. By the time she reached the shoulder of the road the mist had dispersed. She stood still and looked up the hill at the one light in town. Like a beacon on a lighthouse, it was both an invitation and a warning. Carefully, she studied the road and the railroad tracks. From the west there was the distant sound of a train whistle. From the opposite direction she heard the horn of a semi-truck. Hope was quiet but not for long.

Despite the cold breeze she took off her coat. Carefully she removed the bottle from the big inside pocket and dropped the coat to the ground. She looked up at the light in the window of the Soiled Dove Saloon and called out into the night, "Don't start the party without me. Vicky is on her way."

* * *

Molly picked up the second pot of coffee she had fixed since closing. "Sorry, Mike. It don't look good. It's almost midnight and there ain't no woman come through that door. Maybe she is a ghost and you have to be drunk to see her. Hey, Mike, I'm talking to you."

Mike raised his head slowly, looked at Molly and then looked toward the front door.

Molly turned to the other man at the bar. "What will it be, Kurt? Coffee or Whiskey?"

He glanced at his watch. "It's after midnight by my time. Make it coffee." The cup rattled when Kurt pushed it across the bar. "What's that?"

"Just another train coming by," Molly replied. She filled his cup with coffee.

* * *

Phillip switched the headlights to high beam and drove slowly, checking out each house he passed on the left side of the road.

"I've drawn a blank. There is no Hope." He had just spoken those words when the figure of a person on the side of the road came into view. It was a woman and she held her hand up to shield her eyes. He put the headlights on low beams and lowered the window as the car came to a stop beside her.

"My dear lady, don't you know it's dangerous to go walking along the side of a road in the dark?"

She tossed her head to one side and laughed. "It's also dangerous to drive on the left side of the road."

Phillip shrugged "Not where I come from."

She leaned down and looked inside the car. "Poor man. What can you be looking for so late at night?"

"I'm looking for Hope?"

She stood up straight. "You're in Hope, but you haven't found what you are really looking for." With that she walked slowly in front of the car and around to the passenger door on the other side. As she passed by the headlights, he scratched his bearded, appraised her figure and rated it high for such a little woman. He also noticed, with delight, she carried a bottle in her left hand.

She opened the door and slid in the car. "Nice big car." She put the bottle in her lap and ran an open palm across the armrest. "I love the feel of leather. It's so soft."

"What's your name?" Phillip asked.

"Vicky Anna O'Sullivan. My father was Irish but my mother was Scottish. I bet you're Scottish, aren't you?"

"Phillip James McGary III. What's in that bottle?"

She pulled the cork, tipped the bottle and took a long drink before answering. "The best whiskey to ever come down from Canada."

"I'll be the judge of that."

She passed the bottle to him. He took a long draw and then leaned his head back. "Wow that is strong stuff."

Phillip handed the bottle back and leaned toward her. "Now, Vicky my love, let's get down to business. I came to Hope to find some action. Got to relax and have some fun. You're a woman." He paused to look her over. "Where would you find some action on a night like tonight? The whole town seems to be asleep."

Vicky pointed up the hill. "See that light? That's the Soiled Dove Saloon at Hotel Hope."

He leaned toward her, putting his right hand on her knees. "By Damn. That's sounds like just the place for a little fun. How do I get there?"

Vicky put her hand on his. She didn't try to push it aside, but instead pulled a little on the hairs covering the back of his hand. "You aren't going anywhere until the train passes."

Phillip looked out the back window and saw a big bright light coming down the tracks. The high-pitched whistle announced the coming of an old train. The chugging cadence of the steam engine filled the air as the engineer used the engine as well as the brakes to stop the train.

"By God! I haven't seen an old train like that since I was a boy. You people still run steam engines?" He raised his hand from her knee as he watched out the front window.

The train chugged to a stop beside the station up ahead, but the pulse of the engine continued.

"I didn't see that when I drove by," he said.

Phillip watched as a group of twelve men crossed the road and scuttled in short steps toward the last car on the train. They stopped at the flatcar just ahead of the caboose, and one by one the short Chinese men came up from the lake and loaded boxes onto to the flatcar.

"What are they doing?"

Vicky put her hand on his arm and pulled gently until he turned and looked back at her. "Those boxes contain the remains of the Chinamen who died last year. Their friends are shipping them to Seattle where they will be put on a boat and taken back to China for a proper burial."

She held out the bottle to him. "Let's drink to death."

Phillip took the bottle. "This ain't poison, is it?"

"You just saw me drink from it."

He held the bottle up and looked carefully at it. "No label."

"The label washed off years ago. You see, I keep the bottles in the lake where it's cool." Her smile became a grin. "Take a drink, a nice cold drink. We can't go anywhere until the train leaves."

He took a long drink. It burned deeper in his throat. He handed the bottle back to her. "That's strong stuff. Not what I'd expect a lady to drink."

"Maybe I'm not a lady."

"Only a lady would have a proud name like Vicky Anna O'Sullivan. Let's drink to you Anna."

The steam engine let out a long burst of steam. It rose like a small cloud and drifted up the hillside. Phillip felt Anna put her hand on his leg again, this time firmly.

"Most people call me Vicky, but if you like Anna it's okay. I took the name Anna when I was confirmed. The bishop gave me a Saint Anthony's cross; you know, one shaped like the Greek letter tau. On the back he had my name, Anna, inscribed. He told me to wear it always and when I died Saint Peter would welcome me to heaven." She leaned forward and pulled the neckline of her dress out a little. "See, no cross." She sat back and smiled. "I lost the cross in the lake and I've been searching for it every night since. Guess that means I'll never see Saint Peter."

Phillip put one finger of his left hand in the neckline of her dress and peaked down. "You're right. No cross. Just two lovely little hills."

Vicky pushed his hand back, put the cork in the whiskey bottle and tossed it into the back seat of the Cadillac.

"Now, why did you do that? I was just looking."

"I'm moving to the back seat where there is more room. If you want to look you must come back there with me."

Phillip turned off the lights and the engine. He opened the door by the driver's seat, slammed it shut and stepped to the door by the back seat. When he opened it to get in, he saw her dress neatly folded across the back of the seat in front of her.

"Take off your shoes," she ordered.

He leaned against the side of the car and pulled off his shoes, then hurried in and slammed the door.

Chapter 35
Anna: Sunday Morning

I slept in my flannel PJs that night. The top button pulled off when I tried to button it. Even so, it was the most conservative sleepwear I had in the closet. When I couldn't find something to block the door to my bedroom I put a flashlight under my pillow. I had just fallen asleep when I awoke again with a jump. Something was wrong. I slipped out of bed and put on my ankle-length housecoat. With a hammer grip on the flashlight I carefully opened the bedroom door. Just down the hall the door to the guest room was open. The yard light shown in and reflected off the slanted ceiling. I hesitated. What would that cad think if he saw me looking in on him in the dark? I stooped down and peaked in the room. There was a suitcase sitting open on the foot of the bed. I rose up higher and flicked on the flashlight. He wasn't there. Silently, I walked to the window and looked out. I expected to see him standing out there smoking a cigarette as he talked on his cell phone. In the driveway was Lara's SUV, but the Cadillac was gone.

I walked quickly but as silently as I could down the stairs and checked the front door. It was closed but not locked. I locked it. "Now I can sleep in peace."

I went back up to my bedroom and climbed in bed.

Three times during the night I thought I heard someone banging at the front door; twice I went downstairs and checked to see if there were two cars or one in the driveway. I didn't care where Phillip had gone. After hearing Lara's stories— my stories retold— he might have gone to Hope looking for a ghost. Men were such fools. Finally I drifted off to sleep telling myself Kurt had returned and he would come looking for me, but it was Sam's voice I heard.

"Never swim in the lake before June or after September."

I looked back at the dock. Sam stood at the edge pointing at me. I turned back toward the dock, gliding silently between, strong, slow breaststrokes. He had his hands on his hips. Beside him stood Lara. The same pose, the same disapproving look on her face.

"Mother, how could you?"

I glided closer.

Lara turned to her father and said aloud, "Dad, I will never swim in the lake at night. I promise."

I glided to a stop and looked down. My blouse was plastered tightly against my breasts. I looked up at the dock. Where Sam had stood there was now a motorcycle. The rider jumped from the bike, only to fall flat on the dock. I swam quickly to the ladder at the end of the dock. A large hand reached down to pull me up. The red beard wiggled as the giant voice boasted, "Motorcycles are a cheap thrill. Never accept a substitute when you can get the real thing."

He lifted me up onto the deck. The motorcycle and rider vanished. I turned my back to the red-bearded giant, but his hand pinched my shoulder as he tried to turn me around. I pulled my arms in closer and tried to jump back into the river.

"Mom. Mom! Wake up!"

I opened my eyes. Blinding light flashed as I looked back over my shoulder. Lara was sitting on the edge of the bed. Sunlight was coming in the window behind Lara as she stood up.

"You must have been having some dream. It's almost eight o'clock and everyone is here."

I sat up in bed and pulled my flannel nightgown back up over my shoulders. Lara explained that Jim's mother had brought the twins up with her. They were having breakfast downstairs. Lara said her two sisters and their families were driving up from

Spokane also and would meet us at church. The ten o'clock service.

I took a quick shower, dressed for church and went down to greet the family. Phillip's Cadillac was still not in the driveway and no one spoke of him. Jim's mother had taken over my kitchen and fixed breakfast for everyone. She kept a rambling list of things I should buy for a healthy lifestyle all through breakfast. Despite her lecture, I ate only some toast and bacon. Jim took the boys, Jamie and Sammie, both ten, out on the dock to clean up the Good Faith, while Lara rinsed the dishes and started the dishwasher under the watchful eye of her mother-in-law. I sat at the kitchen table with my granddaughter Annette; we both nursed our glasses of orange juice and hid from Mommie Kate, as Annette called Jim's mother. Kate was a natural organizer, but from past encounters she knew not to give Annette a task and to let her enjoy a little time with her other grandmother.

At nine-thirty, Jim ushered the boys inside and to the bathroom to wash up. I took Annette up to the bathroom in the master bedroom and brushed her hair. I was not going to let them hurry me. This was my house not Mommie Kate's.

"You have beautiful hair. Do you want me to put the ribbons back in it, or leave it free?"

Annette looked up. "Make it like your hair."

I brushed my own hair straight back and put a light barrette on each side. Then I brushed Annette's hair back like mine and held it with one hand.

"I just happen to have two extra barrettes that will fit you perfectly."

The girl's eyes shone brightly when she looked at herself in the mirror. "I'm just like you, Grandma."

I smiled back at our reflections and remembered the time when Lara wanted to be just like me. Annette will not be this precious little girl for long. Childhood is a gift to the family as much as the child.

As the two of us walked downstairs, I glanced at Lara with a smile. You did this. It's a conspiracy. Bring all the family together and show me what I will be missing if I stay in Sagle. Lara pointed to her watch and Announced that it was time to go to church.

Annette took my hand. "Can I ride with you?"

"No, it's our turn." The twins rushed forward to claim my other hand.

Mommie Kate stepped forward. "We'll take my car. I have to leave at noon; I can't be bothered to come back here. Anna can ride with Jim and Lara."

"Maybe I should take my motorcycle," I said.

"Do you have a motorcycle?" Annette and the twins raced to the garage door each claiming they would ride with Grandma Anna.

Mommie Kate just stood there speechless. Lara shook as she glared at me. Jim laughed. "Come on, kids. After church Grandma can show you her motorcycle."

I was happy to ride to church with Jim and Lara. The grandkids were sorry they had to ride with Mommie Kate but they didn't say anything. When we arrived at the church parking lot Jim parked near the west end where my other two daughters; Jeannie and Barbara were waiting with their families. Jeannie had two children, a four-year-old Kathy and a two-year-old David. Barbara, who was in graduate school at Eastern Washington University, had only her husband to keep track of today.

Everyone, it seemed, hurried over to help me when I got out of the car. Hugs and kisses were the accepted greeting. Last was Barbara. She hugged me tighter than ever and whispered, "Mom, we did it."

I started to ask, 'Did it?' The answer shown in the look in her eyes. After four years of marriage, Barbara was pregnant. With tears in our eyes we held hands and followed Jim across the parking lot to the open doors of the church.

Jim paused as an old, blue van entered the parking lot and took the last remaining handicap parking spot in the front row. He turned to me. "Is Dennis Peterson still around?"

"No, he moved to Salt Lake City two years ago," I replied.

"Well, that's his van."

I watched as an overweight man with a bushy beard and long hair wheeled out the side door of the van.

"Who is that?" Jim asked.

I shook my head. "I never saw him before. No, wait. I never saw him at church before. I don't know his name but he lives in Sandpoint."

Two motorcycles rumbled into the lot. They took the one remaining parking spot in the front row.

Jim shrugged. "This is really different. Is William G. still the bishop?"

"Yes." I raised my hand to my lips. The riders were too short, too fat and those were Harley-Davidson cycles. It couldn't be Kurt. He wouldn't have changed that much. I glanced around and there at the far end of the lot, away from the rest of the cars, was a lone blue Honda. The rider was carefully locking his helmet in the saddlebag. He turned, took a minute to unzip his jacket and looked around.

"Yes, he did come back."

Chapter 36
Kurt Goes To Church

It was tough to drag myself out of bed Sunday morning. I had stayed at the Soiled Dove Saloon until almost one, drinking coffee and swapping stories with Mike. When we left the hotel we saw two state patrol cars and a sheriff's car down by the lake. Mike took the old road to East Hope with Molly driving. I followed as far as Snell's Hill Road, then cut down to the new highway. I didn't gear down on the hill but used my brakes, trying to be as quiet as I could. After midnight, anyone on the road is suspect to the police. When the alarm went off Sunday morning I had slept only seven hours. That would be plenty on normal mornings, but add a hangover and it was the bare minimum. I was grateful I wasn't trying for a sunrise service.

I parked at the east end of the church parking lot and looked around before taking off my helmet. A big pickup truck backed into a parking spot in the first row. I was glad I didn't park up close to the church. They just don't see bikes in their rearview mirrors. I swung my leg over the bike, leaned over and straightened my pant leg over the brace on my right knee. For a minute I stood straight and surveyed the parking lot. I hadn't come this far to avoid meeting Anna, but last night I had missed Vicky. Maybe this was not my day. The thought of riding back to her house to see if she was home entered my mind, but I dismissed it as an escape. She would be here this morning. Would she remember me? What would her husband think?

I put my shoulders back and took two strides forward, stopped, looked down at the helmet in my left hand and turned back to my bike. I stored the helmet in the left saddlebag and turned back toward the church door. I allowed only a side-glance at the people getting out of their cars and hurrying ahead. There was a mixture of families with many small children and older couples walking alone. I tried to check them out without making direct eye contact. Each time I failed, I was met with a smile and a cheerful "Good morning."

When I reached the sidewalk leading to the open doors, I stopped. Up ahead were two young men who greeted each group. That was it. Everyone came with someone but I came alone. I wanted to turn and leave but forced my legs to carry me up to the door. I would step inside and ask the first person I met if Anna Chapman was here today. They would say something like "I haven't seen her," and I could turn and leave. I had almost reached the doors when I heard my name.

"Kurt?"

I stopped and looked back. A large group of people was making its way between the rows of cars. Ahead ran two young boys. Close behind were three men in dress pants and sports coats. A few steps behind them were four women and one very young girl. Their brightly colored dresses danced in the breeze. The woman with long, blonde hair was laughing. Anna hadn't change a bit; she was as beautiful as ever. The older woman beside her waved at me, or at someone nearer the church.

I took a deep breath. The younger blonde couldn't be Anna; she was too young. But the woman beside her was too old and a little hippy. Anna was tall and thin when I left Hope thirty-five years ago. She would always be that way. I sucked in my gut and tried to stand straight. The older woman ran forward and seemed to be dancing on her toes. I started forward to meet her. If I can talk to her for a few minutes, I can leave.

The closer we came the more confident I was that this was Anna. The blonde hair had streaks of gray. The white sash around the waist of her navy blue dress drifted in the wind to one side as she hurried forward. The other three much younger women caught up with her before we met. I tried to talk and suck in my gut at the same time. It didn't work. I must have sounded like I was out of breath.

"Anna, is that you? Why, you look grand."

She said nothing but gave me a hug. Her head rested on my shoulder. I wanted to kiss her but the look in the eyes of the women standing behind her told me I'd better not. Like an electric shock, the words rushed forward in my mind, 'Where is her husband?'

Anna took a half step back. "Kurt, I want you to meet my girls. This is Barbara and Jeannie." She turned to her left and put her hand out toward the third woman who stood with her arms folded and a stern look in her eyes. "This is my oldest, Lara."

The men and boys who had run ahead came back and Anna continued her introductions. With her family and half the people in the parking lot watching, Anna invited me to join them at church this morning.

I raised both arms slightly in surrender. "Thank you, but I'm not the church-going type."

Anna reached over and took my left hand in hers. "You will be our guest."

She started walking toward the two open doors. Lara, with arms still folded, marched on my right side. The two young boys in white shirts and green ties walked sideways in front of us. One pointed at me and told the other, "He rode a motorcycle. I saw it."

The two almost tripped as one tried to show the other where the motorcycle was parked, yet still hold their place at the head of the procession. The main entryway consisted of two sets of doors and a small vestibule. Anna led the way forward, making more introductions as we encountered people. I wondered how she seemed to know everyone. Perhaps they were all one big family. My short list of new names kept being pushed down until I could only remember the last two I had heard. Anna must have sensed my desire to flee because she never let go of my hand.

As a group, we made our way into the sanctuary. It was a wide room, with a center aisle and pairs of long, wooden but padded pews on either side that would easily seat a dozen people. An older woman with a very stern look on her face and a name I could not remember directed the children to their places. She issued directions to the adults in the group but they, especially Anna, had their own plan. The twins had to move twice before everyone was seated. I found myself sitting with Anna on my left and the two boys who had walked backwards into the room ahead of us on my right. The blonde haired woman who I had at first mistaken for Anna directed one of the boys to move over and she took the seat between them. Only after the boys moved did I recognize they were twins. The woman between was likely the mother, and one of Anna's daughters. A hush settled over the room and everyone, even the two boys turned their attention to the front area behind the pulpit. From a bench behind the pulpit an older man rose and stepped forward.

"Welcome on this beautiful fall Sunday. It is good to see so many here today. Either you have chosen wisely God over hunting, or you are most skillful at the latter and already have your elk hanging in your garage. Either way I'm glad to see you here."

He made the announcement of the opening hymn. Everyone, even the two boys, picked up hymnbooks from the back of the pew in front of them. Anna let go of my hand to hold her book and I scanned the room looking for the quickest way out. We sat for the singing and for the prayer that followed. I began to worry. I didn't remember being introduced to Anna's husband. Where was he? I looked sideways down the aisle. He could not be any of the three men in our pew; they are too young. They must be the husbands of her daughters. I couldn't remember any of their names. I looked the other direction. Twin boys, the stern-looking blonde in the navy blue dress and a tall man who is probably her husband. Where was Anna's husband? I sat back and looked up at the front of the room. Two older men stood before the congregation. One was directing the choir while the other, a tall man with gray hair, was speaking to someone in the front row. That must be him. Oh, no. He's looking directly at me. After the hymn he left the pulpit and walked down the center aisle.

I knew it would happen, as sure and rain at a picnic. The tall man stopped at the end of the aisle, "This morning we have several guests."

I swallowed hard and sat just a little taller. He nodded toward me. Anna stood up and motioned for me to stand also.

"This is Kurt Johnson. He is from Colorado. He came here to welcome our men back from Iraq." She sat down and so did I.

The tall older man said, "Welcome. It is good to have someone come from so far away. Kurt isn't alone. In the back there we have Jeff and Nora Andrew and Will Curley from the Idaho Vietnam Vet Motorcycle Club."

A few other visitors were acknowledged. That was followed by some announcements. I began to relax. At least there were three other like me here. Even if they were probably Mormons, they did ride bikes. The announcements changed tone and the speaker made what sounded like assignments. Most of the adults in the congregation raised their right hands as if voting or approving of the task.

Anna turned to me and said in a whisper, "Now we prepare the sacraments. You would understand if you had read the book I gave you."

"I read enough to know you prepare bread and water, not wine," I whispered back. She cringed and looked down. She must have said a prayer that I would behave and be still, for I could feel the words all through the next hymn. When the bread and water was passed down the pew, the blonde on my right reached out and took it from Anna, bypassing me. Anna took my hand again. The sacraments were followed by a young speaker who looked like he was sill in high school. He talked of the responsibility of each to preach and go on a mission for the Church.

Anna was listening intently to the young man and I felt a hand on my right arm. The young boy next to me pointed at my leg and whispered, "What's that?"

The pant leg had ridden up over the brace on my knee and looked like a lump. I leaned over. "It's a knee brace."

"Why?"

"I broke my leg in an accident."

"Can you ride a motorcycle with one leg?"

"Shush," the blonde next to him hissed.

The other twin leaned forward in his seat. "Jamie, what are you talking about?"

With a few words and stern looks, the woman and the man in the row next to the other boy quieted the twins.

Anna reached over and patted my left knee. "Now, don't you get those boys stirred up."

I tried to flatten my pant leg as best I could without standing up. The boy on my right was moved down one seat and the woman took his place beside me. She looked down once at my knee and shook her head.

The next speaker was much older and talked about the importance of baptism for the remission of sins. I wondered if they had a baptism pool in the building as he mentioned immersion in water.

As the service continued, I noticed how much attention the tall man up front got from Anna and her three daughters. Their faces seem to glow at every word. I turned to my right side ever so slightly and whispered, "Is that your father?"

The blonde woman shook her head and then a smile spread slowly across her face. She even had dimples I'd not noticed before. She leaned very close. "That is Bishop Peterson. My father is a much bigger man. I must warn you my father has a quick temper and no sense of humor." She leaned back a little. "But we all love him dearly."

The next ten minutes were pure agony. My foot tapped like a little boy waiting in line at the bathroom in grammar school. How long will this last? Did Mormons meet for all day on Sunday? I had to leave for Post Falls. I checked my watch twice. The second time Anna took my hand and whispered, "Don't be so impatient. We'll break in a few minutes."

They ended the session singing another hymn. I was tempted to ask if they ever sang 'When The Saints Go Marching In' but I didn't. I closed my eyes for a moment. The singing stopped and everyone stood up and started to depart in several different directions. The blonde smiled and asked, "Would you like to go to Sunday school with the boys?"

"I'm out of here. I mean, it's time I left for Post Falls."

"I'll walk you to the door," Anna said.

The three other bikers in black leather jackets motioned for me to join them.

Anna grabbed my sleeve. "Let me tell you where I live. I want you to come back after the ride. My house is across the river in Sagle. After you cross the bridge go west about an eighth of a mile. It's a two-story white house with green trim. You can't miss it."

I nodded. "I stopped by that house on Saturday but no one was home."

"Go with your friends but don't forget to stop by when you get back. Promise that you will stop by, no matter how late. I have so much to tell you."

The mother of the twins stood behind Anna with a grin but shaking her head as if to say, "You had better not."

I leaned forward and gave Anna a kiss on her cheek. "I'll be there."

As I was leaving the room I heard a term I never expected to hear in church.

"Hey, grunt, remember me?"

I turned and looked across the room. In the very back of the sanctuary a man in a wheelchair gave a salute. I walked quickly toward him. I extended my hand and gave the man a strong shake. "Well, I'll be a son of a – gun. Doctor Brad. What are you doing here? They told me you lost it."

The man in the wheelchair slapped his knee. "Lost most of me."

I lowered my head to the man's shoulders. "I owe you. Doc, you were the best."

The man sat back and pushed me away. "Get riding Kurt. They need you. Those boys who are coming home need you."

The twins and about ten other men and boys followed me and the other three out to our motorcycles. The other three cyclists had Army insignias on the shoulders and a big Viet Nam Vets MC emblem on the back of their black leather jackets. I had only a white, embossed Marine Corps emblem on the back of my jacket. The big Harley Davidson motorcycles fired up with a roar. I pushed the red starter button on my Honda and the bike hummed into action.

"How come your motorcycle isn't loud like theirs?" one of the boys yelled.

"Marines are a little different," I replied, then twisted the throttled and let the big engine race a little. It wasn't the deep, throaty sound of the Harley, but it was far from quiet.

"You can say that again," the cyclist next to me countered.

We rode out of the parking lot in two rows, with me in the back.

Chapter 37
Anna After Church

On the way home from church I rode in the back seat with the twins. They were overflowing with questions about the motorcyclists.

"Grandma, did you know that biker dude has a wooden leg?"

"No, Jamie. He said it was a knee brace, and his name is Kurt, not biker dude."

"I bet he got his leg blown off in the war. He was a soldier and they are always getting hit by roadside bombs. I saw it on television."

I tried to patiently explain. "He wasn't in Iraq. He was in a war that happened a long time ago."

"I bet they still had bombs that would blow up Humvees when soldiers drove by."

Lara poked her head over the back seat. "Let's stop this talk about war. He's not a soldier and he didn't get his leg blown off. He's just an old man. He probably has arthritis or something like that." She looked from her son to me and added, "In a year or two he'll have to use a walker. Now, no more talk about him."

Sammie leaned forward and looked across the back seat at his brother. "Did you hear those motorcycles? Boy, were they cool. Someday I want a motorcycle like that black one. It was really loud. I bet it's the fastest one."

Lara leaned between the front seats with her hand raised. "Stop talking about motorcycles. We came up here to see your grandma. Now, tell her how much fun you had. We would like to see Grandma more often, wouldn't we?"

"Yeah, Grandma. Would you come down next week and see my soccer game? I'm going to be goalie," Sammie asked.

"I'm a forward," Jamie added.

I clasped my hands together. "Why, I'd love to come down and see your game."

On the short ride to my house, the twins, at the urging of their mother, asked me to come down to Spokane for five different events. Since her two sisters left for Spokane after church service, Lara took it upon herself to list a few events in their lives their mother should come down to see, and summed it all up with, "You know, Mom, if you lived closer you wouldn't miss your family so."

I sat back and looked out the window as we crossed the long bridge. Yes, she was right; I should be closer to my family. I wanted to be closer to them. The twins are growing up so fast. I closed my eyes and remembered Sam's words when we moved up to Sagle. "Anna, we can retire up here away from all that city crime. The kids don't need us anymore. In fact, they will grow stronger if we are not there." By retire he meant fishing and playing golf. No concern with what I might want to do. Sam got cancer and I played nurse for three years. Now, what have I got? Two sets of golf clubs and two boats. I looked down the river. Sam, you just stay there. It's time I ran my own life.

Once we reached the house, Jim took the twins down to the basement to watch football with him while Lara made lunch. Apparently he had forgotten about putting the Good Faith up in dry dock. He also didn't say a word about Phillip, and that bothered me. Lara kept me off balance by trying to take over the house. There can only be one queen bee in the hive.

"Really, Mother, why did you move the television down to the basement? It's so far away from everything. The living room looks bare without it."

I opened the vegetable container in the refrigerator. "How about a salad with raisins?"

"Do you have a low-cal dressing?"

"Italian, salsa or ranch?"

"Let's go with the salsa. You make the salad. I'll fix the sandwiches."

Lara quickly fixed the lunch, took trays downstairs for the football fans, and then returned to the kitchen table to eat lunch with me.

"Mom, I'm really glad that man stopped to see you at church. Now there is no reason for you to go to Colorado. He's alive and well. Did I tell you I planned a big dinner for Thanksgiving? I'll fix the turkey. Barbara is doing the potatoes and asparagus. Jeannie will bring the pies, but she'll probably buy them at Albertsons. All you have to do is drive down. Why don't you plan on staying through the weekend?"

I glanced up at the clock above the telephone in the kitchen. One-thirty. He should be in Post Falls, perhaps in Spokane, by now. The Viet Nam vets said they would escort the returning soldiers from the airport in Spokane to the armory in Post Falls. What would they do after that? No doubt there would be some kind of welcome home ceremony. Perhaps Kurt would ride straight back here. Five o'clock? What if he stopped for dinner first?

"Mom, don't look at the clock like that. Are you waiting for me to leave?"

I shook my head. "Just thinking. Wasn't Jim going to put the Good Faith up for the winter?"

"He wants to stay mobile in case Phillip calls. You don't know where he went, do you? No. He left before you got up. Now, how about Thanksgiving?"

"I'd love to come down for Thanksgiving. What would you like me to bring?"

"Nothing. I've arranged everything." Lara said proudly.

Arranged everything. Just like your father. A dozen sailors but only one captain on a ship. I looked out the sliding door past the dock to the river beyond. Don't worry Sam, they don't need us. You were right.

"Mom, you're looking at the clock again."

"No, I'm not. I was looking at the river."

"Well, you are not looking at me. Dad always said you should look at the person you are talking to."

I pointed to the chair across the kitchen table. "Lara sit down. You're as nervous as a cat in a room full of rocking chairs. What's wrong?"

Lara dropped into the chair and put two fists on the table. "What's wrong? What did you say to Phillip? His car was gone when Mommie Kate and the kids arrived this morning. Jim tried twice to reach him on his cellphone. Where is he?"

"I have no idea." I shifted in my chair and looked toward the front door. The car left last night but his bag was still in the guest room. If I tell her that she will stay all day. Maybe he'll return before the football game is over.

"You didn't tell him to leave last night because you knew that man on the motorcycle was coming, did you? I can't believe you invited him to come to your house."

I nodded. "But I did. I want to know more about Kurt."

"You can't rekindle an old flame. Besides, Dad has only been gone a short time."

"You're right. I just want to talk to him. For all I know he's married and has a dozen kids. He met my family. I'd like to hear about his." I raised both of my hands up in the air. "Take a look at your old mother. I'm twenty pounds overweight and I have gray hair. I am not a foolish girl. I'm a wise old woman. I want to know what has happened to him and I want to tell him about you, all my family. You don't have to worry, he's far more of a gentleman than the man Jim brought to the house."

With her elbows on the table for support, Lara put her fists up and rested her chin on them.

"Don't look at me like that," I scolded. "I'm not one of the twins. I'm your mother."

"My stubborn mother." Her face relaxed. Lara spread her hands out across the table. "Give me your hand."

I reached across and our hands enfolded. "Promise me you will call if he comes?"

"Okay, I'll call."

"Then I don't need to stay here and be your chaperon?"

I laughed. "I don't think so."

Lara pushed back in her chair. "Well, keep your cell phone handy. It's the best defense a woman can have. And Mother, change out of that dress before he comes."

"Why?"

"Because it is very beautiful. Besides, it's a church dress."

The game didn't end until almost four. Just as they were getting ready to leave I took the twins into the garage and showed them my Honda ST 1300.

"This is my motorcycle. It's not as loud as those Harleys, but it is big and fast."

The two boys rushed to the cycle, each trying to push the other aside for a closer look.

"Can I climb up on the seat?" Sammie asked.

"No, let me."

Lara rushed forth and grabbed a hand of each of the twins and pulled them back from the bike. I laughed and pushed the button to raise the garage door. Jim, who was loading the station wagon, came running in.

"Hey, I didn't know Sam had a motorcycle."

"He didn't," I asserted. "This bike is mine."

Without asking, Jim swung his right leg over the back of the bike and sat down.

"Mom said not to touch it," Sammie protested.

I watched as Lara quickly gained control and ushered the twins to the car. Jim looked the ST over carefully and said in loud voice, "Nice bike. Looks hot."

"It is hot," I said proudly.

I followed him to the station wagon, and after four hugs and kisses I returned to the house alone once more. I shut the garage door and locked the front door before going upstairs. In front of the tall, doublewide dresser I knelt and opened the bottom drawer. There, under an old miniskirt and my favorite black sweater, was the envelope. I opened it carefully and took out the silver cross and chain. Rising from the rug, I went to the mirror in the master bathroom. The cross looked smaller than I remembered. Against the lacy bodice of the green dress it all but disappeared. I lifted the chain and dropped the cross down under my dress.

Walking slowly back into the bedroom I took off the dress and put it in the laundry basket in the closet. I checked and rejected all six dresses hanging in the closet. My slacks, except for the two new pair I had recently purchased, all now fit a little baggy— the disadvantage of dropping ten pounds last summer. At the far end of the closet were my winter clothes. If they fit last winter, they too would be a little baggy now. I unzipped the ski outfit, I hadn't worn in two years: black ski pants and black woolen sweater with a bright red stripe. The wool was still too warm for this weather, but the ski pants were part spandex and that would help. They would look better still if I had lost that last twenty pounds.

I quickly pulled on the pants and modeled then in the bathroom mirror. I selected two blouses – a white one and a dark red one, both nylon. The gold buttons of the white blouse would clash with the silver cross, so I tried on the red one. I could see the outline of my white bra; I'd have to change it. No, why not go back to something Kurt would remember.

I went back to the dresser and took out the black sweater. I slipped it over my head and pulled it down as I walked back into the bathroom. The boys at college used to kid me about that sweater. It was rayon and fit snugly around each breast. Now it's tight. Maybe if he was looking up here he won't notice my waistline. The outline of the white bra could be seen, but the lights in the bathroom were a little brighter than those downstairs. I walked back to the dresser when I heard the doorbell ring. Kurt is back.

I pulled the chain out from under the sweater, checked that the amulet hung even with my breasts and hurried down the stairs. The doorbell rang again before I reached the door. With one hand I unlocked the deadbolt; with the other I pulled on the door handle and opened wide the front door. The red-bearded giant pushed his way past me into the house.

"Damn poor country where a man gets arrested for just having a drink." He walked into the living room and dropped down hard onto the couch. "Did you know traffic police in this place carry guns? That's entirely uncivilized."

I slammed the door shut and followed him across the living room. His hair was a mess of short curls, in random order. His suit coat looked like it had been dragged in the mud. His white shirt was open and torn, revealing rough, curly hair on his chest.

"What happened to you?"

"I was attacked by those militants in brown uniforms. There were five of them or I wouldn't have been gone so long." He lowered his head. "I didn't get much sleep last night." He mumbled under his breath what must have been a Scottish curse. "That's what they deserve the band of ruffians."

I sat down beside him on the couch. "I'm sorry. Where in heaven's name did you go last night? Jim tried to call you."

He turned his head and his blue eyes grew just a little larger. "I went to Hope." A smile twisted his beard. "For a while I thought I'd found the torrid apex of paradise, a young man's hottest dream come true. But like all such dreams, it ended too soon."

He raises both his eyebrows as he glanced my way. "Well, look at you. Black as coal ready for the fire."

I jumped up off the couch and stepped back. "How dare you talk to me like that? Get out of this house."

He looked me over from toe to neck and chuckled, "Sorry, but in a way that was a compliment."

The red-bearded giant rose slowly from the couch. "I'll have a bath and put on some clean clothes, then I'll leave."

I turned and walked to the kitchen. I heard his slow, clomping footsteps behind me. I picked up my purse, took out the cell phone and turned to face him. "In this country we need only to dial nine-one-one to summon the police. Unless you leave this minute, you will have another encounter with our law enforcement personnel."

He stood there looking at me in silence. I felt myself tremble as his eyes burned a path from the silver cross to my face and back. "You look so sexy in black. Well, put down that phone. Believe me, woman, you'll remember this banquet for the rest of your life."

I turned the phone and punched the numbers, "nine...one..."

"Okay, let me go upstairs and get my bag," he bellowed.

I watched him turn and walk to the foot of the stairs in the next room. Lara was right. My cell phone was my best weapon, but she had the wrong man in mind. I entered the living room and watched him until he reached the top of the stairs. I put my arms out for balance as I walked quietly to the front door. I could go next door and wait until he leaves. Oh, no! What if Kurt comes? I sat down in the chair nearest the front door.

Phillip took much longer to come back down then I thought necessary, but when he walked down the stairs he had on clean clothes. His face looked like he had washed, although I hadn't heard him go down the hall to the bathroom. He wore a white shirt with a plaid vest that matched the plaid on the suitcase he carried. He stopped at the bottom of the stairs and bowed slightly. In a deep but respectful tone, he asked, "Anna, may I trouble you for a cup of tea before I depart?"

"I can do that but you can't stay. I'm expecting company."

I got up from the chair and walked past him and into the kitchen. I glanced over my shoulder to see him put his suitcase by the front door. Before I had the teapot on the burner, he was in the kitchen. He just stood in the doorway watching me. I set a cup and saucer on the table and opened a box of tea bags. "I have only a small selection."

Phillip walked over and sat down at the table. "Let's see … Earl Grey? That will do."

He didn't speak again until I poured the hot water into his cup and set the pot on a hot plate in the center of the table.

"Do you know a woman named Vicky Anna O'Sullivan?"

"I've heard of her," I replied, as I sat down across the table from him. I was not going to tell him she was a ghost.

He smiled. "I've never met a woman like that. In some ways she seemed like a wanton whore, but then she would act like a little lost lassie."

The big man took a deep drink of the tea. "In a town as small as Hope, I bet she is well-known." He shrugged, "I didn't go looking for her; I was looking for Hope. There isn't much to that town."

He put his teacup down and smiled. "You look good in black. Sexy."

"You said that already." I turned the chair slightly to one side to allow a quick exit if he became more aggressive. He put the tea bag back in his cup and refilled it with hot water.

"I must have driven past Hope. Came to a store with a sign that said East Hope, so I turned around and drove slowly back the way I had come. This woman was standing on the side of the road. I stopped to ask directions and she offered to take me to Hope." He dunked the tea bag a few times before setting it in the saucer. "She had a bottle of whiskey. Since a train blocked the road to Hope, we tipped a few."

He shook his head. "We did more than tip a few. I've never seen a woman come on so fast."

The look on his face was that of a man aroused and ready. "Did she tell you her name or did you hear that from someone else later?"

The red beard twitched. "Oh, she told me all right. She told me a story too. That's the strangest part of all."

He sat back and stretched. "Now, don't you run off. I'm just talking. You see, Vicky was dressed when she first got into the car but only a moment later she was out the door, into the back seat and completely undressed. What's a man to do in a case like that?"

Phillip shook his head. "Never had it happen that fast, even in a dream." His beard twisted to match the grin on the rest of his face. "Then the silly lassie got dressed and ran down to the lake. I jumped out of the car and followed her, all the time trying to talk her into getting back in the car."

He put his big right hand down flat on the table and leaned toward me. He was looking again, but not at my face. The fingers of my right hand rose to touch the cross.

"Now, that's an interesting amulet."

I put my hand over the cross. "It's a tau cross." My thumb glided across the letters on the back of the cross. Where is Kurt? I need him now.

In one long drink Phillip emptied the hot cup of tea. He slowly rose to his feet and looked across the table; the table seemed to shrink in size. He was a big man with long, hairy hands. I could feel my legs shaking. If he moved even one step to his left, he would block my path to the door.

Phillip put his right hand on the table and leaned over. His voice was a whisper. "I told you that after our little romp in the back seat of the car she got dressed and ran out into the lake."

I knew I was leaning away from the table and put my arm back to keep from falling off the chair. "Yes, you said that. What happened next?"

He stepped around the end of the table and looked down at me. "I went into the water after her. Vicky kept going out, farther and farther. She was a strong swimmer, that lassie, I can tell you that. I lost sight of her and started to call out to where I had last seen her."

He stood up straight with his hands on his hips. "That's when I made a mistake. Another car stopped on the road near mine. I yelled for him to come down to the lake. I think I said something like 'Get your useless ass down here right now.'"

Phillip rocked back on his heels. "It was one of those damn traffic police. He told me to come out of the lake. I wasn't about to do that but I couldn't find Vicky. She may have swum clear across the lake, for all I know. She certainly wouldn't want anything to do with the police."

I rose carefully from my chair and stepped to the right. "So, when you finally came ashore they arrested you for being drunk and disorderly?"

Phillip put out his left arm to block me from going past him. "I wasn't drunk. I could still stand up. Where are you going?"

"I'm expecting a friend," I replied, and just then, thank God, the doorbell rang.

He dropped his arm to his side and followed me to the front door.

Chapter 38
Kurt Arrives at Anna's House

I raced up highway 41 out of Post Falls. It was a winding, two-lane road built with a motorcycle rider in mind. Tall pines lined the roadside and the small towns were without stoplights. I was torn with the urge to ride faster to get back to see Anna, yet hesitant to meet her husband. I imagined he was the returned missionary she was waiting for back in 1969. No doubt he was an active member of the church. But he hadn't been at church, or at least I hadn't met him that morning. That seemed strange, but Anna's daughter's comment echoed in my ears, 'My father is a much bigger man. I must warn you, he has a quick temper and no sense of humor. But we all love him dearly.' The big man with a quick temper was a warning, and so was the 'we all love him dearly.' Maybe I should just ride on. No. I told Anna I would stop by, so I will. It will just be a quick hello. What have I to lose since, I am not supposed to be here?

At the town of Newport, I stopped to buy gas. It was almost five, so I chose to take highway two on the north side of the river and then cross back at Sandpoint. With the headlights on flashing I rode east, keeping well within the speed limit. Sandpoint traffic was the first stop-and-go riding of the trip. As I crossed the long bridge heading south, I glanced over at the shoreline. One of those houses was Anna's. She would be expecting me. What had she told her husband? Was I to play the old friend role or the jilted lover? We had never done anything, but in those last days it was clear we wanted each other.

I turned right after crossing the bridge and rode slowly past the Landing to Murphy Bay. There was a white Cadillac parked in the driveway. Brace yourself, Kurt, he's home. I turned my bike around and parked it pointed toward the road, and as far from the Cadillac as I could. I got off and started for the front door. After I rang the bell I realized I still had my helmet on. Quickly I unsnapped the chinstrap and pulled it off. The door opened.

She wore a beautiful smile. She took my hand and led me inside. "Kurt, please come in. I've been waiting for you."

A deep voice from within the room bellowed, "So this is the guy you find more interesting than me. Why, if he were a fish, you'd have to toss him back in the lake. Too small."

My first thought was to turn and run but the look on Anna's face stopped me. I stepped forward and looked up at a red-bearded giant of a man. The fingers of my right hand gripped the side of the helmet. With one sweeping blow I could take out a knee that would even the odds.

Anna took a step back.

The giant took a cautious step forward. "He's a biker too. I might have guessed. Anna you need to raise your standards."

I advanced, stepping just to the man's right. "Now that is no way to speak to a lady."

The red beard glanced over his shoulder at Anna. "Don't walk away. This will be amusing."

I let the helmet swing just a little back past my hip. I wanted the best swing I could get. Now, if only the man would look back at Anna like he did a second ago.

"Phillip." Anna's voice was loud and clear. "I am dialing the number. Nine... one..."

"Oh, Hell! Not that again," the giant complained. He stepped backward and shot a glance at Anna. "You win. I'm leaving."

He took a sideways step, picked up a suitcase and marched toward the front door. I stepped aside and watched until he opened the car door, tossed his suitcase in the back and sat down behind the steering wheel.

Anna closed the front door and rushed to me. She put her arms around my neck. I got a kiss and a hug before I could respond. My arms slowly folded around her. "I didn't come here to start any trouble. Maybe I'd better just leave."

She gave me another hug, then stepped back. "Kurt, you were wonderful."

"But he's your husband. No, I'd better leave."

"Kurt, you know me better than that. I would never marry a man like Phillip."

I looked at her. She looked like one of the women in a Black Velvet ad. I reached out and then pulled back my arms. "Okay, Anna. He's not your husband. Where is he?"

"Who?" She slowly put her hands behind her back with a questioning look on her face.

"Your husband. He should be here. He shouldn't let any rough-mannered man in his house, especially not alone with his wife. Well, where is he? I should tell him a thing or two."

She stepped up to my side and took my hand. "That's so gallant. Now let me take your coat."

"No." I said. "Maybe he won't want me to stay."

She squeezed my hand. "Follow me."

I tried to walk tall and not show how much I liked having Anna so close. She led me though the dining room, into the kitchen, and out the back door. All the while I kept the helmet in my right hand. Twice I raised it as if to put it on. At the edge of the dock she stopped and pointed out at the river. "Sam is out there."

"In Sandpoint? Why? Is there some trouble between you two? I didn't come here to cause any trouble." I took a half step to the side.

Anna stepped in closer. She slipped her arms around my waist. "Kurt, my husband died six months ago. He loved fishing and golf, which is why we left Spokane and moved up here. Sam planned every step in his life but he didn't plan on cancer. He never got to really enjoy his retirement. In the end, we were both glad it was over. His dying wish was to have his ashes spread over the river."

I slowly moved my left arm around her shoulder. "Honestly?"

"Now, I wouldn't lie about something like that."

I nodded. "I'm sorry. This is a shock. All the way up here from Colorado I was dreading meeting your husband. Then your daughter really knifed me."

"My daughter? Which one?"

I laughed and turned around to face Anna. "I met too many people today. The woman with the twins. She said her father was a big man with a bad temper. She also said you all still love him."

She smiled, leaned closer and kissed me on the cheek. "That would be Lara; I'll have to talk to her. Now, let's go back inside and take that coat off and put down your helmet. I'll fix dinner. You haven't eaten, have you?"

I sat at the kitchen table as Anna fixed a light dinner of salad and sandwiches. I felt like a burden was lifted from my shoulders, but at the same time I felt guilty. Whenever someone dies I feel guilty. Now, I hadn't really offered an expression of condolences. I didn't know what to say.

Anna sat down at the table, not across from me, but to my right side. She bowed her head. I put down my sandwich and waited in silence as she said a short prayer. The ham and cheese was much better that the bologna sandwiches her mother made, and I told her so.

She took a few bites and then looked sideways at me. "Kurt, I'm sorry. What Lara said had you thinking I was still married. Thank heaven it wasn't to a man like Phillip." She looked down at her plate. "I have a few questions along that line for you."

I raised both hands off the table. "I'm not married."

"Have you ever been?"

I shook my head twice and then bit my lower lip.

"Tell me about it."

I took a deep breath and let it out slowly. "Do I have to?"

"Yes."

"Now?"

"Yes. I want to know about you. You met my family; now tell me about yours."

I took a big bite of the ham and cheese, chewed it up slowly and then took a drink of water. I was trying to calm down, but my heart was racing. "It was about twenty-five years ago. Doesn't seem that long ago. At the time I was driving a cross-country route. Sarah and I were getting along pretty good so she moved in with me."

I put my hands down flat on the table on either side of my plate. I'm not going to take another bite until I tell her. It's just a short story but it's true. "I knew we shouldn't do it that way, but at the time I was only home one weekend a month. She kept asking me to look for another job where I'd be home more. I looked but the money was always less, so I didn't switch. One weekend when I came home she told me she was leaving. I said I'd really try to get a local job. It was too late. She had found someone else."

I slowly pulled my hands back and let them drop to my lap. "I was so upset I just quit my job." I shook my head. "That same week a man at Budweiser called and offered me a job delivering beer in Nebraska."

Anna reached across the table with both hand palms up. "Give me your hands."

I put my hands in hers. She smiled and said, "Now, tell me the rest of the story."

"It's not that bad. Sarah and I are still friends. She married a much better guy than me. She's happier than I could ever make her."

"Keep talking, Kurt."

"What do you want to know?"

"You can start with those men you rode with today. Tell me

about them."

I shrugged. "I don't know much."

"I understand what the motorcycle club is about. They want to give soldiers coming back from Iraq the welcome they never got when they returned from Vietnam. How did you get involved?"

"Yeah, that's what they are about. I met one of the guys in South Dakota a few years back. It sounded like a good thing to do so I tracked them on the internet. Me, I don't fit in there either. Most are Army. Adrian and I were the only Marines there today. We're different, we're a breed apart."

"When I met you, I told Gladys you were a lost soul. I blamed a woman, but maybe it was the war."

I squeezed her hand between mine. "Looking back, it was both. I was just in the wrong place with the wrong dream. I wasn't old enough to handle it. But the war made a big difference too. Before Vietnam, I could study. I was a good student. After Vietnam, I blamed the antiwar groups for my not going back, but it wasn't just them. I knew I couldn't sit still in a classroom for weeks at a time, and that is what it would take. I still read a lot, mostly history now. Today I think I'm too old to go back to school. Hell, I ain't supposed to be here." I let go of her hand and added, "Thanks for listening."

She picked up her sandwich. "I've learned to be a good listener. After dinner you must tell what happened in Vietnam."

I shook my head. "I don't want to talk about it. It's over." They are all dead but me. No that's not right. Doc Brad is still alive. Just me and Doc.

"Okay. If you don't want to talk about Vietnam then you can start with the day you left Hope. How did you get home that winter? I worried terribly about you."

As we ate I told of riding all the way to Pasco in the rain. When I told about going down Meacham Hill she cried. Why? It wasn't her fault. I chose to leave. I chose to ride on despite the advice not to. Each time I stopped talking she urged me to continue. Finally it dawned on me why she wanted to know-she cared.

When I told her about riding with a trucker across Wyoming, she asked, "You trusted a total stranger?"

I smiled. "Turned out all right. He was a real nice guy. His name was Hank Deeming. He had a small ranch outside Pine Bluff, almost on the state line with Nebraska. He raised dry land wheat, ran a few cattle and drove a truck. From Cheyenne, I rode down to Fort Collins. My dad and mom were happy to see me, yet after dinner I checked into a motel."

"Is that when you tried to go back to school?"

"Not there. I went over to Greeley and enrolled at Northern Colorado. For a while I did okay, but as soon as winter ended and the roads were clear I wanted to head out again. It wasn't just riding a motorcycle, it was also traveling."

I had finished the sandwich and took the last drink from my glass. "The stockyards are in Greeley and at times the wind blew the wrong way. That's what I told my major professor. I just dropped out of school. It was the stockyards that brought Hank to Greeley. He had delivered a truckload of Angus down from Nebraska and was headed for Montana to get another load. He asked me to come along. That's how I got started in the trucking business."

Anna smiled. "It appears, Mister Johnson, you have more than one guardian angel."

"He wasn't nearly as pretty as you." I sat back in my chair. "Now, I have an unpleasant question for you. You don't have to answer but I do have to ask. I wrote you a letter before I left and gave it to Betty. She said she'd be sure you got it. Why didn't you ever answer my letter?"

Anna stood up. She picked up the plates from the table and put them in the sink. She turned and motioned toward the living room.

"Kurt, it's a long story. Let's go into the other room and talk. It's getting cool. You can test your skill at building a fire in the fireplace. I don't want to turn on the furnace."

Chapter 39
Anna Tells Kurt Her Story

I watched from the dining room as Kurt opened the flue and crumpled up some newspaper to start the fire. He put his right hand out against the fireplace as he knelt down on his left knee. The knee brace looked like an extra bend in his right leg. When he left the hospital he hopped around for two weeks on his left leg, but once he had that cast off he stood tall and walked straight. It was all an act. The leg must have hurt him back then just as it appeared to now. Now older, he could no longer hide it. He needed a brace just to walk.

"I'll be back in a minute," I said, then turned and hurried up the stairs. I went into the bathroom and closed the door. Tears hadn't waited for me to reach the top of the stairs. I covered my face in a bath towel. He was different but he was still Kurt, the man whose life I had saved. What could I say? I had cried for him but I had not tried to contact him. I had accepted our fate. He had gone back to his Rachel. I had waited quietly for Sam to return from his mission, married him and raised a family. I was so young back then. When Sam returned from his mission he was so glad to see me. He cried and laughed and hugged me so tight. I knew he had missed me, and I knew he still loved me. I had to love him back. It was not until recently I realized I had played the role my family and God laid out for me. If only they hadn't kept his letter from me. But what would I have done back then? The kind of life I would have had if I had chosen Kurt over Sam would have been far different. We would not have lasted, just as his affair had not lasted.

I let myself cry again, with the towel catching the tears and hiding the sound. Suddenly the tears stopped, and I hung the towel back on its rack. I stood up straight, looked in the mirror and centered the silver cross between the curves in my sweater. "I'm not twenty like the girl he fell in love with. I am who I am. After all these years he deserves an answer. I am not in love with him anymore. I still like him but I must tell him I have changed. This won't be easy."

I brushed my hair, wishing it were longer than shoulder length. I washed my face, added a little mascara and fresh lipstick. When I walked down the stairs, he looked up with an admiring look. I tried not to swing my hips, but somehow when walking down stairs I tend to do that. Why did Lara tell him her father was a big man with a bad temper? No wonder Kurt was shocked when he saw Phillip.

"Would you like something to drink?" I asked.

"No, I'm fine."

"I could make some tea. I don't have any wine or beer."

"I didn't expect you would."

He was seated in the chair to the right of the fireplace, leaning forward a little. I moved to the love seat and sat at the end nearest the fire. He relaxed and sat back against the overstuffed chair. His legs were spread apart slightly and the brace on the right knee rotated out like an extra joint in the leg.

I leaned back and pulled my legs up on the cushion next to me. Oops! If I kicked off my shoes that wouldn't look polite. He was smiling at me. I bet he can't curl his legs up like this, not with that brace on anyway. I wish he were over here sitting beside me. I had better get right to the point; I never wrote him or tried to contact him. My left hand rested on the armrest and I pushed back a little more.

"The short answer to why I didn't write is I didn't get your letter until years later."

His eyebrows rose. They were thick, dark eyebrows that stood out in contrast to the short, white hair on his head. At least he hadn't gone bald. In a way he's a more handsome man than when he was younger. Age gives a man's face character and dries a woman's up like a prune.

I raised my head slightly, smiled and took a deep breath. He blinked. What had Phillip said? 'You look good in black. Sexy.' Phillip was no gentleman; still Kurt may be thinking the same thing. He came all this way. He deserves to know what happened.

"I don't know how he got the letter, but my husband Sam had it. I found it after he died when I was going through his personal records. He kept records on everything he did, for the church, for his business and his family." I looked down at the floor for a moment. I can't bite my lip or touch them with my tongue; I've got fresh lipstick on.

"You see, it was in a way a conspiracy. My mother was behind it. Moving to Hope was the start of her plan." I looked up. On their own, my eyes opened wider as they met his.

"Mother wanted me to marry Sam Chapman. I told you about Sam." I sighed. "I didn't tell you how in love with him I was. I understood he had to go off on his mission. He had to do it. My dad shouldn't have died when he did, but that happened too. Mother didn't want me to stray while he was away."

Kurt's head nodded slowly. Stray was the wrong word to use just then. "I wanted to go back to college. All my friends would be down in Moscow. I was in a sorority. You were in college. You know what that means."

He didn't say anything and his expression was almost blank. Perhaps he was thinking of his college years, or was he thinking of the time he tried to return to school? He wouldn't be thinking of the day we made out on the couch in his little house and I was late for work.

I turned my body to face the fire. The wood was crackling as the flames rose high in the hearth. I could feel the warmth on my face but there was another warmth building beneath the snug, black sweater. I had better speak quickly. "I felt lost in Hope. I know that sounds odd, but I wanted to go back to school. I pleaded with my mother, but she was firm."

A side-glance told me he was watching me closely. I leaned toward the fire. "All my friends were miles away."

I paused a moment. The heat within me was greater than the fire in the fireplace. This was a feeling I hadn't experienced in years. No, don't think that way, Anna. Who are you fooling with this provocative pose? You're flirting again. You know it and he knows it. I felt the sweater tighten across my chest, and yet I hadn't taken a deep breath. I wasn't sure I was breathing at all. I turned my face back to look at his eyes Dark brown pupils filled Kurt's eyes. I leaned back, moved my right hand to the back of the love seat and extended my right leg over left.

"I was told we moved to Hope to live with Aunt Gladys because we needed to save money. Much later I learned that wasn't true. Mother moved us to Hope to keep me from returning to college."

His eyes looked so big and dark I had to look away.

"After raising three girls to womanhood, I understand. There is a time in a woman's life when she is ready to fall in love. Mother feared if I returned to college I'd fall in love with someone else and not marry Sam Chapman. Well, half of her plan worked."

I leaned back until my head rested on the top of the love seat. He was looking, staring not at my body but at my eyes. I had best be careful how I say this. "A stranger came to town. He didn't plan on staying. He was just passing through. Thanks to a moose he spent the next two months in Hope, and just as Mother feared, I fell in love."

"So, it was just a matter of timing," he said. "I can understand that."

"Can you understand if I had gotten your letter the day you left, I would have followed you? Kurt, I was in love with you. I'd have left everything. I'd have ridden all the way to Colorado on the back of that bike."

He shook his head. "Guess your mother did the right thing."

I looked back at the fire. The flames were leaping high above the split logs. The heat came in waves. This wasn't the way to tell him. He couldn't believe my mother was right. I looked into the flames and they seemed to advance across the room. I felt his hand on my leg, his lips on my cheek. Despite the heat I froze, unable to respond to his advances. Then he spoke softly.

"Anna, I was so in love with you—too much to take you with me. At the time I was drifting. I didn't have a job and didn't believe I had any future at all. A man can't ask a woman to go with him if he has no idea of where he is going. Gladys was right. You deserved better."

I held my head stiff and only my eyes turned his way. His face was so close I could feel his breath as he whispered.

"I can't say anything or do anything to change the past. If we look at it clearly, you had a better life with Sam than you'd have had with me."

"And what about you? Were you better off?"

He chuckled. "I don't count that much. I'm not even supposed to be here."

His fingers glided through my hair and gently turned my face toward his. His lips were gentle but so warm. My arms circled his chest and pulled him closer. I rolled over until my back was resting on the arm of the love seat. My head extended toward the fire but his hand held it steady. Soft kisses spread from ear to ear. A peppy tone sounded from across the room. The kisses stopped. I wanted to shout but he leaned back away from me. I pulled myself forward into a sitting position. He moved into a sitting position on the love seat next to me. The peppy tone sounded again and I jumped up, crossed the room in quick steps and snapped open the cell phone.

"Hello. I thought it would be you." I turned and looked back at Kurt. "Yes, he came back. I know it's late. My dear daughter I know what I am doing." I smiled at Kurt. "Now, let me worry about that. He is not. Lara, please. I can't believe you asked that. I'll call you tomorrow."

I snapped shut the cell phone and walked back to where Kurt was sitting on the love seat.

"Sorry, I got carried away," he said sheepishly.

"That was my daughter, Lara. She wanted to know if you were staying tonight."

"Anna, I have a cabin at Red Fir and I should be on my way." His eyes surveyed me from toes to lips as he rose from the love seat. I took a step backwards from him.

"Sorry, I just want to remember just how beautiful you are."

I shook my head. "Don't say I look sexy in black."

He laughed. "Okay, I won't say it."

I walked him out to his bike. I knew the bike was over thirty-five years old but he had it shining like new. I didn't cry until he had ridden away and I was back in my house sitting in the love seat and roasting in the warmth of the fire.

Chapter 40
Kurt: The Soiled Dove Saloon

I stopped outside the Soiled Dove Saloon but it was closed. I assumed Molly made Mike close up early after staying up until after midnight the night before. I rode on to my cabin at Red Fir. As I walked down the gravel path to the cabin, I looked across at the Hope. I swear there was a light in the window of one of the second floor rooms. I got my binoculars and checked it out from the deck. Through the binoculars none of the windows appeared lighted on the second floor, but when I lowered the binoculars and looked there was a light. The place must be haunted; Vicky must have come a day later than Mike figured she would.

I dreamed of sex, which was no surprise. Anna had ignited a fire in me hotter than the one I lit in the fireplace. I was so hot it felt like the whole room was burning around us. Then, just in a flash, she changed into Vicky. We rolled off the love seat into a lake of warm water. We fought to keep from drowning and yet kept making love. The bed was wet from sweat when I got up the next morning.

I checked out of the resort and rode over to Hope for breakfast. In Hope, I strolled into the café with a steel thermos in my left hand. I sat down at one of the many empty tables and waited. The cute waitress wore a too-large sweatshirt with a huge moose head on the front. I imagined she was wearing the same tight, hip-hugging jeans, but the shirt came down past her hips.

"Breakfast burritos are the special today," she said.

"Sounds good enough for a Monday. And I need coffee," I took the top off my thermos. "One cup here and two to go."

She picked up the thermos, lifted it high and looked inside. "Ooo! I had better wash this."

I silently rebuked myself for staring at the moose head. It was Anna's fault. I was riding away again.

"Hey, Kurt! What brings you back?" Molly called from the front door.

I turned toward her, pushing my right leg out so I wouldn't twist the knee brace. "On my way back home. I needed a jolt of coffee. Good coffee."

Molly walked over and sat down in the chair to my left. "Let me tell you about our late night vigil."

I smiled. "What's to tell? I was there and Vicky didn't show up?"

"No. Well, at least not here." Molly shook her head.

"Where was she?"

Molly nodded. "Down at the lake. You see, she met this Scotsman, a big obnoxious fellow."

"Scotsman?"

"Yeah, with a dark red beard and a voice that rattled the windows." Molly raised her finger and waved it at me. "You know, the kind of man who wants everyone to look at him when he walks into a room. Well, this phony was parked down by the lake. In fact, he was swimming in the lake. Drunk as a skunk. It took two deputies to pull him out of the water."

"Maybe they shouldn't have done that."

Hip-hugger brought the thermos to the table. I must admit, I looked at the moose.

Molly waited until the girl had left, then whispered, "This Scotsman claimed he was trying to save a woman named Vicky. They had just been having a good time in the back seat of his Cadillac when she decided to go for a swim."

I jerked my head back toward Molly. "Vicky?"

"Mike was right. Midnight, a full moon and October. She showed up right on schedule."

"So, next year Mike will be down at the lake at midnight?"

"A pack of wolves couldn't keep him away. But that's not all. I talked to the two deputies who pulled the blowhard from the lake. They said he was damn indignant." Molly put her hand on my arm. "The Scotsman told them Vicky was looking for an amulet she lost in the lake. She needed it to protect her from harm and it was her passport to heaven. She said she lost it in the lake years ago."

I nodded. "Let me guess. This amulet, as you call it was a silver cross that looked like the Greek letter tau, and on the back is inscribed her name."

"Well, he didn't say all that, but now Mike thinks he knows why Vicky comes back. She's looking for her amulet."

Hip-hugger brought the breakfast burrito to the table and again Molly paused in her story until she was gone. I shook my head. "That story does not make sense. If this ghost spends her time looking in the lake for a lost cross, no one would ever see her. Besides, even a ghost knows you can't find anything in the lake at night."

"Then why does she come back?" Molly asked.

I smiled. "She is looking for me. Don't tell Mike, but I just might come back this way again next fall."

Molly laughed so loud everyone in the room turned to watch. "Men. I will never understand them. Dreamers. That's what they are."

I said it softly, trying to remember the exact words. "The reason they return is they are lonely. They were lonely in life and now they are lonely in death. They wander between the two worlds looking for someone or something. Do not fear them, but treat them kindly."

"Now that sounds familiar," Molly said. "Who told you that?"

"An old woman named Betty." I said with a smile, "When Betty talked of Vicky she spoke as if she knew the woman, while Gladys talked as if she had only heard the stories about Vicky. She probably heard them from Betty. Now, if Betty knew Vicky back in the nineteen twenties, how old would Betty have been in nineteen-sixty-nine?"

"Why don't you ask her? She is still down at that little house on the road below."

I rubbed my fist across my chin. Yes, Betty is still here. I wonder what she would say if I asked her why she didn't give my letter to Anna. I dropped my fist to my side and shook my head. "If I stopped to talk with Betty, I'd be there for hours. That woman is a spellbinder. I'm headed back home to Colorado. I've got enough to think about."

I decided not to go back through Montana, but to head down through Idaho on Highway 95. It was a road I had never traveled. I stopped at the Mobil station in Sandpoint to buy gas and checked the phone book. My next stop was at a small trailer court in the north end of town. A deep voice answered my knock on the door. "It ain't locked."

"Well, good morning to you too, Doc," I said as I pulled open the metal door.

"Hey, Kurt! Good to see you. How was the ride? You give those boys a proper welcome?"

I came in and closed the door. "Yeah! It was a good show. We weren't official, of course, but I think they were glad we came."

"That's what counts. It's about them this time. Don't forget that. It's about them. Have a seat."

I squatted on a wooden box that also had served as an end table. We talked of the war in Iraq and other current events. Slowly the topic changed to that other war and the men we had served with.

"Ever hear of Billy Jackson?" Brad asked.

"He's dead." I bowed my head. "They are all dead but you and me. Billy had it all, or so I thought the last time I saw him. The next thing I knew he died in an auto accident." I shook my head.

"A one-car accident at three in the morning. Ran right into a tree. I guess that's a quick way to go."

"Don't do it, Kurt. Don't even think about it."

I grinned. "You know we both have thought about it. They all died. Some in Nam, some shortly after we came back. Why wasn't I killed? Why weren't you? Ever think about it? We don't deserve life more than they did."

Brad shook his fist. "Don't think that way. It's not about us anymore. Maybe it never was. It's about those who died; they must be honored. It's about those who will die; they must be supported in the fight. They are fighting for us." He leaned back and laughed. "Hell, Kurt. Who was the fancy lady who dragged you into church the other day? You got someone like that on your line, you don't want to die."

I nodded and took a big red handkerchief from my back pocket. I don't know why but there was moisture in my eyes.

"Glad you stopped by, Kurt. Have a safe ride back home."

I went outside and fired up the bike. Brad really hit the nail on the head when he mentioned her. A woman, a woman like Anna gives you hope.

Chapter 41
Anna: After Kurt Leaves

As love letters go, this was not an outstanding one. Not very eloquent or very passionate, but it was honest. It was surprisingly formal and yet warm. He wrote of how grateful he was for the kindness he received from Gladys and my mother. He said he didn't deserve the kindness and he was going to repay it by going back to Colorado. It was not until the second page that he really addressed us. This page was different, as if he had written it later just before sealing the letter.

I am in love with you. I didn't plan it, it just happened. You are truly beautiful, too physically attractive to ignore and on top of it all, you're an angel. You are also a saint. Now, in the Catholic religion they say that and saints are different, but then they call Michael the Archangel, Saint Michael. I wish I could be a saint, but I know in my heart I cannot. Nor can I ask you to shed your wings. Gladys observed we were becoming too close. She said it is best I leave before we do something that will bind us together. At first I thought she was way off base. We weren't having sex, so how could you be pregnant. I was wrong.

As I pack my things to leave, I know I will always love you. Falling in love is something that will bind me to you forever. It is time for me to leave. You have a much better life ahead of you with that missionary she told me about than you could ever have with me. I am not even supposed to be here. Still, I do want to know I did the right thing.

Please write me in a year or two and tell me you are

happy. This is all I ask. You can send the letter to my
father's address because I have no idea where I am going.
Love always, Kurt

If only I had received this letter thirty-five years ago I would
have known what to say. I would have answered with my heart,
not my adult mind. I'd have told him how I watched his room at
night with the telescope, how I longed for another loving session
on the couch in his house. I shivered just thinking of those fond
but short expressions of passion. He wanted me so badly. I
shivered again and then realized the phone was ringing downstairs.
Hurrying down the stairs and I got the phone just before the
answering machine started.

"Mom, you didn't call. You said you would call me and tell
me what happened. The bum didn't stay the night, did he?"

I walked back to the stairs as I replied.

"No, he went back to the cabin he'd rented in Hope."

"Would you believe I stayed up half the night waiting for you
to call back and tell me he left town? I hope no one saw his
motorcycle parked in your driveway. What would they think?"

I reached the top of the stairs. "Relax, Lara. By the way, I
forgot to tell you last night but Phillip also stopped by late
yesterday afternoon. He was a real bore. It seems Saturday night
he got drunk, went for a swim in the lake, got arrested and spent
the night in jail. You won't believe the story he told me."

"Mother! Don't change the subject. Where is he now?"

"Phillip left last night about six. I assume he drove back
to Spokane."

A long few seconds of silence preceded my daughter's reply.
"Mother, I know what you are doing. I can see right through you.
You were all hung up on this Kurt. He was the return of an old
flame. Now, what happened?"

I had to smile. I had run all the way downstairs thinking the
call might have been from Kurt. "Let me put the phone down for a

minute. I need to change loads in the washer. Be back in a minute."

I quickly gathered up the sheets from my bed and the bed down the hall where Lara and Jim had slept. The sheets from the guest room went into the dryer. After reloading the washer, I hurried upstairs to my bedroom where I had left the phone.

"Hi, hon, still there?"

"Yes. What took you so long? He isn't still there, is he?"

I sat down on the bare mattress, looked at the pile of fresh bedding and decided a break was in order.

"He isn't here but I was thinking about him. He left last night. By now he is halfway across Montana. The news reported a storm in Montana today. I hope he is all right."

"Mom, let him go and don't plan to go to Colorado. There is no reason to. You have seen him and he is alive. Now, about moving to Spokane. That would be a great change."

I slid the stack of fresh sheets down to the foot of the bed, lay back on the mattress and looked up at the ceiling. "I still dream of going for a long ride on my bike. I could go alone or with someone, like Kurt. We'd ride as far as we wished and stop when we wanted. We'd see the country and enjoy riding."

"Mom, you can't do that."

"No, not this year. In fact I worry about Kurt getting home alone. The weather can turn bad any day." I touched the tip of my tongue to the roof of my mouth. It was fun to tease Lara and it was fun to think of Kurt. I wondered where he would be sleeping tonight. I raised my head and glanced over to see the letter was still on my dressing table. "He invited me to come visit him. I'm curious. I'd like to see his house. He told me he has a dog named Charlie."

"But you just said you weren't going."

"I told him I had to be here this winter. Maybe next spring or summer we'll talk about it again. Don't worry; I'll keep you informed. It was nice of him to invite me, don't you think?"

"Mom, I don't like this. You'd be alone. Men behave differently when they have you alone."

I rolled up and off the bed. Lara continued to protest, mentioning several problems that might arise if I were so far away. Most of her rambling I dismissed as nonsense, except for one question: "Mother, do you know what he did in Vietnam?"

"He was a Marine."

"But what did he do? Was he one of those guys that Kerry talked about? You know, war crimes?"

"I can't believe my daughter, the vice president of the Pachyderm Club, would put any credence in what that man said."

"My point is you don't know this man. You don't know what he did in Vietnam and you don't know what he's doing in Colorado."

"Okay, I'll ask him. But most Vietnam vets don't talk much about that war. Now, I must get back to my laundry. I'll call you tonight."

* * *

It was Wednesday when I drove to Hope with fresh flowers for Gladys' grave. The weather was cold and wet. This would be the last time I would bring flowers this year. I took the new bouquet of bright yellow French marigolds called carefully out of the paper bag. Gladys always loved bright yellow flowers. I stopped at the grave and picked the wilted red and white flowers from the basket. "Now who put these here?"

I placed the marigolds in the basket and slowly stood up. "He came here, didn't he?"

I didn't expect a reply as I stuffed the dead flowers into the paper bag. "Those yellow flowers won't last long if it starts getting cold at night. Gladys, tell me you liked him. He was a good man. I know you sent him away, but he came back. Maybe we were meant to be together."

I looked out toward the lake. Only a few blue spots could be seen between the tall pine trees. A light breeze wandered up the hill and shook the tops of the pine trees. "I'm going now, Gladys. I'll let you know what I decide to do."

I knelt down on the rough ground and said a prayer before leaving. On the way back though Hope I stopped at the Soiled Dove Saloon. A buxom brunette in a black sweatshirt came down the bar. "Can I get you something to warm your spirits?"

"No thank you. I was just looking." I glanced around at the few old men in the place and walked out the door. For a long time I just stood outside the bar looking down the street at the little house where Kurt had stayed. Finally, with the breeze in my face, I walked down to the house. Time had stood still here. It was just as I remembered it the last time I came to see Kurt. I walked up to the front door. A voice like a parrot called from upwind, "There is no one home. They left for the winter a month ago."

I glared at the old woman sitting in a rocking chair on the porch of the house next door. I could forgive Gladys and my mother for hiding that letter from me, but if Betty had seen it first I bet she would have read it. I turned and walked to the porch in long strides. The old woman's voice rushed down wind. "Everyone has left for the winter except for a few ghosts. Don't be afraid, for they mean no harm. They just have no other place to go."

I stopped at the edge of the porch and replied, "You don't remember me, do you? My name is Anna. I used to live here."

Her old head with the heavy scarf on it turned as if consulting with someone sitting beside her. "We remember you. Oh, yes. You're the young girl who used to look out at Cottage Island and wish you were there. You came looking for Kurt, didn't you?"

Again she looked around as if gathering assurance she was right. "Well, you had your chance. You didn't get him. Now he belongs to Vicky."

"Nonsense."

"One night is all it would have taken. Vicky didn't fail her test and now he will return to see her. Not you, but Vicky."

I turned and walked back to where I had parked my SUV across from the café.

*   *   *

Friday I spent in the basement. I pulled Sam's old treadmill out of the small room he used for exercise in the winter. I dusted it and pulled it out into the family room in front of the television. The last twenty pounds is going off. Most people gain weight in the winter; I'm going to lose weight. I went back and cleaned everything in the exercise room. Confined spaces were like jail cells, so the weight bench and some of the free weights were moved to the larger family room. Sam's big recliner went into the smaller room to balance things out. I put off starting an exercise program until Monday and went upstairs. That night I weighed myself on the bathroom scale.

"No, I can't have gained five pounds in a week." I glared at the scale. "You wait and see. Before I go down to Colorado I'll be back to my weight. I won't be a fat old lady when he introduces me to his family. You watch."

I made up a menu for the week; I refused to use the word diet. I also wrote up an exercise schedule. It was Monday before I put either into action. The next two months rolled by slowly as I tried to adjust to my new busy schedule. I alternated early mornings between aerobic exercises, an hour on the treadmill or walking the long bridge, as weather dictated, and strength training. The first month I told myself I was not losing weight but gaining muscle. The second month I lost ten pounds.

I decided to keep the Good Faith and had it put up for the winter over in Sandpoint. I couldn't wait any longer for Jim to put it on his busy schedule. Three weekends in a row he had promised to come up to do it. When he called with his fourth excuse, I told him it was done already.

When I offered him Sam's golf clubs, he was up the next day. He said he'd give them a try next spring, but I knew he would work some trade for golf clubs that better suited his fancy. I had a few boxes of Sam's clothes I had asked him to take to Goodwill. Larry, Barbara's husband, had already bought Sam's truck for a reasonable price. I would have given it to him but Barbara insisted she let Larry buy it. Larry recognized he had married into a richer family. I thought about that for almost a week. Larry was a poor but proud man. Kurt too was a proud man. No doubt my home at the lake had made an impression on both men. Kurt had invited me to visit him but made no other contact since his departure. Proud men need to be pushed sometimes.

I sat down at the computer and did a people search for Kurt Johnson in Colorado. I came up with a lot of prospects, including one who lived in the little town of Ault. I started an email to Kurt, revised it three times, deleted it and picked up the telephone. The phone rang four times before a brief greeting, "You have reached the home of Kurt, Charlie, Billy and Bonnie. We cannot come to the phone at this time. Please leave a message and we'll get back to you."

I lowered the phone from my ear and looked at it. Billy and Bonnie? He lied to me. No, he wouldn't lie. He said his dog was named Charlie and there was no Rachel. Who was Billy? More importantly, who was Bonnie? What do I really know of Kurt? What did he do in Vietnam?

Chapter 42
Kurt in Colorado

I followed highway 95 south toward Boise. It was a highway designed for the biker in all of us. The road followed the hills as it crossed the high prairie country and then down into the canyon country. The road twisted and turned as it followed the steep canyon walls along the fast moving river. It was a road that kept you alert. At New Meadows I took highway 55 into the McCall Valley and Payette Lake country. The trip up the McCall Valley was beautiful, but the bigger reward came with I reached the canyon of the Payette River as it flowed west to Boise.

My one-day adventure ended at Boise. There I stopped for the night at a hotel near interstate 84 so I could get an early start heading east. I soaked in the hot tub at the motel after dinner. The hot water felt good as I massaged my right knee. This was my last long ride of the summer.

From Boise to Rock Springs, Wyoming, was a long ride. I stopped for dinner and decided not to travel farther that night. The high country of southern Wyoming is cursed with winds so strong they often tip trailers. The next morning I followed some semi trucks east and used the smoke from their stacks to anticipate the wind's power and sudden changes in direction— touring at its worst.

When I got home I called Dr. Grey and his nurse found a time slot for me to see him the next afternoon. Dr. Grey sent me to the hospital to get some X-rays. Later that week Dr. Grey called and told me my right knee had gotten worse. The meniscus on the outside of the knee was split, and fragments of bone were floating under the kneecap. He suggested I have an operation to remove them and insert some material to replace the lost cartilage.

"Kurt, when you went for the knee brace a year ago, I told you it was not a final solution. I think we'd better do some repair now before the surface of the joint is damaged further."

"But I haven't had much trouble until now."

Dr. Grey nodded. "Perhaps it was the bike ride. It's harder on you than driving a truck. You could quit riding and see how it feels. You don't want to ride in winter anyway, do you?"

I shrugged. "Don't ride much in winter, but I do some. How long would an operation keep me out of work? I've got to drive to make a living."

"We can do a partial knee replacement this winter, and you could be back driving in four to six months. Let me know if the pain gets worse. I'll leave some information about the surgery at the desk. Read it over and we'll talk about it in a week or two. In the meantime, rest that leg as much as you can. Wear the brace when walking but take it off while you rest the leg."

"Thanks, Doc." I hung up the phone and looked down at my leg.

I kept the information about the knee surgery on the kitchen table for a week. I went to work and rested the knee when I got home. My biggest problem was getting into the truck. I had to open the door, climb up, balance on my left leg and turn around clockwise to sit back into the driver's seat. The first time I did it at the brewery I felt everyone was watching. After a few days I did it so smoothly I was no longer self-conscious about getting into the cab.

I started to write Anna a letter when I got home but tore it up. She was a widow dealing with the recent passing of her husband. Now was not the time to mention my minor medical problems. Just after Thanksgiving I received an email from her. No one hides on the internet. I printed out the message and took it with me to reread later. Visions of Thanksgiving at Gladys' home visited me all day as I drove my truck. Anna wrote mostly of her family gathering in Spokane for Thanksgiving. I remembered kissing her on the way home after Thanksgiving in Hope, as well as our sessions on the couch. I knew it was dangerous to try to rewrite the past, so I wrote her a short but friendly reply mentioning only a little of the trip back to Colorado and nothing of my medical problem. I began planning my return to see Anna again. I would not be in a wheelchair or leaning on a cane.

I wore the brace most of the day. Getting in and out of the big Kenworth was still a problem, but so was hiking around the barn and pasture taking care of the donkeys, Billy and Bonnie. My plan was simple—make as many runs for other drivers during the holiday season as I could, then let those drivers take my route when January came. I'd have the surgery and be back on the road before spring. My boss agreed to my plan and helped me coordinate it.

"Kurt, you are one of the most dependable drivers I have. I want you to keep running until you're an old man."

"Hey, isn't sixty old?" I joked.

"It was twenty years ago, but it isn't any more. The younger drivers are so unreliable. What you need is a partner."

"I got one, and his name is Charlie."

I was surprised to receive an email from Anna the day after Christmas. She wrote about several visits she made to Spokane over the Christmas holiday to see her daughters and grandkids. I quickly became disinterested until I read:

This was the second strangest Christmas I've had. The first Christmas in Hope was the strangest. Sam was off on his mission and you rode off in a snowstorm. I remember sitting at my widow looking out at the lake and wondering if either of you would ever return. This year I felt that way again. I think I'm the only widow in town under seventy.

I reread the email slowly from the top again. The formality of the earlier correspondence was gone. This was the Anna I knew years ago. Wiser now, but so honest and open. I took a pen and underlined a few sentences planning my reply.

She not only told about her family gatherings but also of the impending sale of the Chapman family farm. She asked my advice.

She wrote:

To be frank, two things bother me. I am not a poor woman, thanks to Sam. But this amount of money is more than we ever talked about and I have an obligation to manage it for the family. The other reason is the man behind the money. You met Phillip James McGary III last fall. He is a big braggart, forever boasting of family wealth and Scottish machismo, if there is such a thing. Jim says such behavior is common among the movers and shakers in the financial world.

I read the detail she included about the proposal for the development of the McGary Castle. A very cold chill filled the room. Anna was being taken for a ride by that Scottish Bull. I pounded my fist on the desk. "Don't do it."

I started to simply send a reply telling her not to do it. But what did I know about investments? All I had was a truck, an old house and four acres of dry farmland. I said *I don't play golf and I don't understand that kind of money. I only met this man for a few minutes but I would not trust him.* I logged off the computer and hobbled out to feed the donkeys.

She wrote back the next day:

Don't be intimidated by money. It is a family trust. I must consult with all my children before making a decision but I think they all want to sell. What if I sold and then put the

money in a trust fund? There is a lot of pressure on me to
do something next month. What would you do if you were
me?

I thought a lot about her question before I sent a reply. This
was about money, but it was also about relationship. Anna was
living alone up there by the lake. She needed someone. No doubt
she would have preferred Sam, but he was gone. I knew so little
about money and was afraid to give advice. That night I called a
veterinarian whom I worked for at Colorado State University.

Karen Anderson retired to raise horses on a small ranch just
north of Ault. She was also the one who talked me into taking
Billy and Bonnie to keep them from becoming dog meat. She
didn't give advice over the phone, but made arrangements to stop
in Ault on Sunday. Of course she stopped to see the donkeys first.

Karen leaned over the rail to pet each of them. "Bonnie seems
to be getting along just fine. Billy, he's a little on the heavy side.
He needs more exercise and less food."

"They fight over the food if I cut it back. Bonnie here is just
too docile; she lets him eat and drink first."

Karen leaned forward and Bonnie raised her head and snorted.
"Bonnie was smelling my breath. I don't know why horses and
mules do that, but animals pay attention to odors much more than
we do. Like people, donkeys are happier in pairs, even if one eats
too much. These two are doing just fine. Good job, Kurt "

"You get the blame for that. You're the one who talked me
into adopting them from the BLM."

"As I recall, it didn't take much talking to convince you. In
fact, I remember you saying it was a way to repay a debt."

I laughed. "Did I say that? Well, I have a problem dealing
with people, but these two I understand. But only two. I'm not
going to take any more."

"Okay, but what debt are you repaying by taking care of
two donkeys?"

"I was in an accident and these people helped me. They saved my life and then they gave me a place to stay while I recovered. I wanted to pay them, but instead they said I'd just have to do something for someone else in need. They were very religious so they had in mind I would help someone, but not a donkey. Guess I never got the hang of religious ways."

"Don't be so sure. 'He prayeth best who loveth best, all things both great and small; For the dear God who loveth us, He made and loveth all.'"

"Hey, I heard something like that before, but not in church."

"It's from Samuel Coleridge's The Rhyme of the Ancient Mariner. You likely read it in high school. Now, about these two donkeys. They were not in such good shape when you got them. You should have been a vet; you have a compassion for animals. Now, what is this high finance deal you want to tell me about?"

As we walked back to the house, I tried to explain the offer Anna had for the Chapman farm. Karen was not only a successful veterinarian; she had invested her money well and was financially independent. Over coffee, she told me to advise Anna not to get involved in any partnership or co-development deal. These often involved silent partners who would back a part of the project and then sell their interest off to someone else. She cited two ski development projects and a dude ranch in Wyoming that did just that. All three folded when the investors withdrew their support. "You see the wording for such contracts often favors the investor. If they finance the initial phase part of the project, they have the option of retaining stock in the next phase. They often sell that stock to someone else who would then restructure the whole project to their advantage. Unless you are a developer, sell for cash."

I smiled. "I'll relay this advice to Anna in my next email."

Karen raised her hand. "Be careful, Kurt. When a woman asks such advice of a friend, she is also saying he is more than just a friend."

"I can handle that."

Karen shook her finger at me. "It sounds like this is a family matter to her and she just included you in it. Kurt, are you ready for that?"

"Sure."

"Do you share with her your family problems?"

I shrugged. "I would if I had any."

"We all have problems, Kurt." Karen looked down at his right leg. "When are you going to have the knee surgery?"

"Next Monday. The Doc says I'll be hobbling around the next day."

"You may be hobbling around your hospital room but you won't be home. When you get home you will need a great deal of help. Have you made arrangements for a nurse to come see you? How about physical therapy?"

"Hey, I can take care of myself."

"Check your medical insurance. They must cover some kind of physical therapy. Look, you want to get back to work as soon as possible, right? I'll stop by and check on you." She stepped back from the fence. "Okay, Kurt, what's her name?"

"Anna. Anna Chapman. She lives in north Idaho."

Karen winked. "I want to meet her when she comes to Colorado."

I walked Karen to her pickup truck and watched as she drove away. How do women understand so much from a simple conversation?

That night my email to Anna was several pages long. I included not only Karen's advice, but I also laid out the surgery scheduled for my knee.

Chapter 43
Anna Goes To See Brad

It was the Sunday after Christmas when I went to church alone in Sandpoint. Bishop Peterson left those he was talking to and came to greet me.

"Anna, how are you. I have not seen you in weeks."

I smiled warmly. "My children have been keeping me busy. It seems every weekend they have some grand event. It's all a conspiracy to get me to move to Spokane. This week I simply said 'no.' Twice in the last few weeks I've had to drive home in the snow."

"Perhaps they are right. You should move to Spokane. It might be better for you than living up here alone."

I shook my head. "I'm not ready to move yet."

"Then we will be seeing you more often?"

"Of course." I looked around the room. "I know so many people up here I feel I'm home." My eyes stopped at the back of the room where a man in a wheelchair sat alone. Bishop Peterson turned to leave and I put my hand on his arm. "Wait a minute." I nodded toward the back of the room. "Who is that man in the wheelchair?"

Peterson raised his head a little. "He's my latest project. I am going to need a lot of help from the Lord to make him see the light."

I tilted my head slightly. "I bet life looks different from a wheelchair. I'd like to know more about him."

Peterson smiled. "We'll talk after services."

During the break, not one but three different men came up to ask if I was back for the winter. One man was even bold enough to ask if he could drop by some day to chat.

"Be sure to call first. I have a busy schedule," I told him.

"I bet you do," he winked and walked away. I felt everyone was watching me especially the women in the room. I was no longer the grieving widow women felt they must comfort. I was something else. Later, I met Bishop Peterson in a small room off the main hall.

"Anna, I can't tell you how glad I am you will be here for the winter. I assure you I am not alone in those feelings." He smiled. "I also have a dozen little projects that could use your assistance."

"I'm not looking for a job. I'm still sorting out my own life."

"You're new life will be much different from your past," he said. "It has to be that way. You and Sam were married in the temple."

I laughed. "I assure you I am not looking for a husband. You can tell the ladies not to worry."

He nodded slowly. "I understand, but men are bold and you are an attractive woman, an attractive rich woman."

"I find the richer you are, or people think you are, the more problems you have." I folded my arms and turned my head slightly to the right. "A man has offered to buy the Chapman family farm for a great amount of money. Suddenly everyone in the family is advising me about the deal."

"Is the farm yours to sell?"

"Yes and no. It is in the family trust, but I am the executrix of the trust."

"Why don't you want to sell?"

My hands tightened on my arms. "I don't want to give up the farm. It's been in the family for four generations." I looked down. "I don't want to fail Sam. He always made such decisions in the family. The rest of the family is already counting their share of the sale."

He raised his right hand. "Get some advice. You may be able to sell the farm and put the money in a trust, a family trust." He pointed at her. "I can recommend a very good investment firm." He took out his wallet, searched through it and pulled out a business card.

I took the card, read the name and then looked directly up at him. "If I call this man will everyone in church know I called him next week?"

"I assure you no one will know unless you tell them." He smiled. "Now, what is your interest in Brad?"

"Brad?"

"The man in the wheelchair. His name is Brad Lundstrum. What is your interest in him?"

I took a deep breath and then spoke quickly, "We have a mutual friend, Kurt Johnson. He was here this fall with the Vietnam vets motorcycle group. He's back in Colorado now. He invited me to come down and visit him this summer, but I want to know more about Kurt before I do that."

"Well, Brad is not an upstanding member of the community, not yet anyway. He had a number of friends who dealt in drugs. He's put that behind him but he still has a drinking problem. I spotted him one day last winter trying to cross First Avenue. He got stuck in the slush. I helped him get going again. He didn't want to go to the sidewalk, but instead, to his car parked there. I was impressed as I watched him open the door to the car, lift his body into the driver's seat, fold the wheelchair and push it past the steering wheel to the passenger side. A man with that much determination is worth saving."

The smile on Peterson's face broadened. "It took a while, but when Dad decided to trade in his old van. I offered to buy it. 'What use have you for a van modified for a wheelchair?' he asked. When I told him about Mister Lundstrum, he gave it to me."

Peterson laughed. "I really took a chance on that one." He shook his head, "I saw Brad's car parked outside Eichardt's one night. I parked the van next to his car and waited until he came out. Then I went into my pitch. 'This was my father's van. It's fitted with a ramp for a wheelchair. You can wheel right in and lock your chair in place behind the steering wheel. Now my father doesn't have any use for it. Why don't you give it a try?' He was a little tipsy but he had no trouble wheeling up and into the van. Dad's old chair was in there. I needed that to drive the van downtown. I wheeled dad's chair out of the way and Mister Lundstrum wheeled right in place.' Peterson chuckled a little before continuing. "That man found a dozen things he didn't like about the van, but I persuaded him to take it for a test drive. Told him I was going to junk it because it cost more to put it back as a standard van than it was worth."

"So he took the van?" I asked.

"Oh, it took a bit of talking to get him to take it home just for a week, he did. He promised to pay me when he got some money. I waited two weeks and then I stopped by to see him." Peterson grinned. "I wouldn't take his money. Instead, I wanted him to promise he'd stop drinking. He threatened to throw me out of his trailer. It was his life, not mine. He'd drink if he wanted to and I could take the van back with me."

Peterson shook his head. "I couldn't drive the van back because I had driven my own car over to see him. So I told him I'd let him think on it for a month, and then come see him again. Well, one month led to another. We argued about this all summer." The grin returned to his face. "In the end I won, or God won. Mister Lundstrum stopped drinking and I had some boys just back from their mission check in on him once in a while. This fall he started attending services but he's not made a full commitment."

He folded his hand and looked at me. "Mister Lundstrum is the kind of man who will tell you something good about one of his friends, but might conceal the bad."

264 | Michael Andrew Marsden

"I'd still like to speak with him."

Peterson nodded. "I can give you his address. He doesn't have a phone. Would you like someone to go with you?"

"No. I want to speak to him alone."

I drove to the trailer court in Sandpoint. It was easy to spot the van. I parked behind it. Lundstrum had been to church that morning, so I reasoned he probably had not had anything to drink yet today. The slurred voice that answered my knock on the door indicated I was wrong.

"It ain't locked."

I opened the door and looked inside. The room was cleaner that I anticipated but the furniture was all wrong or mostly absent. Trailers have chairs and tables made for them, but this one was mostly open space. A small television sat on a wooden table, and just a few feet in front of it the wheelchair and Mister Lundstrum.

"Hi! My name is Anna Chapman. May I come in?"

He tilted the beer bottle, drained it and then dropped it into the trashcan beside the table. "You can tell Peterson I'm still a sinner. If he wants his damn van he can come get it."

I stepped inside and closed the door. "We are all sinners. I didn't come here to talk about the van. That's between you and Bishop Peterson."

He grabbed the remote and muted the telecast of the football game. "What do you want?"

There was no chair to sit on so I took just a step closer and began. "Last fall a friend of mine came to visit— Kurt Johnson. He stopped to talk to you before he left church."

"Yeah, I know Kurt."

"What can you tell me about him?"

He put his hands on the wheels of the chair and turned it to face me. "What's this about? You trying to convert him?"

His eyes looked angry and yet they were looking me over, not looking at my face. Well, a man's weakness can sometimes be used to a woman's advantage. I put my hands behind my back and stood tall. After he had time enough for a good look I answered his question. "No, I like him just as he is."

"Then why ask me?"

I took another step forward and tried to keep a smile, but it was forced. "How long have you known Kurt?"

"Kurt? Not long." He shook his head, "Can't tell you much about him."

"What can you tell me?"

He looked down at the floor and then slowly up at me. It was a toe to head inspection and he made no attempt to hide it. "You like him?"

I nodded. "We met over thirty-five years ago. He stayed in Hope for a few months and then he left. I was surprised he came back. It was just for a short visit, but he did come back. Maybe it was to ride with the others down to Post Falls." I noticed a smile slowly warmed the man's round face.

"You like him."

"We have written each other a few times since he left. Were you in the Marines with Kurt?"

The man shook his face. "Do I look like a grunt?" He laughed. "I wasn't a Marine. I slept with them, ate with them and watched them die, but I was different. I was Navy, a corpsman."

"Kurt called you Doc."

"Marines called all corpsmen Doc. He pointed down to where his feet should have been. Couldn't save all of me. I stepped on a mine and a damn corpsman bandaged me up and hauled me out of there. Some days I wonder if I should be grateful or angry." He looked up. "He could have let me die. No one wants to die, but I never wanted to live like this."

"Did you help Kurt when he was shot?"

"Yeah, all three times. How did you hitch up with Kurt?"

I shook my head. "I didn't hitch up with him. He had an accident. He and his motorcycle ended up in the mud flats down by the Pack River." I stood tall and folded my arms across my chest. "I pulled him out. He stayed until he could ride again and left town."

He looked around the room as if searching for the answer. "He told me he was accepted in vet school and planned to go back once he got out of Nam." He looked down where his feet should have been and mumbled, "I was carrying him out when I stepped on that damn landmine." Lundstrum never raised his head as he spoke. "Gary, another medic, got me to the helio-copter and then went back to get Kurt. The next time I saw him he was on a cot next to mine, waiting to be lifted back to Okinawa."

I stepped closer. "Where was he shot?"

Lundstrum glanced in my direction but never raised his head much. "The big hit was his right leg. Shattered his fibula. They put a steel rod in its place. They didn't have enough steel rods to replace my legs."

He was looking at my legs. Men are often attracted to women with nice legs, but what attraction did they hold for a man without legs? I was glad my dress came down below my knees. I put my feet together.

"Tell me about Vietnam. I want to know what Kurt did and what happened to him there."

He looked at where his feet should have been. "I can tell you but you won't understand."

"Try me."

Part III

2006

Chapter 44
Kurt Comes Home From Hospital

I arrived at the hospital ten minutes after five, Monday morning. The nurse informed me Dr. Grey would be here shortly. I suddenly felt cold and hungry. I told myself I need not be afraid of the surgery, but I was. From the MRI Dr. Grey had shown me, this would be more of a mechanical operation. He was dealing with bones. Cutting and filling bones. Screwing metal and plastic parts into the bones, then sewing it all back together. God, I hoped the man had small fingers.

"When did you eat last?" the nurse asked.

"Noon."

"What did you have?"

I looked up and winked. "Burgers and beer."

"Not a balanced diet, Mister Johnson." She read the entries I had made on the admissions form to be sure I was the right person.

"You are allergic to pain medications? Which ones?"

"Most pain medications have too much of an impact on me, especially Demerol. I try to stay away from morphine-based drugs."

"You need to talk to the doctor about this when he gets here." She turned to the man standing at the foot of the table. She didn't have to introduce him. Only an anesthesiologist would be smiling this early in the morning.

I hated to lie flat on my back. I asked for a second pillow to prop up my head. I tried to look at my feet as the anesthesia began to take effect. The bed seemed to float up and down as we rumbled down the hall. I saw another bed rolling in the opposite direction. Dead men floating on a lake? The anesthesia had me now. My left foot turned and looked back at me. Anna was never so lovely—wet hair plastered against her head, rosy cheeks and that saintly smile. A wave splashed her face. The woman on the right with eyes that shown like a cat's eyes floated toward me. "My name is Vicky Anna O'Sullivan. What's your story, Kurt?" The closer she came the farther away Anna drifted. I tried to swim but my arms and legs just floated in the water. Strong, cold hands pulled me backwards down the river. Dark, green eyes appeared close to my head. Betty whispered in my ear, "Don't go, Kurt. It's not your time yet."

My head kept bobbing, the cold water washing over my face. I turned my head, spit out the water and tried to swim. My arms were strapped close to the sides of my body. Betty leaned over and pushed down on both of my shoulders.

"Be still. Watch. Your turn will come. "

Anna spread wings like a white swan and flew off. I felt those cold hands pulling me back into shallow water where the wave action was greater. It was so cold. Suddenly, I rose straight up. I was being lifted from the lake in a warm blanket. Below, light flashed. Above, the rattling sound of helicopter blades shook the stretcher. I felt the copter rumble off into the night sky. Gases in my belly rose to my throat. I struggled to sit up.

"Relax Mister Johnson. We're just changing those pillows. Here, let me wipe your face."

There was light, a bright white light. I squeezed my eyes closed and then ever so slowly opened then again. She pulled a warm blanket up over my shoulders. It was Gladys. No, it couldn't be. The woman stood up straight. She was not Gladys nor was she Anna. She was a nurse. When I really needed a woman I get a nurse.

The blanket felt warm and she tucked it close to both sides of my body.

"You must have had some wild dreams. It's all over now. Just rest. This will be your room for the next few days. My name is Marie." She wrote it on the board near the foot of my bed.

I felt limp, like a deflated tire. My leg from the hip down was like a log. Dr. Grey finally came into the room. He adjusted the level on the pain medication that was being fed into my left arm. "I am increasing this a bit; the operation took a little longer than I thought it would. I used artificial joints. When you're healed, the right knee will be stronger than the left."

That day was painful. I was hungry and afraid to eat. Tired and afraid to go to sleep. The only control I had was to lower or raise the back of the bed. I could feel the pain, and despite my protests, Marie brought me some pills to take every four hours. Finally I fell asleep, without the ghosts from the past invading my rest.

I enjoyed one day and night alone before a roommate was wheeled in. He spent his first day in a daze while I learned to use a walker to get to the bathroom. Removing the catheter was a painful affair. I pissed blood that day. The third day I was walking the hall with my walker, hiding the pain and crying to go home.

Finally, Karen and the woman who lived down the road from my house came to take me home. A man from the physical therapy unit of the county health agency was there with a truckload of items. I protested, and my neighbor told me to just endure what my tax dollars are paying for. As it turned out later, my insurance picked up the bill for most of the items. The most useful was an extra tall seat for the toilet. I never realized toilet seats were so low until I was hopping around on one leg.

I was happy to be home, but now I had to manage the pain. The neighbor brought me some sandwiches the first day and said her son would continue to check on the animals. I made the couch my bed. Charlie became my companion. I hated the pain pills, but the pain was too much to handle without them. I tried to keep track of when I last took one, but I lost my notes. The highlight of each day became the visit from the physical therapist. She was a pleasant woman and amazingly strong. She was also disciplined. She arrived at ten-fifteen each day and left after one hour. Most of the exercises were done lying on the couch. After four days she had me walking, with help from a cane.

Nighttime was the worst time of the day. I'd struggle to get up off the couch and hobble to the bathroom in the dark. I could never remember when I took the last pain pill. The first night I must have lost track completely. I made it back to the couch and laid there staring at the ceiling, waiting for the pain traffic light to change to from red to green. Each time I closed my eyes a different scene appeared, like a movie on the ceiling above. I was back in Nam and mortals were dropping in the trees around me. I told myself to lie still; you never see the one that gets you. I choked on the smell of blood, the smell of morphine. Why wasn't there something else to kill the pain? Clouds raced across the sky and all was dark. The darkness was not of night, but of death. The killing had stopped because there was no one else to kill. In the morning we would count the dead and do it again.

I rolled over on my side. Two ears perked up beside me, followed by two eyes. "Be still, Charlie. I want to dream of something else. You wouldn't understand this dream."

The next dream came as soon as I closed my eyes. I knew I was still awake, yet I was dreaming. There was Anna, dressed in white and with angel wings. In her hands she held a large whiskey bottle with no label on it. She held the bottle up to the candle on the table. I could see a woman trapped inside. Dressed in black, Vicky was like a tadpole swimming in circles. Anna pulled the bottle back and tossed it out into the lake. I rolled off the couch and into the water after it. The water was like a blanket of ice as I swam down looking for Vicky. Up above, Anna flew on her white wings. I dove deep into the cold water. My hand closed on the bottle and I swam for shore. There stood Gladys and Betty, watching in silence. I tried to run when I reached the shallow water, despite the waves splashing at my legs. My motorcycle was lying on the rocks just out of the water. I tried to swing my right leg over it, but I fell backwards with the motorcycle landing on top of me. Anna landed and lifted the bike upright. In my hand I held the broken bottle. Vicky rose to full size and jumped onto the bike. The rear wheel spun and the bike raced across the rocks toward the highway. I ran as fast as I could to catch up.

"This way," Anna called, as she flew like a swan up in the crimson sky. Vicky stopped at the shoulder of the road. I jumped right through her and grabbed the handlebars. I felt her breath on the back of my neck.

"No, you must stay," Betty, yelled.

We raced, not down the road, but back to the lake. Water sprayed wide from the front tire and we raced across the lake. I felt the bike tip to one side and reached back to hold Vicky. Then we rolled.

A sudden yelp jerked me back from the water to the rug in my living room. Charlie pulled back out of my grasp. Then with a whimper, licked the hand that still held some of his fur. I pushed myself into a sitting position on the floor.

"Sorry, Charlie. I told them I don't do well with pain medicine. Give me whiskey any day."

Chapter 45
Anna Learns of Kurt's Operation

After I read Kurt's email I called his house. The phone rang four times and then that welcoming message came on again: "You have reached the home of Kurt, Charlie, Billy and Bonnie. We cannot come to the phone at this time. Please leave a message and we'll get back to you."

I tapped the desk with both hands. Charlie was his dog, but who are Billy and Bonnie? If he had three dogs, he'd have said so.

"Kurt, this is Anna. Please call me after the surgery and let me know how it came out." I hesitated as if expecting a reply, and then added, "Thanks for the advice about selling the farm. Bye now."

I hung up the phone and gasped. "I almost said 'Love you.' I can't say that. No I can't."

I closed the phone and sat back in my chair. "Who are Billy and Bonnie? Why doesn't one of them answer the phone?"

I read the email again and figured Kurt just might be still in the hospital. If so, Billy and Bonnie would be in town checking on him. I printed out the email, turned off the computer and hurried downstairs. Too uptight to sit down, I pulled on my ski jacket, walked out on the dock and looked at the river. The breeze from downriver whipped the surface, making it appear like sailor hats bobbing upstream. Underneath, the waters rolled slowly west toward the Albeni Falls Dam. Kurt was like the river. He looked like he was headed one direction and all the time he was going another. He wore a brace on his knee but never mentioned needing an operation. He was in Vietnam but never told me what he did. Men…they just don't talk. No one at church knows Brad

Lundstrum was a medic in Vietnam. It's nothing to be ashamed of. Why do I imagine the worst? Bonnie is his live-in girlfriend and Billy is her son. He wouldn't have told me if they were. One day one of them will answer the phone and I'll not hesitate to ask them.

I flopped down in the only deck chair left out for the winter. The email was still in my hand and I read it once more. The breeze tried to take the page out to the river.

"Stop that." I looked out at the river. "Sam, stay out of this. I can do this myself. I can handle my personal life and the family business too. I wish you were here but you are not. Now let me run my life."

I folded the paper twice so it would fit in my jacket pocket. I went back to the kitchen, picked up my purse, opened it and found the business card Bishop Peterson had given me. I flipped open my cell phone and called the number. A cordial feminine voice answered the call.

"Frank Snow Investment Company. How may I help you?"

I didn't recognize the voice and hoped she was not someone I knew.

"My name is Anna Chapman. Bishop Peterson suggested I contact Frank about an investment possibility."

"Frank is on another line. May I have your number and he will call you back."

I gave my number and closed the phone. I walked back out on the deck, to the very edge of the dock. "See, I can do something myself."

* * *

"Don't men ever consider others? I was really concerned about him," I complained to Lara. "He didn't call back. He sent another email."

"Forget him. He's just a bum who can take care of himself. He doesn't have a family so he doesn't understand things like caring."

I read the email aloud. "See? He really has a problem. I bet it takes a lot more to drive one of those semi-trucks than an ordinary car. I wish I could go see him."

"No, Mom. He is not your problem. Your problem is the family. Did you look at the new proposal Jim sent you?"

"Yes. I asked Jim to set up a meeting with McGary next time he's in town."

"Why not let Jim handle it?"

I sat back in my chair. This was Lara's house, Lara's living room. It was not the place and likely not the time to tell her Jim had made a mess of the whole thing. He may know something about selling real estate, but he knew little about a major capital venture like this. The first rule was to know enough about the investment partners so you could trust them. Jim had been hoodwinked by McGary. He was not nearly as successful a businessman as he pretended to be. The problem now was how to get out of the agreements Jim had made without damaging Jim's reputation.

The phone rang; Lara raced across the room, fumbled through her purse and took out her cell phone. "Hi, Hon...At home...Oh, you're right...It's almost two-thirty; I was just about to leave...No, they don't get out at three...They have band practice today...I love you too. Oh, wait a minute! Mom drove down this afternoon...No, she doesn't want to go out to dinner...She wants to know if you straightened out that deal with the farm...All settled."

"No," I said. "Give me that phone."

"Now, Mom, don't be so rude. Honey, Mom is upset about something. Maybe you'd better talk to her."

I marched over and took the phone from Lara. "Jim, do NOT sign another agreement with McGary."

"Now, Anna, I thought we agreed I would negotiate this."

"Jim, my last instructions to you were to do a credit check on McGary and inquire with the Better Business Bureau about his company. I haven't seen either report." I heard Lara stomp out of the room.

"Anna, this is my job not yours. I know the man. This is big money. You can't treat him like someone who just came out of bankruptcy. Just calm down and let me handle it."

"I am the manager of the Chapman trust. You cannot sell one acre without my signature. Now, Jim, make those inquires I asked for and after we have them we can discuss this latest proposal."

"Anna, get off your high horse. The Chapman farm is part of the family trust. Sam should have named a man to take charge before he died. Now I don't want a family fight, but if you don't sign this agreement I'll file in court to have you removed as executrix of the trust."

I felt my body tremble. I held the phone away from my ear. Lara stood in the doorway to the dining room watching me. I took a deep breath, then almost shouted, "You don't know what you are doing."

"And you do? How many houses have you sold this last year?"

I put my right hand on my left so I held the phone with both. "Jim, I will not sign that contract. If you will not get those reports to me, I will get them myself."

"Anna, just stay there. I'll be home in ten minutes."

Lara smiled as if she had heard what Jim said. I walked over to Lara and handed the phone to her. "Tell Jim I left for home and he should not bother calling me until he has the reports I asked for."

That night I sat on the deck in the cold and cried. Four times the phone rang. The first two times Jim left a message; the last two times the line just went dead. The cold wind pushed the clouds away and reflections of the lights from the city across the river danced on the water. When I die, I want my ashes dumped in the river. That way I'll be with Sam and my bullheaded son-in-law can't stomp on my grave.

At eleven thirty the phone rang again. This time Jim left a message.

"I talked it over with Larry and Mark. We decided to avoid a court fight. I will get the reports you asked for. We also plan to have a meeting next week at my office."

I smiled out at the river. "I think he will cancel that meeting after he gets those reports. What do you think, Sam? When he learns what a risk taker McGary is, will he still want to sign that contract? You know you were a strong man. They all respected you. No one challenged your decisions. Am I so weak or is it just that I am a woman?"

I got up and walked to the back door, stopped, turned and said, "I'll let you know how it all turns out."

Chapter 46
Kurt Recovers

For a week I hobbled around the house but refused to use the crutch or the cane the county nurse had given me; I was going to tough it out. Thursday I admitted this recovery would take time. Later, I used the crutch to hobble out of the house. I hadn't seen Bonnie and Billy for almost two weeks. I got a handle of an old shovel from the barn and used it as a cane. Bonnie and Billy were stretching their necks over the fence and baying a donkey song. I went back to the house, left the crutch by the front door and got two carrots from the kitchen.

I was petting Bonnie, after the two had gobbled down the carrots, when Karen Anderson drove up.

"Hey, how is it going?" She jumped from the big four-wheel drive pickup. "Maybe you should be riding one of those donkeys."

I laughed and waited at the gate. When Karen got there I took the keys out of my pocket and unlocked the padlock on the chain. "I keep this locked, not to keep people out, but to keep Billy in. He has figured out how to open all the gates on this place."

Karen pulled the gate open and held it as I hobbled out. I stopped to lock the gate behind me and asked, "Care for a cup of coffee?"

"No thanks. I just stopped by to see if you needed anything. I'm going into the Fort."

"Thanks, I'm not supposed to drive yet. Let me go back to the house and check my list."

As Karen walked beside me she studied my legs like checking out one of her horses. "You walk like it hurts. Did the doctor give you pain medication?"

"Yeah, but I hate those things. It hurts less today than yesterday."

"It's not just for pain. They control inflammation too. If you are going to play macho guy, it will take longer for your leg to heal."

"What would you prescribe for a lame horse?"

Karen followed me into the house. "This is no joke. Let me see what they gave you."

I pointed to the cup of pills on the counter. "It's over there. I haven't taken anything this week." I picked up my grocery list from the table, added beer and cake, then checked the refrigerator.

Karen looked at the two small envelopes of pills and the two prescriptions in the coffee cup. "Well, at least you didn't throw these away."

She held up the first small envelope. "This is for pain. Why aren't you taking it?"

"It makes me feel dizzy but that's not all. One night I must have taken too many, and it took over a day to recover."

She opened the second envelope. "This is an antibiotic. Take it now. While taking care of your animals, you are exposed to all kinds of possible infections. Kurt, you know better than this. I'm filling the prescriptions while I'm in town."

I filled a glass with water and took one of the pills. When she opened the first envelope I backed away. "Don't want that."

"How about half?" She took a step forward. "You are in pain. Admit it. Take half a pill."

I handed her my list in exchange for the pill. Under her watchful eye I cut the pill in half and washed it down with a glass of water. "How many of these am I supposed to take?"

"As needed."

"Then I won't need another today."

Karen pulled a chair out from the kitchen table. "Drop your pants and sit down."

"What?"

"Pretend you're a donkey. I want to take a look at that knee."

I followed her instructions, glad I had changed my underwear this morning. She looked at the incision and checked the knee for swelling. Then, despite my objection, she washed the leg and put on a clean bandage. Before she left, I was lying on the couch with an icepack on my knee.

That night I must have been feeling better because I sent an email to Anna. I told her my leg was doing great and I was under the care of a veterinarian, the same woman who had given me the advice about not selling the farm. *She came over to check on Billy and Bonnie, but spent most of her time fix'en me up. Let me call her my third guardian angel. The doctor told me I couldn't drive for a least a month, perhaps two. Thanks to Karen, I think I will be driving again in one.*

I got a reply the very next day in which Anna told of fight with her son-in-law. It ended with two questions: *How old is this new angel? Who are Billy and Bonnie?*

I had to laugh. "Look at that, Charlie! I think Anna is jealous. What should we do?"

Charlie barked twice.

"Keep her guessing? Okay, I think I can do that. Let me see, Billy is 16 and Bonnie is 19. That's true, and they both are country folks that don't like city life. Neither finished high school. Now what else can I say?"

Chapter 47
Anna Deals With Phillip

Jim's office was a small one, so we met in the real estate company's conference room. Phillip claimed the chair at the head of the table, forcing Jim to sit across from me. The Scotsman flipped through his purchase offer to the last page.

"There, Mrs. Chapman is where you sign your name."

"No, Mister McGary. I do not accept the terms of this contract."

The giant shook his head and looked over at Jim. "Are you going to let this woman sink this venture?" He folded his arms across his broad chest and glared first at Jim and then at me.

"Must I go to court to force you to live up to our agreement?"

"I don't think that will be necessary," Jim said quickly. "We have begun an effort to change the administration of the Chapman trust, and hence the right to sell the farm, from Anna to me. Just give me a little time."

He pounded a fist on the table. "What kind of family is this?"

I reached over and pulled the contract toward me. The giant smiled. I flipped it to the first page and looked back at the red beard.

"We are a family much like your own. Some members are conservative and will not enter into such a speculative venture," I nodded across the table at Jim, "while others are too eager to do so. The best policy lies somewhere between."

I put my index finger on the letterhead of the first page. "Is this the family crest or the corporation logo?"

"What difference does that make?" Phillip thundered back. "We have a contract for several million dollars. You'll not get a better offer anywhere. Sign the damn thing."

My eyes opened wider and I looked across the table at Jim. "Did you get the reports I requested?"

"No, Anna, I did not." He smiled at Phillip. "Mister McGary was kind enough to supply me with credible references. Now, would you sign the contract?"

I put the document down and opened my purse.

"I have a pen," Jim said.

I pulled a letter out of my purse, opened it and placed the top page next to the contract. "This letter has the same logo as the contract."

"Where did you get that?" Phillip's voice thundered. He reached across the table but I pulled the letter back too quickly for him to grasp it.

"The letter is from your father. In it he says you are not an agent for the McGary Company in Scotland, and you have started your own independent development company. While McGary Company of Scotland has considerable assets, a company by that name in California is operating on, as we say in this country, a shoestring."

"You spoke with my father?"

"Yes, and on his advice I decline your offer."

"No! NO!" Phillip pounded the table. "He's always doing this to me." He shook his fist at Jim. "We had an agreement."

Jim rose to his feet. "Those golf courses in Scotland and in Ireland...does your company own them or do they belong to your father's company?"

Phillip sat back in his chair and flung his arms around like he was swatting flies. "He owns them all. He owns everything. It's a family business but he's cut me and my brothers out." He glared at me. "He treats us like incompetent children. I moved to California to start my own business. I can do this. Just give me a chance."

I shook my head. "Business deals are based on trust. You deliberately deceived us." I pushed the contract to the middle of the table. "This gives you the right to develop the land in any way you wish. We get only a small payment the first year and after that," I looked over at Jim, "we wait, like all the other investors, until the last of the development is completed. You talk of millions, but you say nothing about the money needed to make this work."

Phillip shrugged. "There will be other investors. Everyone is looking for a good way to make a few million. You just got no guts."

I folded the letter and put it back in my purse. Jim sat looking down at his hands. Phillip got up and walked silently out of the room. I tried to speak to Jim after the giant departed but he turned away.

There was no word from Jim or Lara that week. I felt I had been barred from the family, and for what? Not falling for that buffoon? I turned to Kurt for support. At least he listened. We exchanged email daily for a week. I prayed more often and pushed my diet and exercise program to the limit. Late Saturday morning, after I had walked the long bridge, I went up to the bathroom and stepped on the scale–125. Just five pounds away from my goal. I took off my shoes and stepped back on the scale–123. I stripped for my shower and then weighed myself again–122. I looked in the mirror and complained, "Where is a man when you really need one?"

I went to the office and sat in front of the computer. What started out as a simple greeting to Kurt rambled on. I asked about his health and the weather in Colorado. I told him about the beautiful spring we were having and I boasted, yes boasted, of meeting my weight goal and setting out to buy new clothes for summer at the lake. Then I asked what Billy and Bonnie looked like and how old they were. Last, I ended on a more serious note telling him about my encounter with Phillip and how Jim still does not see what I did was best for us all.

Chapter 48
Kurt Goes Back to Work

I climbed down from my truck, a 2004 Kenworth T600, and Charlie jumped over into the driver's seat. I looked up at him and smiled. This rig cost more than my house, but I owned it free and clear. Not many truckers can say that. Most need to keep them rolling to make the payments. I reached up and pulled my cane down from behind the front seat. It was a limb from an apple tree that Karen had given me. On one end there was a notch where the branch had forked. With the two ends sanded and rounded it formed a nice handle. The other end was thicker and cut flat. Karen said it was not a cane, but a shillelagh. It was too long for a shillelagh, but I kept it and after a few days grew to like it. This was my first run since the operation. I had lied through the last medical exam to get Dr. Brian to tell them I could drive again.

It was five fifteen that morning before my truck was loaded. I had kept a close watch on the process. Monday's run was the longest in terms of miles. Chadron, Nebraska, was also the northern-most point on my route. It was a small town just south of the Black Hills and west of the Sandhills in Nebraska. It was the kind of town I'd like to retire to, but it does get lots of snow and cold weather, much more than Ault. The population was less than six thousand and it had a college and a Wal-Mart store. There were more bars than grocery stories, and I stopped at the bars first. Wal-Mart was last stop and the biggest delivery. I was moving slow when I got to Wal-Mart. Driving was not the problem; climbing in and out of the cab was. I had to check each load taken from the truck and supervise the operation. The beer wasn't theirs until it was in their store. Some of the clients hired lumpers, and they were not used to dealing with flats of beer. Wal-Mart had regular employees do the unloading but they were different people every time. Before noon I had climbed down out of the cab and back up five times. I tried to ignore the pain in my right leg, but it hurt now even as I was sitting in the cab driving.

One thing you could say about Chadron was the people there liked their steak, and so do I. After unloading my truck we stopped at Helen's Steak & Pancake House. 'Stay here,' I told Charlie, 'and I'll bring back a T-bone.' It was two in the afternoon but the waitress didn't bat an eye when I ordered blueberry pancakes and a T-bone steak. I laid the shillelagh across the table and propped my right leg up on a chair as I ate. After dinner I climbed into the cab, gave Charlie the bone, pulled down my pants and rubbed the leg with Deep Heat. I wasn't about to take any of those pain pills when I still had to drive back home.

The next two days went by without incident. These routes were right off the Interstate 80 and there were reliable crews to unload the beer. On Thursday, it was back to Chadron. Getting out of the truck, I put my left foot down on the first rung, and then turned around to climb down backwards. My left foot slipped and I landed hard on the asphalt parking lot. Luckily my left leg took most of the shock. The manager of the store, a burly man of short stature but enormous strength, hurried out and lifted me to my feet.

"Hurt bad? I can take you to the doctor."

I patted the man on his broad shoulder. "I can take care of myself."

"Hope so. You know what we do around here with a horse when it breaks a leg? We shoot it."

"Don't shoot. I'll be fine."

It was not until I was putting Deep Heat on my leg before heading home that I noticed my left ankle hurt more than my right leg. By the time I got home the ankle was badly swollen.

That afternoon I took a pain pill, set my alarm for four o'clock and went to bed. Sometime later, I had no idea when, I got up and took another pill. That was a mistake. It all came back that night. The ambush, the mortar shells, the sniper fire and most of all, Brad Lundstrum. The squad had jumped off the trail and down the slope into the brush. No protection from the sniper's bullets, but concealment. I felt the jab of pain in my right leg. I tried to crawl forward but the pain raced up to my hip. Someone nearby call out, "Corpsman Up!" In a flash, Brad landed just a few feet away. He quickly put a tourniquet on my leg and jabbed me with a vile of morphine. The squad was returning fire and the North Vietnam Army faded into the brush at the top of the hill. Brad pulled me up and carried me back down the trail. The sniper fire began again. Brad jumped off the trail, and then we both flew up in the air. I didn't even feel it when I rolled down the hill. This was the end. I knew I was dead. Up on the horizon was the shadow of a man looking back down at the two of us. I closed my eyes, cursed and screamed. Flashes of pain rattled around in my head. Then I felt hands pull my arms up, lifting me off the ground. They dragged me back up the hill. Sniper fire or not, they would bring me home or die trying. I felt my body being passed on to another man to carry. I was farther down the hill now, out of the line of fire and safe from the snipers, but still hearing the mortars fall.

The noise was so deafening I couldn't hear the men near me speaking. It was like a silent movie. All I could do was look up at the jungle and the sky and wonder where I was being taken next. A face leaned close to mine.

"Hey, man, you're bleeding like crazy. Who put the bandage on you, some grunt who just got here?"

I could not focus on him. I tried to answer, "It was done right but we fell back there. Must have slipped. Where is Doc Brad?"

"On the stretcher beside you. We had better get both of you out of here fast."

The man broke open a capsule of morphine and shoved it in my left leg. "If you want to walk again, you got to go back to the Helipad."

I turned my head and spat. "If I lose that leg, shoot me."

The morphine was taking effect. I could hear and see better as the pain floated away. Scenes flashed by too fast to recall what was happening. The loud slap of the chopper blades cutting through the air almost freaked me out. If I hadn't been strapped down I would have climbed off the stretcher. All went dark and I don't remember the copter landing.

I do remember being moved around a lot. Finally the steady vibrations of yet another machine brought me back to consciousness. The voices were suddenly loud and clear.

"He can't be Johnson. Johnson is on the next flight. So is Lundstrum."

"They are here and now they are yours. Take them on to Okinawa."

I felt the stretcher being lifted.

"Okay, Johnson. We're putting you and your friend here by the door. If it sounds a little noisy, just remember you ain't supposed to be here."

I awoke to the sound of the alarm, holding my leg and crying, "If I lose that leg, shoot me."

Charlie came to the side of the bed and put a paw up beside me. I sat up and carefully tested both legs. I could stand and I could walk. The swelling in the ankle had gone down. I wasn't going to take any pain pills; I had a run to make today. I searched the bathroom cabinet until I found an Ace-bandage. I wrapped the ankle and put on my boots. One more day, one more run. I was alive. I could walk. The run was painful but I had the next two days off.

That night I sat down at my computer and read the latest email from Anna. The part about reaching her goal with respect to weight, begged for a reply.

It is time to buy new clothes. Even the clothes I bought last fall don't fit anymore. From dresses to swimsuit, I am going to replace them all.

I tried to picture Anna in a bikini, reclining on her dock, looking out at the river. I cherished that image for a while and then read the rest of the email. She ended with complaining about her encounter with Phillip McGary and how she felt she had alienated her son-in-law.

Men are so dominating. They never take advice from a woman. Sam was like that. He so established himself as being in charge; no one ever challenged his decisions. Everyone thinks they know better than me. How can I make Jim listen to me?

I replied to the message right away, dealing with the money issue first before getting personal.

We all have our own wars to fight; it sounds like you are winning yours.

I also tried to explain that Jim may never understand. *Some men want to be in charge, let's call them the officer corps. Others want the job done right, and I'm one of them. Call us the NCOs. It sounds like you were married to a general and now he has stepped down. Colonel Jim wants to be promoted. My guess is General Sam treated you like a private and Colonel Jim intends to do the same. You have two choices—assume the rank of general or resign.*

I added a few words about being happy to be driving again, then ended with *Can't wait to see you in your new bikini. Black is my favorite color but if you get a nice tan, a white one would look great too. Sent me a photograph of the one you buy; I'll put it on the visor in my truck. As for Billy and Bonnie, they are excited that I have a girlfriend. They can't wait to meet her. How about setting a date to come out and visit for a few days?*

Chapter 49
Anna in the Riverfront Mall in Spokane

I walked almost on my toes away from the mirrors, turned and walked back toward them. I could see Lara in the reflection, holding the other two dresses I had picked out. She had an impish smile on her face.

"Well, what do you think?"

"It's nice. You look great in that color but it's not for you." Lara replied.

I looked in the mirror. It was a silk skirt set in light orange with bright red and yellow flowers printed on both the blouse and the skirt. The outer skirt was silky with a split handkerchief hem with georgette lining. The top was of the same pattern but the polyester lining stopped at the bust line. I'd have to buy a new strapless bra to wear with the dress.

"I like it. Of course, I'd have to buy new shoes to match."

"Mom, it's indecent. You can see right through it. We aren't even out in the sunlight."

"It has a lining." I pulled up the outer silk skirt. "See, it's very modest."

"I can see your underwear."

"I wouldn't wear dark panties with this light-colored skirt." I dropped the hem of the outer skirt.

"Doesn't matter. I can see your silhouette. No, Mom, it's not for you. Let's go back to look at slacks and blouses."

I went into the dressing room and changed out of the dress. When I returned I found Lara had left the dress section and was looking at swimsuits. She had two selections she was holding up next to each other. The blue one had a tankini top with a skirted bottom and the red one had a halter bra top and hip-hugging bottom.

"Oh, is my daughter reliving her younger dreams?" I teased.

"Dreaming, yes. Wouldn't this drive Jim wild?"

I took the blue suit from her. "Try on the blue and I'll be your judge."

"Okay."

Lara changed into the blue swimsuit and strutted in front of the mirrors. It didn't take much urging to get her to try on the red combination too. She balked when I selected a white bikini with black spots on it.

"Mom, I could never wear something like that. What would people think?"

I held the bikini top up. "Look, it ties, top and back. One size fits all."

"No, Mom, I'm a little too hippy for a bikini. Why there is hardly anything to the pants. Let's look at one-piece suits."

After trying on several suits Lara selected a swimdress for me. It had a scoop neck, princess seams, and tank straps. The little imp had the nerve to point out it also had swim pants underneath with tummy control. It was however black, and looked pretty good on me. Lara was off looking at shorts and tops when I paid for my two dresses and the swimdress, so I returned to the counter with the one-size-fits-all bikinis and got the white one with black spots.

At home, in the basement, I paraded back and forth in front of the mirror beside the exercise bike. The black swimdress looked attractive. What I hated was Lara pointing out it had tummy control pants. Daughters can be cruel at times. The bikini was embarrassing, even in the privacy of my own home. I was in great shape but I was over fifty, and it showed. I set up my digital camera and took three pictures. None of them looked very good. I changed back to the black swimdress and took two pictures. These looked much better; I even noticed the exercise equipment in the background. I went upstairs to the deck, and after several tries I managed to take three pictures of myself in one of the deck chairs. For a long time I sat there in the afternoon sun in my new swimdress, wishing I was twenty again. Finally, I walked to the edge of the dock and looked out at the river.

"Well, Sam, this is the best I can do. I'd like to have shown you the bikini but that time has passed me by. It's Kurt's fault. He got me thinking young and foolish. He does that to me. Even at fifty a woman likes a man to flirt with her." I looked down at the black swimdress. Here I am, over fifty and dreaming again. Kurt is dreaming about being young again too. This has got to stop. If only I were twenty for a week, I'd go down to Colorado.

I turned and leaned on one leg and looked sideways at the river. "See, I still have curves. I don't need tummy control either." I spread my arms out wide. "Don't worry about me, Sam. I will write to Kurt just one more time, and then it's over."

Chapter 50
Kurt: The Last Letter

A week passed and I hadn't received a reply from my last email and thought perhaps Anna was down in Spokane visiting her family. With the aid of the shillelagh I was able to make my runs. I was more careful and didn't care anymore when the other drivers watched me getting down out of my rig. Karen said it takes longer for an old donkey's leg to heal. Her bit of humor helped me deal with the pain.

Saturday I received a large envelope in the mail from Anna. Thinking it was a photo of her; I tore the envelope open right away. No picture, just a short letter and the amulet that looked like a tau cross on a silver chain. I put the letter and cross back in the envelope and walked back to the house. By the time I sat down at the kitchen table I had crushed the envelope into a ball. With Charlie sitting by my side for support, I unfolded and read the letter.

It was over; she wanted to end it without offering me any hope. She took time to explain something about being married for time and eternity to Sam. Hell, what was that supposed to mean? Sam was dead.

I held up the silver chain and looked closely at it again. It was a beautiful piece of art. I had meant it to be a complement to her beauty. So much for good intentions. This woman was married for time and eternity. A nice thought, but it also meant she was married to a ghost. Well, there was more than one ghost in Hope... if you believed Betty's stories.

I looked down at Charlie, "Charlie, I am going back to Hope.

Not right way; I need to be able to ride first. Hope is where it all started and Hope is where it will end."

I went back to doing my therapy exercises. It was like spring training for football. No games planned until fall, but you work as hard as if they were next weekend. To my surprise the pain in my leg vanished and my leg slowly got stronger. It was mostly focus. I didn't see myself as an old man with a bum leg trying to still do his job. I was training to be Kurt, the wild motorcycle man. Well, not wild, but independent. The lone wolf that traveled the back roads.

In early June I made my first ride to Fort Collins. They say you never forget how to ride a bicycle; well, you never forget the thrill of riding a motorcycle. I was back. On the bike I felt like I was twenty again. This was what I needed to recover. A woman would have been better but with none I still had the open road. The following week several of the other drivers commented on my change in attitude. I attributed it to the end of driving on snowy roads.

It was not until the end of July I made my first long ride. I headed up toward the Black Hills. I stuck to the back roads and was on highway 71 headed to Ardmore, just across the South Dakota state line, when a thunderstorm raced up from the south. A sudden tailwind and a bolt of lightning were my first awareness of the storm. This was the badlands, with no shelter anywhere. I twisted the throttle and raced forward. Only a fool would try to outrun a thunderstorm. An old fool I was. A curtain of rain passed over, drenching the road. I sped up and soon reached dry pavement. The rain continued the chase. As if the storm was upset I was outdistancing it, a bolt of lightning crashed onto the highway up ahead. Like a fool, I raced on. The tailwind changed to a side rush, and I knew I was in the sights of the storm. A bright blue flash erupted and I went soaring up into the sky. I saw the bike continue down the road without me. Death was not what I had been told it would be. I flew like a kite in the wind before drifting down to earth. Once at ground level the wind tossed me along the side of the road like a leaf from an aspen tree. I finally came to a stop where my bike lay in a ditch not far from where I went air-born.

Chapter 51
Anna Settles the Family Relations

I sat back in the deck chair and looked past Jim, out to the river. "So, what did you want to talk to me about? I hope it's not another fight over the family trust."

He shook his head. "Peterson firmly rebuked me for trying to take over the family. You are in charge of the family trust." He shrugged. "I'm just a little too competitive. I didn't mean to cause any trouble."

I looked away. You aren't going to admit I was right either. McGary was a fraud and today you are buttering me up for something. "What is it this time?"

"Lara is very upset about your friend."

"She was being a protective daughter. Nice thought but I can take care of myself. For the record, it's over. We have not had contact, not even an email, in four months. Tell Lara to let it go. I have."

He leaned forward and then back in his chair as if he couldn't make up his mind. "Well, Lara planned this weekend."

"She planned what this weekend?"

"It's a surprise party. She's driving up tomorrow afternoon as soon as the twin's soccer game is over. It's to be one last cruise on the Good Faith before it is put up for the winter. The boys are excited. I told her we should ask you first, but she wants it to be a surprise for you too."

I closed my eyes. My fingers curled into fists. Why this weekend, the weekend of a full moon? I do have memories. I looked past him. The water in the river was still as glass. It looked like one could walk across it. This was a strange fall day. Fog all morning and no wind this afternoon. There were days like this the year I lived in Hope.

I turned and looked at the tall, young man my daughter had married. He was so like her father. Smart but strong-willed to a fault. He sat there looking at his hands, like he had something to give me.

"What time on Saturday?"

"The game won't end until after three."

"Good. Plan on coming. You know, you could have just called. Now you have to drive all the way up here again tomorrow," I said.

He leaned forward and put his elbows on his knees. "I came up today because there is something else. This is my idea. I haven't discussed it with anyone else."

My hands opened and my fingers grasped the arms of the chair. Here we go at the family trust again. This man never gives up.

"As you know, Larry and Barbara are renting an apartment in Cheney. She has a teaching assistantship at Eastern."

"I know that, Jim. Get to the point."

He sat up straight and gave me that superior look. "You probably don't know Larry hasn't found a permanent job yet. Rent is high in Cheney because of the all the students."

I nodded.

"Anna, you could ask them if they want to stay at the farm. It's only a fifteen minute drive from the university." He nodded, swallowed hard and then continued. "In fact, Larry was raised on a farm. He could . . ."

I finished the sentence for him, "run the farm next summer and make more money than working part-time in Spokane. He would have to take care of the baby too."

"He does that already."

I watched him. He had that confident look. Men are masters at hiding their fears.

"Have you discussed this with Larry?" I asked.

"No."

"What about Lara?"

He shrugged. "I haven't told her about it either. It just occurred to me the last time we drove out to see how they were doing." He tilted his head slightly. "Think about it and let me know. I won't say anything to anyone. The ball is in your court."

I waited as he rose from his chair. The ball is in your court. You think like a man. He reached the back door to the house and I got up quickly.

"Wait, Jim." I walked to his side. He held the door and I entered the kitchen first. "Let me say this is a grand idea, but not a simple one. We have a farmer who has leased the land the past five years and commitments to sell the wheat. These are not written agreements but ones I don't want to break without talking to him first."

As we walked through the house, I explained the arrangements in more detail ending with, "Using the farm for benefit of the family is a good thing to do. I'd rather see it as a farm than as a golf course."

I closed and locked the front door behind us as Jim walked to this car. He looked back. "Okay, you need to give Larry a call sometime and talk to him. Like I said, I haven't talked to anyone. I came to you first."

I smiled. Don't act so smug. I don't believe for a second you didn't talk to Lara.

He opened his car door and nodded. "I'll tell Lara this Saturday is okay. We didn't mean to interfere with your plans for the weekend. What were your plans?"

I took the garage door opener from my jacket pocket and pressed the button. "Oh, nothing important. I was just was going up to the Casino and hope to get lucky."

"You don't gamble."

I shook my head. "We all gamble in one way or another. Instead, I'll settle for a quick ride. It's all the excitement I can allow myself."

Jim smiled. "On your motorcycle?"

"Yes. Now don't tell me I'm too old."

Jim grinned. "Hey, I envy you. I bet it is a real charge." He shook his head. "I told Lara I wanted to buy one and she had a fit."

I walked into the garage, took off my jacket and put on the leather one strung across the back of the bike. I snapped on my helmet and backed the bike around to face out the door. Jim backed his station wagon halfway up the driveway. The ST started with a roar. I popped it in gear and jetted past him. At the road I hesitated just a second before turning left.

Rumbling across the long bridge, I spotted Jim catching up in my rearview mirror. The old station wagon fitted my daughter's image far more than it did Jim's. I knew it; Jim knew it and Lara would never admit it. Everyone is trying to control someone else.

For a few minutes I rode through Sandpoint and out the west end of town. Once past Dover, I opened up the ST and rode with the wind. By the time I slowed for the town of Priest River, I knew I had left Jim far behind. Another burst of speed and I was crossing the bridge into Oldtown. Here I turned off on highway 41; Jim would drive on into Washington and take highway 2 down to Spokane. On the map, 41 looked like a straight line with but one long sweeping curve. In reality it was a narrow, two-lane road that turned, rose, dropped and turned again as it wound its way through the tall timber. For someone who loved the woods, this was the scenic route. For someone on a motorcycle, this was a challenge and a thrill. By the time I reached the town of Rathdrum I was on a high. I didn't have a man like Kurt to share it with but I had my ST and the open road.

Chapter 52
Kurt Returns to Hope

There was a mist over the east end of the lake as Megan walked down to the café in the hotel. Up on the hill the sun shown, but a cloud sat over the water. Unusual for this time of the year, there was not even a hint of a breeze from the lake. She paused at the door and looked back. She could not see the cabins at Red Fir, only the tall steeples of the trees on the hill above where the resort should be.

She was not a young teenage girl, but a woman in her late twenties. An attractive woman, even wearing gray slacks, a casual off-white blouse and no makeup. Her pale complexion fit with her clothes, except for the bright red apron tied around her waist. This morning there were few patrons and she hovered near the large front windows and stared out at the strange gray world.

When a young man finally stopped for breakfast, she rushed to his table.

"Kind of gray today," he said.

"I just moved here last month. It's been warm and windy up until today. This morning when I walked to work all I could see on the highway were the headlights of cars as they went by. Betty told me this would happen. We're due for a full moon in a few nights."

He glanced around the room to find he was the only patron. Good, he didn't need people watching him. Not today. It was the break between breakfast and lunch. He smiled up at the waitress. She had to be nice to him. If not, she got no tip.

"The fog will clear out shortly," he said.

"How do you know?" She crossed her arms in front of her chest.

"Sunshine. If you watch, you can almost see the cloud pushing back across the bay."

She shivered, lowered her hands, then took a pad and a pencil from her apron pocket— an admission she was not confident of her skill at the new job. "What can I get you this morning? We're still serving from the breakfast menu."

"I'd like corn beef hash and eggs."

"To drink?"

"Coffee. No make that coffee now and a glass of milk with the meal," he replied.

He noticed she finished writing on her little pad before she departed. He put his elbows on the table and rested his chin on his fists. People are so insecure when in a new place. Women can act insecure, but that's taboo for a man. And dammit, women were the source of man's insecurity. He reached in his pants pocket. The engagement ring was still there. He should take it out and throw it in the lake.

The coffee came quickly and the nervous waitress peered out the window before returning to the kitchen. His breakfast arrived in good time and the waitress made a trip to the front door and stepped out. She returned with a smile on her face. He assumed the fog had lifted, or at least retreated to the other side of the bay.

Before he finished his breakfast, a few new customers arrived seeking an early lunch. The waitress kept his cup filled with coffee. He wondered as he watched her take orders at the other tables ... now what was her story? How did she end up in a little town like this? Everyone has a story. She had a pleasant looking face but no outstanding features. Her lips were thin, but lipstick could change that. Her eyes were light brown, as was her hair. In general it was a washed-out watercolor painting of a face.

"Hey, are you Wally?

He shivered and then looked over his shoulder. Standing just inside the front door stood an older woman in a tight-fitting black sweatshirt with a pair of owls on the front. The message printed below was NIGHT HUNTERS. He smiled as she approached and noticed the twinkle in her eyes and dimpled smile. Dark red lips and a little eye shadow drew his attention to her face despite the inviting shape behind the owls. The new waitress could take a few lessons from this old broad.

"I'm Wally. Who are you?" he asked.

"Name is Molly. My sister works down at the resort. She said she hired a young man to do some painting during the off-season. Welcome to Hope. By the way, the Soiled Dove will be open late tonight if you care to stop by." She walked over and patted him on the shoulder. "Can't stop. I'm on this shift." She winked and went off into the kitchen.

Wally nursed his coffee for a short time and then got up to pay his bill. Molly hurried over to the counter. "Where are you staying?"

He nodded. "I got myself a room down at the resort, as long as I'm working there. That way I can start early in the morning."

"And work late at night. Those people are smart. They will get a lot more work out of you that way." Molly took his money. "Say, I know I don't have to say this, but don't forget a tip. Megan here needs the money."

Molly leaned forward and whispered, "Poor girl. Her man just up and left her here at the café one night. I put her up at one of the small houses that are empty all winter anyway. She's a nice girl who got mixed up with a jerk."

Wally took out two dollars from his wallet.

"Come back and see me later tonight," Molly said. "Mike and I will be up late. You know what night this is?"

"No. What happens tonight?"

"Anything you can dream of," Molly replied.

* * *

It was dark when Kurt motored to a stop at the Hotel Hope. There were two trucks parked across the road from the Soiled Dove Saloon. He motored on slowly down the street. A light was on the Waldron house. He rode up as silently as he could and peeked in the window. Every light in the house was on but the shades were drawn.

"Now don't be a peeping Tom," a husky female voice called from the porch of the house next door.

Kurt rode over, stopped his motorcycle and walked up on the porch.

"So, you came back," Betty, said. She nodded and looked around the porch. "I told you he would."

Kurt stepped back and raised his fists. He could see them; twelve young men huddling around the old rocking chair where Betty sat.

"Don't act so surprised. You're one of us now."

He lowered his hands to his side. "I don't get it. I can see you. I could always see you, but who are they?"

Betty opened her eyes, those deep, dark green eyes that seemed to wander as she spoke. "They are all seekers of Vicky. They couldn't swim in the cold water but they wouldn't leave her. She led them to a watery grave. You were lucky. You were saved by that angel of yours."

"Anna? Anna saved me?"

"Yes. She went looking for you that night. She found the two of you. Once she arrived Vicky had to vanish. That is the rule. Anna took you home from the hotel that night. You should have gone to the lake with Vicky." She looked around and chuckled. "Then you could stay here with us."

Kurt folded his arms across his chest. They were all young men in their prime, just as he had been some thirty-six years ago. He was so much older now. Would that make a difference?

"Why did you come back, Kurt? To see that angel of yours?"

He reached in his coat pocket and pulled out the silver chain with the tau cross. "I came to give this back to Vicky. The story I heard is she lost it in the lake long ago."

Betty nodded. "That she did. This is the night." She again looked around for the nodding approval from the young men on the porch. "Tonight at midnight."

* * *

The moon never looked so large as when it sits in the sky over the deep south arm of Lake Pend Oreille. The ridges of the Green Monarchs looked like a sleeping giant staring up at the night sky. To the west, a wall of darkness pushed over Bald Mountain.

Wally parked his pickup across the road from the hotel. He walked up and peeked in the tall window before going in. Molly wore a white turtleneck sweater tonight. He took notice, as he was sure every man did in the Soiled Dove Saloon. There were two tables of men drinking and complaining about something he couldn't hear well enough to understand. At the other tables couples sipped their brew and whispered to each other. At the bar two old men drank and shared a bowl of chips. Old Mike lingered behind the bar, letting Molly wait on the customers at the tables but watching her as she did. Wally sat down and ordered a Scotch on the rocks.

* * *

There was a steady breeze from the west when Vicky's head broke the surface of the lake. Short gusts of wind from the north whipped the water into hundreds of little waves, each seeking its own destiny. She glided toward the north shore of the bay with long, strong strokes, like a swimmer alone in an indoor swimming pool. The wind and waves continued their fight as if she was not there at all. Only when she reached the shallow waters close to the shore and stood up to walk did the crashing waves make her alter her course. She stopped and waited for the next two waves to roll in and the backwash to start before she moved swiftly to the rocky shore.

There she shook her clothing and the water vapor raced off like a spray from a wave against a dock. She looked back at the big orange moon and then at the fast advancing clouds. Nights like this she hated, for on such a night many years ago she went for that fatal swim to save the whiskey less it be washed up on the rocks. She had done it, but at a price. That greedy man. He had sent her on one last dive and then he rowed away. She lifted the bottle in her left hand and looked up at Hope. Who will share my whiskey? Who will share my night?

The wind whipped at her dress and coat as she walked up the rocky slope to the road. A bright light came on just down the road. Vicky hurried forward and stepped over the guardrail, lifting her skirt just a little higher than necessary to do so. She had seen motorcycles change through the years. This one was cleaner and quieter than most. It pulled slowly to a stop. The rider turned off the engine and removed his helmet.

"Good evening, Vicky."

She raised her right hand to her lips. "Have we met?"

His voice was friendly and calm. "Yes. We met some thirty-six years ago at the Soiled Dove Saloon."

"You lie; no one ever comes a second time. What's your name?"

"Kurt Johnson. The year was 1969."

She held up the whiskey bottle. "I remember the name but you look too old to be Kurt."

He laughed. "You forget. We age while you do not."

She nodded to the west. "There is a storm coming. Do you have a place where we can go?"

He smiled. "I have no place to go. That is why I came back. But I didn't come to share a drink and good time with you tonight."

"You lie; men always want more."

He unzipped his black leather jacket and reached inside. "This time I have something to give you."

She watched as he took his hand from inside the jacket and extended his arm with his palm turned up. Cautiously she stepped forward. He turned his hand and the silver chain unfolded as it fell. At the very bottom the tau cross jerked to a stop. Vicky took a quick step backwards.

"I think this cross and chain is yours. It was found in the lake many years ago." He raised his hand slightly so the cross was at her eye level. "The name Anna is etched on the back of the cross. Is it yours?"

"Yes." Vicky put down the whiskey bottle and took the chain in her hands. She held the chain open above her face, as if to put it on, and then suddenly lowered it. "What happens next?"

He zipped shut his jacket and lifted his helmet. "I have no idea what will happen. I'm just learning to adjust to my new role— haunting the back roads and byways."

She again slowly lifted the chain. She shivered when it touched the back of her neck. "I haven't felt something cold in a long time. The lake is never cold, nor is the night air."

She smiled. "Thank you."

The motorcycle engine started with a low rumble. He turned in the saddle and gestured with his right arm to the saddle behind.

Vicky came up and climbed on the motorcycle behind him. "Take me to the hotel but let me off just down the road. I want to check it out before I go there."

Chapter 53
Molly and Mike

"Damn, if that isn't the strangest Vicky story I ever heard," Mike swore.

Molly grinned. "I told you only a young man, a drunken young man will meet Vicky. Wally was plenty drunk when he left last night." She laughed. "Something good did come from it. You remember he said when he left the bar he was going down to the dock and throw that ring in the lake. Well, he still has the ring."

Mike shrugged. "So, Wally met Vicky when he left here."

"Said he met her as soon as he closed the door behind him."

"I bet they had a wild time too."

"As wild as a young man's dreams," Molly replied.

"But who was that other woman?"

Molly shook her head. "He didn't ask her name. Wally said he was swimming after Vicky. They were going to Cottage Island. He got a cramp and almost drowned. Just in time this pontoon boat appeared and the woman on board threw him a life preserver. Then she helped him on board, gave him a towel and motored over to the dock. She also called ahead and had the police come down and get him."

"Who was she?" Mike asked.

"Wally said she was an angel to have saved his life like that. Now do you want to hear a stranger tale yet?"

Mike shook his head. "Can't be a story stranger than that."

Molly put her hands flat on the bar. "You know that young woman who works at the café ... Megan?"

"Yeah, she's a strange one too."

"Well, when she came to work this morning she told me a man on a motorcycle picked her up last night."

"What?"

"That's what she said. About midnight she heard a motorcycle outside her house. She went out to see what the guy wanted and he asked her to go for a ride."

"She didn't go, did she?"

Molly grinned. "She went. Lonely women can dream dreams even stranger than the ones young men dream."

"What happened?" Mike asked.

"She didn't tell me all that happened. She did say they went for a wild ride. Faster and more exciting than anything she had ever done before." Molly cocked her head to one side. "When I asked what happened when she got back to the house, she only smiled. I asked Betty if she heard anything last night. Guess what she said?"

Molly clapped her hands together.

"You may see a ghost or two while you are in Hope. They return for many different reasons. Most come back because they are simply lonely. They were lonely in life and now they are lonely in death. They wonder between the two worlds looking for someone or something."

Chapter 54
Anna At Home

The news of the strange events at Hope traveled fast to Sandpoint. I never told anyone I was the woman in the boat who rescued that foolish young man. How could I? What would I say was my reason for being alone on the lake in the middle of the night? People might think I was strange. My daughter would insist I move to Spokane if she knew. The other part of the story was nonsense. Some young woman had a dream of riding off in the night with a handsome stranger. Who hasn't? She didn't say his name was Kurt. It could not have been him. But now Hope has two ghost stories to boast about. What could be more absurd than a ghost on a motorcycle?

It is getting dark and I can feel a cool breeze blowing off the river. Last weekend when Lara was here, I told her I wanted to stay in my house by the river to be near Sam. I hope this Indian summer continues until Thanksgiving. It never does. What is that? A motorcycle on the bridge? Yes, with these binoculars I can see it as soon as it rounds the bend in the bridge. There it is and the rider is sitting up tall in the saddle. The Honda has a sound of its own, not at all like those other cycles with only two cylinders. No, not a second motorcycle. Kurt always rode alone. He was lonely all his life and now he is lonely in death. He wanders between the two worlds looking for something or someone.

The End

Other Novels by
Michael Andrew Marsden

Midnight in Hope is the fourth of my north Idaho ghost stories. The other three are *The House in Harrison* (2003), *The Man in the Closet* (2005), and *The Black Dog Bed & Breakfast* (2012).

Each of the novels is quite different in their representation of the ghost or in this case ghosts. I do not consider any of them to be a horror story but *The Man in the Closet* comes close to being one. *Midnight in Hope* has the most ghosts, some romantic some dangerous and all I hope interesting.

By contrast the other three novels have only one ghost. *Midnight in Hope* has a love story within it as have two other of the ghost stories – *The House in Harrison* and *The Black Dog Bed & Breakfast*. Each of the stories takes place in a small town in north Idaho and thus I have come to call myself *The North Idaho Ghost Writer*.

If ghost stories do not interest you, even with a love story included, I have two other novels you might consider. *A Walk in the Rain* (2006) is a love story without a ghost. *Sam d'Bear* is a mainstream novel, the tale of how a big Newfoundland dog changes the life of a young man in Colorado. Gray Dog Press in Spokane, Washington published this novel.